Pivot Point

Pivot Point

A NOVEL

Betsy Brannon Green

Printed in the United States of America
First Printing: October 2012

ISBN-13: 978-1480129573
ISBN-10: 1480129577
BISAC: Fiction / Suspense

Prologue

On the television screen two tennis players faced each other over the net. In hushed tones, the announcer reminded viewers that it was the title match at the US Open. The number one seed, Ian Lauder from Sweden, was playing a young American, Ty Randall.

Just as the American began his serve, a woman came running out onto the court. She tried to hug the young man – crying that she loved him. He warded her off with his tennis racket.

"I miss you!" she cried in front of the stunned audience. "Our son misses you! Please come back to us!"

"I don't even know you!" Ty Randall insisted as several security guards swarmed onto the court.

The woman fought them as they dragged her off. Her hand was extended to the young tennis player and her pleadings could still be heard even after she was out of sight.

"Well," the announcer said. "That was odd."

"I've never seen anything like it," his co-commentator agreed.

"Ty seems shaken. I wonder if this incident will affect his play here at the end of such an important tournament."

"It's a mystery. Something people will be talking about for weeks."

"One thing is for sure. It will make the *ESPN Not Top Ten* list."

Chapter One

Dr. Meghan Collins sighed in relief as her interview with the host of *Today in Atlanta* ended. She unclipped the microphone from the lapel of the expensive suit her mother had insisted she purchase for the occasion and handed it to the technician who was hovering nearby.

"Good job," the technician said. "The camera loves you. Maybe you should have gone into show business instead of medicine."

Meghan couldn't tell if he was flirting or trying to give her a sincere compliment, but it didn't really matter. She had no interest in flirtation and she had never taken any pride in her appearance, since it was nothing she had earned. The credit went to her Scandinavian ancestors.

The morning show host, Windy Meeks, was a little less effusive in her praise. "Yes, it was a very good interview."

"You deserve the credit for that," Meghan told her honestly.

Windy flashed a professional smile. "Congratulations on your award."

Meghan nodded. "Thank you."

Windy smoothed her short, tight skirt. "Now, I don't mean to rush you off, but Dr. Pierce Morrow is our next guest and we have to prepare the set for him."

"The Nobel Prize winner?" Meghan asked in surprise.

Windy nodded. "It's a real honor." Belatedly, she seemed to realize that this could be taken the wrong way. "Not that it wasn't an honor to interview you too!"

"I understand completely." Meghan stood and several crew members rushed up to swap out furniture and add a flower arrangement to the coffee table.

Meghan stepped away from the set transformation and once she was out from under the bright studio lights, she could see that Chase was there. He had taken off his suit coat, loosened the tie at his neck and rolled up the sleeves of his dress shirt – achieving a business-casual look. Even after a long day his dark shiny hair was still perfectly in place and his bright blue eyes looked amused as he waved her over.

She walked to her husband and pressed a quick kiss to his lips. "You left the office early today."

"I did," he confirmed.

"So the DA didn't have enough work to keep you busy?"

"I had plenty of work as usual," he corrected with a smile. "But it's not every day that a man's wife is interviewed on television. I wanted to savor it. And I thought you could use some moral support."

"You were right about that," she muttered with a glance back at the studio set.

His eyes admired her. "You look fantastic."

She grimaced. "Mom picked out this suit."

"I knew that," he assured her. "If it had been left up to you – you'd still be in scrubs."

"I'm not a fashion idiot and I wouldn't wear scrubs on television," she said. "At least not without a nice crisply starched lab coat."

He laughed. "I'm glad you let your mother pick the outfit."

There was some commotion at the studio door and Meghan turned as Dr. Morrow, followed by several other people, walked into the small room. He was in his late forties, perhaps early fifties. His longish brown hair was laced with gray, his skin was tanned, and his physique was trim. She'd never been attracted to older men, but Dr. Morrow was quite handsome.

Windy approached her important guest with giddy enthusiasm. "Thank you so much for coming! I can't wait to get started on our interview."

"Thank you for the invitation," Dr. Morrow said graciously. Then he turned to Meghan and extended his hand. "If I read the schedule in the hall correctly, you are Dr. Collins, Atlanta's Woman of the Year."

She shook his hand. "I'm Meghan Collins."

Windy put a proprietary hand on the doctor's arm. Then she addressed Meghan. "Dr. Morrow is doing some fascinating research with dream therapy. Pretty soon there won't be a disturbed person left in Atlanta."

His entourage laughed politely, but the Nobel Prize winner himself, did not.

"My research is not only for the disturbed," he corrected Windy. "It is also for healthy people and I believe in the near future it will revolutionize life as we know it."

This was a bold statement and Meghan found herself intrigued. "I'd like to hear more about your work."

Dr. Morrow smiled. "And I'd be delighted to discuss it with you. Perhaps after my interview we could get some dinner and talk about my research."

"I'd like that, but I'm not sure what our plans are." Meghan moved a little closer to Chase and he put an arm across her shoulders. "I'll have to ask my husband."

Dr. Morrow's eyes drifted over to Chase. "What can I say that will convince you to stay and have dinner with me?"

"Nothing," Chase replied coolly. "But we'll stay if Meghan wants to."

Dr. Morrow nodded. "A wise husband." He lowered his voice and said, "This won't take long." Then he walked over to the set where Windy was perched on a little green chair.

From the corner of her eye Meghan could see the technician putting a microphone on Dr. Morrow. Windy was batting her eyes and blushing.

Meghan whispered to Chase, "Thanks for accepting Dr. Morrow's invitation."

He frowned. "You're welcome, although I can't understand why you want to eat dinner with him."

"He's a Nobel Prize winner," she pointed out. "That alone is enough to make me accept the invitation. But besides that, I'm interested in his new dream-therapy research."

Chase whimpered. "Great. I get to spend the evening listening to a bunch of medical talk."

"It's not like I haven't spent plenty of evenings listening to you and your colleagues discuss boring points of law."

He acknowledged this with a shrug. "Okay, but let's try to make it home before too late."

Pleased, Meghan gave him another quick kiss. "We won't stay out late, I promise." Then she turned her attention to Dr. Morrow, who was now settled in the spot she had recently vacated. With a microphone clipped to the collar of his shirt he looked composed and prepared for the interview ahead.

Then the technician walked over to Meghan and said, "I'm sorry but Mindy is afraid you'll be a distraction during Dr. Morrow's interview, so you'll have to wait in the hall."

Meghan frowned and Chase grinned. "That's what you get for being so distractingly gorgeous," he whispered as they walked out of the small, crowded studio.

She rolled her eyes. "Windy is being ridiculous."

They waited in the hallway until Dr. Morrow emerged, followed by his own personal parade.

"All finished," he declared. "I hope you're hungry."

"We are," Meghan replied for both of them.

"You name the restaurant and I'll meet you there."

"How about Minelli's Buffet?" Meghan suggested. "It's right around the corner."

"Sounds perfect," Dr. Morrow agreed. "I'll see you there in a few minutes."

Chase and Meghan rode in his car to the restaurant. They were seated at a quiet table discussing their day when Dr. Morrow walked in – without his entourage.

"So, are we ready to eat?" he asked.

"We're more than ready," Chase replied. "Meghan looks like she's about to disappear."

"I am hungry," Meghan murmured, slightly embarrassed.

They walked over to the buffet tables, laden with food. Everything looked delicious and Meghan hadn't eaten since breakfast so she filled her plate. Chase was a health nut so he made his choices more judiciously, avoiding fat and tending toward fresh vegetables.

For the first few minutes of their meal there wasn't much conversation as they enjoyed the food. But when Dr. Morrow finished his dinner he pushed back a few inches from the table and said, "Dr. Collins, how does someone so young get named Woman of the Year in a city like Atlanta?"

"It was a great honor," Meghan acknowledged, "Although I don't deserve all the credit. I started a program in conjunction with Children's Hospital that provides assistance to teenage mothers including, but not limited to, prenatal care and parenting classes. The idea was good but *Mom*entum has become a huge success thanks to remarkable community support."

"She's too modest," Chase inserted. "She worked herself to death generating that remarkable community support. And the program she developed is now being used as a model for similar programs all across the southeast. And she still donates twelve to fifteen hours a week to *Mom*entum in addition to her rigorous private practice schedule."

Dr. Morrow seemed impressed. "Now I understand why you have risen above the pack. You're beautiful, you're smart, and you work very hard."

Meghan was uncomfortable with the praise so she deflected attention from herself by pointing at her husband. "I'm not the only one who works hard. Chase is a very up and coming assistant district attorney and he puts in long hours as well."

Chase rolled his eyes. "I'm an assistant DA – but I'm not sure about the up and coming part."

Dr. Morrow acted politely interested in Chase and his career, but after a few intelligent questions, he turned his attention back to Meghan.

"Because of your medical knowledge, I would love to give you a tour of my lab and get your opinion about my work. Your husband too," he included Chase in the invitation as almost an afterthought.

Chase asked, "So what is it you do at this lab?"

"We manipulate dreams," Dr. Morrow said. "I call it dream therapy and it can help people solve problems – like phobias or addictions. But the applications are much broader than just that and the possibilities are almost endless."

Meghan twirled shrimp Alfredo onto her fork. "What kind of possibilities?"

"Most people have points in their lives – we call them pivot points – where they make a decision that sets the course for everything that comes afterward. Things like what school to attend, what career to pursue, who to marry." He glanced between them. "Even things as simple as whether to play little league baseball or take piano lessons can make a huge difference in life. For instance, what if Tiger Woods had taken swimming lessons instead of learning to play golf?"

"He might have been a great swimmer," Chase said. "Maybe the greatness is inside him and the sport didn't matter."

"Maybe," Dr. Morrow said. "Our technology would allow him to find out. We take people back to those pivotal moments and let them make a different choice – just through dreams – and see what might have happened if they'd taken another path."

"You're kidding." Chase's tone was skeptical.

Dr. Morrow shook his head. "I assure you I'm completely serious."

Meghan put her fork down. "How do you do it? How can you manipulate people's dreams to recreate a scene from the past and then project it forward on another path?"

Dr. Morrow said, "First, we recognize that the brain is an amazing source of stored knowledge. Every experience you've ever had is locked there in perfect clarity – just out of reach."

"But how do you reach these perfect memories and then change them?"

"We begin with an in-depth exploratory session with the client. We glean as much from their conscious memory as we can and determine the new path they would like to take. Once we have this information we can use computers to flesh out their memories and make the adjustments."

"Flesh them out?" Chase repeated.

"We combine the information about the client, including pictures, with actual data from the time that their pivot point took place – like the weather, the music, architecture, clothing styles, popular models of cars. Then using a technique similar to the ones used in sophisticated video games, the computer creates an alternate life – starting with the pivotal moment. We anesthetize the client to keep them in REM sleep, and give them a combination of drugs . . ."

"Drugs?" Chase asked with a frown. He wouldn't even take an aspirin, so this portion of the therapy earned his immediate disapproval.

"All perfectly legal and harmless in moderation," Dr. Morrow assured him. "And the final component is something similar to subliminal imagery – only much better. That is how we impress the alternate reality – if you will – on the client's sleeping mind."

"And that works?" Chase was still frowning.

"It does," Dr. Morrow claimed. "Let's say for instance your pivotal moment was the day you chose between two college scholarships – one baseball and one academic. If you chose the academic course but wanted to see how your life would have been if you played baseball – the computer would start at your pivot point. It would take all the variables – the schedule played by the college, broken down into individual games, and then it would predict what effect your presence would have made based on your strengths and abilities at the age of eighteen. It would create an alternate path using the cities you would have visited, other students who would have been in your classes, and – of course – incorporating any desires you mentioned during the exploratory session."

"Like if I said I preferred redheads my wife in this new reality would have red hair?"

"Perhaps," Dr. Morrow said. "Or if during exploration it was determined that the woman you married in your real life is your one true love, the computer would find a way to introduce her into your dream life. Everything doesn't have to change just because you picked a different career path."

"So it's not what would have happened," Chase said. "It's what could have happened."

"Exactly," Dr. Morrow told him. "We just give our clients a possibility - preferably one that they will be pleased to explore."

"What if the client isn't pleased to explore the scenario generated by the computer?" Meghan asked.

"Then we can make adjustments to the scenario and let them have the dream again."

"And what is the point of all this?" Chase wanted to know.

"From a clinical standpoint, it can help people with problems. Smokers can visualize the benefits of a life without cigarettes and that gives them added incentive to stop. It can be used on both criminals and their victims, on soldiers who suffer from post combat distress syndrome, and to help people with neuroses to conquer their fears."

"Maybe." Chase was not convinced.

"Definitely," Dr. Morrow insisted. "We've seen great success in our chemical dependency group of test clients. Also victims of violent crimes benefit from the dream therapy. They can relive the horrible moment with a different outcome."

"That sounds like hiding from the truth," Meghan said.

"It might sound that way, but actually it's very therapeutic. It seems to help them let go of the pain from the past and move forward."

Chase shrugged. "If you say so."

"Obviously there is a lot more research that needs to be done to determine the clinical benefits of the therapy, but I have high hopes," Dr. Morrow continued. "However this level of science and technology is not cheap and there is a limit to how much money I can raise from wealthy donors. So I'm shifting gears."

"What gear are you shifting into?" Chase asked suspiciously.

"Commercial," Dr. Morrow replied. "I'm looking to create revenue from the process itself that will fund continued research."

Meghan frowned. "How?"

"I'm hoping that people might find it amusing to take a walk down a different Memory Lane." He winked at his play on words.

"So you want people to pay for the opportunity to dream a different life than the one they actually chose?" Meghan confirmed.

"Yes."

"You want to create a new industry," Chase said. "Recreational dreaming?"

Dr. Morrow nodded.

"It sounds like a hard sale to me," Chase told him. "I wouldn't take drugs and let a computer mess with my mind just to try out an alternate life path."

Dr. Morrow raised an eyebrow. "Then you are a rare man with no regrets. You're sure you made all the right choices."

Chase stared back, silent and maybe even a little angry. "I'm sure there's nothing I can do about any wrong choices I made in my past."

Meghan inserted herself into the awkward moment. "If you could make the cost reasonable and guarantee that there are no negative side-effects, I think there would be a market for your dream therapy. It would be like personalized escapism – watching a fictional movie staring yourself."

Dr. Morrow seemed pleased. "Exactly! And there would be practical applications for healthy, well-adjusted people as well. If a man and woman want to marry they could do dream therapy first – to make sure they are compatible. They could experience years of marriage together before they ever say 'I do'."

"That's amazing," Meghan was fascinated by the possibilities.

Encouraged, Dr. Morrow continued. "If the leader of a country wanted to know if they should start a war with an enemy – he could try it through dream therapy first and make sure the outcome is worth the loss of life before a single shot is fired."

"Think how many senseless wars could be avoided if leaders were given hindsight in advance!" Meghan said with enthusiasm.

Chase looked unhappy. "But the computer can't tell anyone what would happen for sure – it's just a guess."

"A very good guess," Dr. Morrow amended.

"But still a guess," Chase insisted. "So what if the dream indicates that a couple will be unhappy and they don't marry – but really they would have had a long and compatible relationship?"

"We make sure that our clients understand from the beginning that dream therapy is just a tool to help them make life decisions," Dr. Morrow said. "They are all required to participate in counseling before and after their sessions."

"So you already have clients?" Meghan asked. "You've been practicing these techniques on *people*?"

15

"Oh yes," the doctor said. "We've been using human clients for almost three years now."

Meghan's mind was racing with so many questions she wanted to ask, but before she could pose another one, Chase stood.

"Well, it's late and we need to get home," he said.

Dr. Morrow stood as well. "I'm sorry that I kept you so long. When I get talking about my research I have a tendency to get carried away."

Meghan frowned at her husband and then addressed Dr. Morrow. "Your research is fascinating and it was wonderful to meet you."

"I consider myself the fortunate one to have spent the evening with someone both beautiful and intelligent. Your husband is a very lucky man."

"That is one thing we can agree on," Chase said with a semi-smile.

Dr. Morrow insisted on paying for the meal.

So with a grudging, "Thank you," Chase headed toward the door.

Meghan added her thanks and moved to join her husband.

But Dr. Morrow put a hand on her arm to delay her departure. Then he leaned in close and said, "Because of your medical background my research is much more interesting to you than it is to your husband. I would love to show you my research facility and explain my dream technology in depth. Would you come for a tour tomorrow? I could answer any other questions you might have then."

Meghan found that this offer was just too tempting. "I would like to do that," she responded. "I'll have to check my schedule, but I can probably break away for a little while during lunchtime."

He pressed a card into her hand. "Here are several numbers where I can be reached. Just let me know."

"Meghan?" Chase called to her from the door.

His voice had a little edge of annoyance so she smiled at Dr. Morrow and said, "Good night."

Then she hurried to the door with Dr. Morrow's card was clutched tightly in her hand.

***

Meghan slept fitfully, her old recurring nightmare disturbing her sleep. So when she heard her alarm the next morning she groaned, knowing she would pay the price with a day of fighting fatigue.

Chase put his arms around her and pulled her close. Then he whispered in her ear, "Wake up."

"I'm trying."

She smiled as his lips began a journey along her shoulder. "If we don't get up now we won't have time for our morning run."

He continued his kisses. "Then I say we forget the run."

Chapter Two

When Meghan was dressed and ready for work she rushed into the kitchen where Chase had a glass of orange juice and a bagel with cream cheese waiting for her. She sat down on a stool at the island and devoured it gratefully.

"You didn't sleep well last night?" he asked.

She shook her head. "The same old nightmare was back. I hope I didn't keep you awake."

"No," he said thoughtfully. "But maybe you should start going to see your therapist again."

"No, that was a waste of time and money. There's nothing she can do to help me."

He leaned his elbows on the counter across from her and asked, "So, what does your day look like?"

"The usual," she said between bites, "Rounds at the hospital this morning, patients this afternoon, and then a couple of hours at the *Mom*entum clinic before I come home."

"Yep, that sounds pretty usual."

She traced the pattern in the granite and casually added, "I'm thinking that during lunch I might see if Dr. Morrow will give me a tour of his research lab."

Chase's eyes widened in surprise. "You took all that stuff he said last night *seriously?*

"Not completely," she hedged. "But I did find his claims fascinating. If he really can do what he says he can do . . ."

"He can't," Chase said flatly. "It's impossible to change the past, even through dreams."

"Well, I would like to see the lab for myself." She drank the last of her juice. "Do you want to come?"

"I'll be working through lunch today to make up for leaving early yesterday. If you can wait until the weekend I'll go with you then."

She smiled. "You don't want to go anyway. I'll just go by myself today."

He grinned back. "You're right. I don't have any interest in that fancy voodoo doctor. But call me and let me know how it goes."

She promised she would and kissed him goodbye. After he left she called the office number on Dr. Morrow's card. To her surprise, he answered personally.

A little unnerved she said, "This is Meghan Collins." Then afraid that a famous person like Dr. Morrow might not remember her, she added, "My husband and I went to dinner with you last night."

He laughed into the phone. "Good morning, Meghan. Of course I remember dinner last night and I never forget a pretty face."

She blushed like a silly teenager. After clearing her throat, she said, "I would like to come tour your lab today. Would about eleven o'clock be convenient?"

"I will make it convenient," he replied.

They said their goodbyes and she hung up the phone feeling like she was sneaking around on her husband and beholden to Dr. Morrow in some way.

***

Meghan did her rounds at two hospitals before arriving at the pediatric offices where she worked. As usual, her desk was piled with patient files and the phone was ringing insistently. Her assistant, Penelope, followed her into her small office.

"I watched your interview last night!" Penelope said. "You looked great by the way."

"Thanks." Meghan sat down behind the desk.

"And I can't believe Dr. Pierce Morrow was interviewed right after you! Did you get to meet him?"

Meghan nodded. "Chase and I went out to dinner with him."

"Oh!" Penelope cried. "If I had known I would have asked you to get me his autograph."

"I'm going to see him again at lunch. I'll try to get your autograph then. Now, do I have any messages?"

Penelope's eyes widened. "That would be so awesome!" She put several computer generated message slips on the desk. Meghan thumbed through them and divided the slips into two stacks – ones that could be dealt with later and ones that needed to be handled immediately. The immediate stack she kept and the others she gave back to Penelope.

"Show me these again this afternoon."

Penelope nodded absently. "You're going to lunch? With Dr. Morrow?"

"Well, I'm taking a tour of his lab during lunch," Meghan corrected. "Why do you seem so surprised?"

"You've never taken a lunch break in the entire year we've worked together," Penelope explained. "So Dr. Morrow must be as charming as he looks on TV."

"My visit to his lab has nothing to do with his charm," Meghan told her assistant firmly. "It's more like a business meeting. Now let me make these phone calls and then I'll start seeing patients."

Penelope walked out, still looking a little stunned.

Throughout the rest of the morning while Meghan examined patients, her eyes kept straying toward the clock. Time seemed to crawl, but finally the lunch break arrived and it was time for her to leave.

She was taking off her lab coat when Penelope came into her office. "Oh, I was coming to remind you, but I see you didn't need any help being on time to *this* appointment." Penelope eyed the black slacks and gray silk blouse Meghan was wearing. "And we're dressed up too, I see," the assistant teased. "Promise you'll let me know if your gorgeous husband is about to be single again because I want first shot at him."

Meghan didn't try to hide her annoyance. "Chase is definitely not going to be single - ever. And I'm not dressing up for Dr. Morrow. I usually wear scrubs all day because I'm either at the hospital or here or at the clinic. But if I was meeting *anyone* for lunch – I would wear regular clothes. Really Penelope, sometimes your outrageousness goes beyond what is professionally acceptable."

"I'm sorry," Penelope said quickly, and she did look contrite. "I didn't mean to be unprofessional."

21

Meghan knew she'd hurt the girl's feelings and might have even apologized if she hadn't been in such a hurry. But she didn't want to be late for her appointment with Dr. Morrow so she grabbed her handbag from the desk drawer and headed out the door.

***

Dr. Morrow's lab was located on the south side of Atlanta and when Meghan arrived she was surprised. She expected to see a tall, modern building made of glass and steel – stark and a little edgy – like his futuristic research.

But the lab was in an old dentist office made of yellow brick. It was squat, unassuming, and understated to the point of boring. The grounds were simply landscaped with plants that required little maintenance. Despite the unstylish exterior, the building was strangely inviting.

She parked in one of the spaces marked 'visitor' and walked up the sidewalk to a large wooden door. She wasn't sure if she should knock or just go in. She decided to try the knob first. It turned easily under her hand the door swung open.

Meghan stepped inside and looked around. There was nothing old or boring about the interior of the building. It was very modern and immaculate - the type of sterile environment to which she was accustomed. The butterflies in her stomach disappeared. She was on familiar ground.

Meghan was welcomed by a very professional receptionist and invited to sit on one of the chairs in the small lobby. She was kept waiting only a few minutes and then Dr. Morrow himself came out to greet her. He was as handsome in a white lab coat as he had been in his suit the night before. He greeted her warmly and then took her on a quick tour of the facility.

"Our first stop," Dr. Morrow told her, "is a room where a client is undergoing a dream session."

Meghan felt a little like a voyeur as she watched a middle-aged woman on a hospital bed in a darkened room. The client was sleeping peacefully. An IV pole was near her head with a bag constantly dripping fluids into her body. ECG electrodes were visible on her upper chest. A woman dressed in scrubs was checking the vital sign monitors that glowed in the dim light.

"At least one member of our staff is always with clients when they are dreaming," he told Meghan. He kept his voice low as if they could disturb the sleeping woman through the thick glass window separated them. "We want them to relax and trust that they are being well cared for. If the client chooses, a family member or friend can be present also. And if the client exhibits any signs of distress we wake them immediately."

"How long do your clients dream?"

"The times vary," he replied. "Twenty-four hours is our maximum limit. I personally believe that a person would be safe much longer but want to err on side of safety."

"And how do they feel when they wake up?"

"They feel very relaxed and rested."

"No one ever hates the experience?" she asked.

"Out of approximately two thousand clinical tests not one person has hated the experience," he confirmed. "The only complaint we've had is that some of our clients didn't want to leave their dream."

She smiled. "I guess that's a good complaint – if there is such a thing."

He nodded. "Leaving your customers wanting more is definitely a good thing – from a marketing standpoint at least."

"I can see how dream therapy could be interesting and maybe even helpful – in a controlled environment with mentally stable people who can separate reality and dreams."

He smiled. "Yes, that would be the optimum conditions." Then he waved for her to follow him. "Let's continue the tour." He showed her a large computer room, a medical lab, a pharmacy, a laundry and what he called a cafeteria but looked more like a five-star restaurant with floor-length tablecloths, fresh flower arrangements, and soft music.

He stopped there and said, "I'll bet you're hungry. I happen to know you didn't eat much of your dinner last night."

"I am hungry," she admitted.

"Then let's continue our discussion over lunch. I have a wonderful chef here."

The smells coming from the cafeteria, dominated by freshly-baked bread, swayed her. "I can't stay much longer, but I would love some lunch."

23

They walked inside and he helped her navigate the various food options. She chose a Caesar salad with breadsticks for her main course and let Dr. Morrow talk her into a little chocolate mousse for dessert. He led her to a quiet table in the corner of the room that faced a peaceful courtyard out back.

Then while they ate she said, "You received your Nobel Prize for your research in sleep deprivation. What made you change your focus to dreams?"

"I've always been fascinated with dreams," he replied. "Why we dream, the significance of dreams, and if it's possible to interpret them. My entire life has been dedicated in one way or another to their study. That is what fuels all of this." He waved to encompass the complex.

"It is an amazing facility," she said.

"That means a lot coming from you – since you're Woman of the Year and your *Mom*entum clinic is state-of-the-art."

It was unnerving to realize that he had researched the clinic and, no doubt, Meghan herself.

"I do love the modern technology we have available at the clinic, but I regret winning that award. It has been a constant source of distraction. Maybe I should try your dream therapy and reset my life to the time before I won and then withdraw my name from consideration."

He smiled. "You don't need dream therapy for that, but perhaps you have other questions and the answers are only a dream away."

She stared back at him uneasily. "I prefer working things out while I'm awake."

"But some things can only be worked out in dreams," he said. "If you're concerned about the safety of this technology, I told you my procedures have been in the testing phase for years. We have copious amounts of data. There are no negative health effects. However up to this point we have depended on paid clients, so most of people we tested have been poor, often with chemical abuse problems in their past or present. Some were not even emotionally stable – and as you pointed out – to reach optimum success, we need our clients to be healthy mentally as well as physically. So now we want to test a more normal segment of society – not just desperate people who will do anything for money."

"That sounds like you've been taking advantage of the underprivileged."

"Believe me, Meghan, these people do a lot worse things for money than what I asked – to come into my lab and dream about a better life."

She had to concede this point. "I suppose that's true. But I'm uncomfortable with the idea of experimenting on people who can't adequately judge the consequences associated with what they have agreed to."

"I respect your reservations and in a perfect world I would have other options. But I had to work with what was available to me. And these people were both treated and paid well."

"I don't like it but I do understand the necessity," she admitted.

He smiled. "That's the scientist in you. I've got a DVD showing before and after interviews with some of our clients and I think you'll be quite impressed by the difference the therapy has made in their lives."

Meghan checked her watch. "I'd like to watch it, but I start seeing patients soon so I can't stay . . ."

He waved this concern aside. "I'll send a DVD home with you. Just promise me you won't show it to anyone except your husband and that you'll return it soon. As with any new technology we're vulnerable to thieves."

"I won't show it to anyone except Chase and I'll bring it back to you soon," Meghan promised.

The doctor seemed pleased. "Now before you leave, I want to mention one more thing. I told you last night that I'm anxious for this incredible technology to start paying for itself. And that's where I can use your help."

"You want me to make a donation?" she guessed.

"No," he said slowly. "I want you to try the procedure – representing the emotionally healthy, intelligent and able to pay sector of society."

Meghan laughed. "Even if I wanted to try your dream therapy, which I don't, I haven't got the time. I usually work eighty hours a week – so I can't invest twenty-four hours of my scarce leisure time in dreaming of how things could have been – especially since I love my life as it is now!"

"Twenty-four hours is the maximum," Dr. Morrow said. "You could do less time."

"Is dream-time equivalent to real-time?"

"Oh no," Dr. Morrow replied. "During a twenty-four hour period of dream-time the average client covers almost a year in their alternate life."

"A whole year?" Meghan was intrigued even though she didn't want to be.

"In your dreams you don't sleep, you rarely eat or shower or change clothes or get caught in traffic. The brain edits out the minutia of life – so time passes quickly."

"I see."

"If you wanted to dream for only one hour you could probably cover two to three weeks in dream-time. Surely even someone as busy as you are could spare one hour in the name of science."

It was true. She could spare an hour. And although she knew she was being manipulated by the charming Dr. Morrow, his research really did appeal to her on a very personal level. "There are no negative affects?"

"Not in years of testing."

"I would still keep all my memories and be able to distinguish between what was real and what happened in the dream?"

"You absolutely would," he assured her. "The dreams are very vivid and you may want to believe in the dream, but the second you wake up you'll know you're back to reality."

"If I did decide to try the therapy for just an hour," Meghan said cautiously. "What would I have to do?"

"Well, the first thing would be to choose a pivot point. It can be something inconsequential or it can have life-changing implications. That part is up to you."

"So once I had a pivotal moment in mind – then what?"

"You'll meet with a research specialist who will get all the background information. The specialist will enter your memories into the computer, along with all the historical and geographical data and the computer will create your dream. Then we'll set up a time for you to come in for your actual dream session."

"It would have to be on a Saturday so I wouldn't miss work."

"Of course. In fact, that would be ideal."

"And in my one hour session I will cover about two weeks of dream-time?"

"It's different for each person, so I can't guarantee you a time frame. I believe it is because some people dream in more detail than others. For instance, I am a detailed dreamer and one hour of dream time would only cover about a week for me."

"So you've participated in the dream therapy?"

"I wouldn't ask my clients to try something I hadn't experienced myself."

"May I ask what your pivot point was?"

"You may." For the first time since she'd met him the doctor seemed to drop his charming, sales-pitch manner and became more genuine. "It's very personal, but if you agree to participate in this clinical test you will be providing us with a great deal of personal information as well. If I expect you to trust me – I must trust you."

Meghan nodded.

"My wife died ten years ago in a car accident. My pivotal moment is that morning when we were leaving home. Instead of letting her drive her car in my dream I took her to work."

"And avoided the wreck."

He nodded. "So in my dream version of life she is still alive."

"Still?"

"I update my personal data frequently and the computer keeps generating continuations of my dream life. I limit myself to one session a month and only for one hour," he told her. "It's the purest form of escapism – like reading a good fiction book. I know my dream is not real, but that doesn't keep me from enjoying every moment of it."

"And how will you feel when, or if, you can't dream about her anymore?"

"Then I'll grieve again, but I'll survive. Just like I did when she died."

Meghan checked her watch again. Startled by how quickly time had passed, she pushed back her chair and stood. "I'm sorry to rush off, but I really have to get back to work."

He stood as well. "So, will you try a dream session?"

"It's interesting and I might be willing to do an hour session. I'll talk to Chase and let you know."

"I'll be waiting anxiously to hear from you." He handed her a copy of the DVD and they started for the door.

Then Meghan stopped and said, "One more thing."

"Anything," he offered magnanimously.

She smiled. "Can I get your autograph? My assistant is a big fan of yours."

***

Throughout her busy afternoon, Meghan found her mind drifting back to Dr. Morrow and his research. She couldn't help wondering if it would work. Could the combination of technologies he'd described really direct her, in dreams, along an alternate life course? And if it was possible, would it be wise to know how things could have been?

As she drove home well after dark, she rehearsed in her mind what she would say to Chase. She wanted to tell him everything she'd learned and convince him that trying the dream-therapy would be at the worst harmless and at the most fun. But she knew that no matter what Chase said, she was going to do it. The draw of the 'possible' was too strong. She was pretty sure Dr. Morrow knew that she wouldn't be able to resist. And there is no doubt in her mind what her pivot point would be.

Chapter Three

Chase had Chinese takeout on the kitchen table when she got home. They fixed their plates and then she convinced him to watch the DVD Dr. Morrow had given her while they ate. It was divided into three sections – one for each of three test clients. They were interviewed before their dream sessions – all pretty sad characters. Dr. Morrow was the guide on the DVD, just as he had been for her at his lab earlier that day. He led the viewer to the dream therapy room and explained the set up.

Next were interviews with each of the clients at the end of their sessions, describing their dreams. As Dr. Morrow had promised, they all considered the experience very positive.

After a brief interlude with Dr. Morrow detailing all the precautions and client-counseling that was built into his dream-therapy, the DVD showed the three clients months later. They were well-groomed and looking into the camera with clear eyes.

Then the last part was a series of short clips with the clients praising the therapy and giving Dr. Morrow credit for helping them to break out of the cycle of defeat and make something of their lives. The whole thing was well done and after seeing it, Meghan was positive that she wanted to try the therapy.

Chase seemed less enthusiastic. "Well, that was interesting," he said as he cleared away their empty food containers.

"It's more than interesting," Meghan disagreed. "It's fascinating."

"I'm going to get myself another bottle of water," Chase said. "You want one?"

"No thanks." When he returned from the kitchen she said, "So you really don't think much of Dr. Morrow's dream therapy?"

"Not much." He sat on the couch and draped one arm across her shoulders. "He struck me as kind of a nut."

She smiled. "He's intense – but most people who believe strongly in something are. His lab is very impressive and he's got years of data to back up his research." She waved toward the television. "And real people giving testimonials."

"He paid those people to say that stuff," Chase said. "Which means they are far from credible witnesses."

"Thank you, Mr. Assistant District Attorney."

He took a long swig of water. "Never say I spent all those years in law school for nothing."

For the next several days Meghan was plagued with nightmares. She watched the DVD repeatedly and researched Dr. Morrow on the Internet. Finally on Sunday night while Chase was watching TV she told him that she was going to return the DVD to Dr. Morrow the next day.

"Good," he said. "I'm tired of you watching it over and over. I'll be glad when you forget all about him and his crazy dream therapy."

She cleared her throat. "Actually, I think I'm going to do it."

"Do what?"

"The dream therapy," she replied. "This Saturday if possible."

Chase sat up straight and turned off the television. "You're kidding."

"No, I'm completely serious."

"You're going to let that quack mess with your mind?"

"He's not a quack and he won't be messing with my mind. He'll just be manipulating an hour-long dream. There is quite a difference. "

Chase shook his head. "I can't believe you'd even consider it."

"I've done a lot of research on Dr. Morrow. He's well-respected and his lab is state of the art. I've watched the DVD several times and, well, I trust him."

"Well, I don't," Chase said.

"You understand the premise of directed-dreaming, right? I get to pick a pivotal moment in my life and then see what would have happened if I'd made a different choice." She looked away not quite able to meet his eyes as she continued. "I have lived with it for ten years. Time hasn't helped, therapy hasn't helped, and working myself to death for other people's children hasn't helped. Maybe this will help."

His lips were pressed together – not angry, but upset. "And what if it doesn't? What if you do this crazy dream therapy and it doesn't help at all?"

"Then I'll be no worse off than I am now."

"I strongly advise against it," he said in his best lawyer tone.

She nodded. "I know."

"But if you've made up your mind, I'll go with you and watch over your unconscious body while Dr. Morrow plants computer-generated dreams in your mind."

She turned in his arms and held him close. "Thank you for your support. It means so much to me."

He stroked her hair. "You're welcome, I guess."

She laughed, relieved now that this final hurdle had been cleared. And she already had an alternate plan, involving her best friend since elementary school.

"I appreciate your willingness to sit with me during the session, but I think your negative energy might taint the results. So I'll get Caldwell to go."

He didn't object. "Just one hour on Saturday?"

"Yes, if it can be arranged that quickly."

Chase stood and walked into the kitchen to throw his water bottle away. "The sooner you get it over with so we can move on with real life, the better."

***

The next morning Meghan called Dr. Morrow while she was driving to the hospital. He was pleased with her decision to try the dream therapy and arranged for her to come in after work to get the process started.

"If you'll give me your fax number at work I'll send over some release forms so we can get your medical records. Then we'll tentatively plan on Saturday for your session but there is a lot to do before then so they might have to wait a week."

"I hope not. I hate suspense."

He laughed. "We'll go as quickly as we can – but I won't jeopardize the quality of your dream by rushing."

Reluctantly she had to admit that no matter how anxious she wanted to try the dream-therapy – she did not want to sacrifice dream-quality.

The day was busy with little or no time to think beyond the immediate needs of her patients. But finally it was time to leave and she rushed to Dr. Morrow's office with a sense of anticipation she hadn't felt in years.

She was taken into a room that looked more cozy than clinical. A research specialist, who introduced herself as Ms. Jernigan, was seated behind a desk. She told Meghan to make herself comfortable on the large leather recliner that dominated the small room.

Feeling like she was lying on the couch in a psychiatrist's office, Meghan did as she was asked.

Ms. Jernigan said, "Most of our clients find it easier to remember things with clarity if they lean back and close their eyes."

Meghan settled into the chair and closed her eyes. Then they began the initial interview. Ms. Jernigan already had a lot of information on her including her medical history and a detailed biography.

"What I need for you to do is fill in memories along your lifeline as I prompt you," Ms Jernigan said. "Even if these memories are not specifically related to your pivot point they will help us prepare your dream."

"That's fine," Meghan agreed to these terms.

"Then I'll begin with your childhood. Tell me about your parents."

"My parents were older when they had me – in their early forties. My father is a heart surgeon and my mother is a professor at Emory University. I'm an only child."

"Tell me your first memory."

Meghan complied, describing her second birthday. At first it was unnerving to be asked so many personal questions, but Ms. Jernigan was very businesslike and soon Meghan relaxed.

They moved through her childhood with Ms. Jernigan asking leading questions and Meghan providing the answers in more detail than she had expected. Eventually they arrived at the present day. Then the research specialist asked if she had identified a pivotal moment.

Meghan's mouth felt dry. "Yes."

"How old were you?"

"Eighteen."

The researcher made a notation on her laptop. "Up to this point you have been telling me what you could remember generally. Now that we have your pivot point we are going to get very specific. I am going to try and pull out every tiny memory associated with this time. It may be tedious – it may even be painful. But you must tell me everything. It will help us create a realistic dream for you."

Meghan nodded. "I understand."

"Tell me about your pivot point, please – everything you can remember. I will interrupt with questions if I need more detail. And if you mention names please give me their relationship to you, if any."

Meghan nodded again. Her nervousness had returned.

"Go ahead," Ms. Jernigan encouraged. "I'm ready."

"I told you already that I started dating Joey Patrone during my senior year."

Ms. Jernigan nodded. "He didn't live in your school district but came to your private high school on a football scholarship, correct?"

"Yes, his family lived in Old Mountain, a small rural community a few miles east of Atlanta. His father, Troy, owned a construction business with his two brothers as partners. His mother was a stay-at-home mom. He had three brothers, all younger. They weren't poor, but they could not have afforded for Joey to go to Meadowbrook without the scholarship."

"So you and Joey started dating during your senior year," Ms. Jernigan prompted.

"He actually started at Meadowbrook in the tenth grade but we weren't friends until our senior year when we were matched up as partners in AP Physics."

"And then you started dating?"

"Yes." Meghan cleared her throat. "My parents aren't exactly snobbish, but they are very well-educated and they have money and I'm their only child . . . They wanted the best for me and Joey didn't fit into their plans. They discouraged me from dating him but when they realized that I couldn't be dissuaded, they endured his presence. But they never really accepted him."

"Joey wanted their approval. He tried to convince them that he could be the kind of man they wanted for me. Of course no matter what he did he couldn't impress them. We had been accepted to different colleges so they hoped that once we were apart geographically, an emotional separation would follow. Then just after graduation I found out I was pregnant."

Ms. Jernigan didn't comment, but kept quietly typing into her laptop.

"Since my parents had never been very happy about my relationship with Joey, I knew they would be extremely upset about a teenage pregnancy. I had a scholarship to Vanderbilt – my father's alma mater. Joey had an athletic scholarship to play football at Georgia State and he wanted to be the first member of his family to graduate from college."

"But now our dreams were at risk and I didn't know what to do. I kept the news to myself for a few days, but I finally I realized I had to talk to Joey. It was his problem too. So I asked him to meet me at the football stadium. We were sitting on the bleachers, looking down at the field where he'd been a high school star, when I told him."

"Was that your pivotal point?" Ms. Jernigan asked.

"No. I'm still setting the scene."

"That's fine," the researcher said. "The more details we have the better."

"Joey was shocked, of course. He said he'd have to think about it and we would talk more the next day. He didn't want me to tell anyone until we'd come up with a plan, but when I got home my parents could tell I'd been crying. They asked me what was wrong and, well, I told them."

"They didn't over-react the way I expected," Meghan continued. "They listened and then calmly began discussing the options. So by the time Joey got to our house the next day – it was all settled. I would have an abortion and our lives would go on just like we'd planned."

"He reminded them that he was Catholic and didn't believe in abortion. They reminded him that he was not the one who was pregnant. I sat there in silence and let them discuss me and my future. Finally Joey said he had another plan. He held out his fist." She paused and pressed her hand against her trembling lips. "Slowly he opened it and resting on his palm was a wedding band."

She took a deep breath. "Both my parents laughed and I did too, a little. They said it was ridiculous and I had to agree. We had scholarships to different schools – in different states. We could not be married under those circumstances, let alone raise a child. I'll never forget the look on Joey's face. He was humiliated and embarrassed and furious and desperate. 'I'll take care of you!' he promised. 'I'll give up my scholarship and get a job until you're through with school. I can take night classes or something. We'll make it work. Please!' he begged me."

Meghan took a deep breath. "At that point my father stepped between us and told him to go. He called out my name wanting me to side with him. He wanted me to tell my parents to, well, leave us alone. But how could I do that? How could I trust an eighteen year old kid to provide for me and a baby?" She sat up straight, wringing her hands. "So I didn't say anything. His shoulders slumped in defeat. He allowed my father to push him to the door. But just as he stepped outside he called to me, 'Please Meg – don't kill our baby!'"

She paused for another breath. "That was the last time I ever saw him. I don't know what happened to him because he would never speak to me again. I had the abortion and went to Vanderbilt for my undergraduate degree and then I was accepted into their medical school. I finished near the top of my class and had my choice of internships. I chose Children's Hospital in Atlanta so I could be near my parents."

Meghan forced herself to continue. "Sometimes while I was in college I watched Georgia State football games, but I never saw Joey or heard his name announced. So I don't know if he kept his scholarship there or not. After medical school I met and married Chase Collins. I have a great job and run a clinic for teenage mothers. I have a full, happy life, but I am haunted by that one decision I made. Was it the right thing to do? Or was it a choice I made just because I was so young and was I overly influenced by my parents? I don't blame myself or them. But often I think about how old the baby would be – how different my life would be. And now I just want to know."

Meghan stopped talking, thankful her disclosures were finally over.

Ms. Jernigan nodded. "This is good. The more compelling the memory the more vivid the dream will be. Now we're going to go back and I want you to tell me what the kitchen looked like – every detail you can remember. What everyone was wearing, that kind of thing. I'll pull some pictures off the internet, but if you have any old photographs of yourself and the other people involved from this time period – that will help as well. What you can't remember we'll fill in with things that logically could have been – since you don't remember them anyway it won't negatively affect your dream."

Meghan garnered her strength, closed her eyes, and pictured herself in her parents' kitchen nearly ten years before. And then she began describing it all.

***

When the session with the research specialist ended Meghan felt drained, almost like she'd experienced the whole terrible ordeal all over again. She was surprised to see that it was nearly nine o'clock – which meant she'd talked about the past for almost two hours.

As she walked down the hallway toward the front entrance she saw Dr. Morrow waiting for her by the big wooden door.

"I thought you would have gone home long before now," she said to him.

36

He smiled. "There are many nights when I don't go home at all. You know how it is to be married to your work."

She frowned. "I am *married* to my husband. I am *dedicated* to my work."

Dr. Morrow didn't argue the point. "I looked through the data we've collected and I was able to listen to part of your interview with Ms. Jernigan. I think your dream session is going to be very realistic."

Meghan's heart beat a little faster but she tried to sound casual as she replied, "I hope so."

"If we have any questions we'll call you," Dr. Morrow said. "Otherwise, we'll see you on Saturday morning."

"Eight o'clock?" she confirmed unnecessarily.

He nodded. "Your life will never be the same again."

***

There was no dinner waiting when Meghan walked into the condo that night. Chase usually got home first so even though no specific assignment had been made, it was understood between them that he handled dinner. Sometimes he cooked and sometimes he picked up takeout on his way home. But he always had a meal ready to eat when she got home. So the dark kitchen spoke volumes. He was too mature to pout and too refined to argue. Apparently, however, he wasn't above making her get her own dinner when she had annoyed him.

Two years of marriage had taught her how to handle Chase when he was in a mood – she just didn't acknowledge it. Walking into the living room where he was watching television, she leaned over the back of the couch and kissed his neck.

"Miss me?" she whispered.

"You're late," he responded. "Even for you."

"What did you have for dinner?" she asked.

"Cereal," he replied.

"Mmmm, sounds good." She walked into the kitchen and flipped on every light. Then she made a big production of getting out a bowl, choosing which cereal she would have, pouring it into the bowl, and finally dousing it with skim milk.

37

Chase tried to ignore her but eventually gave up and came into the kitchen.

He pulled out a stool and sat down beside her. "So, how did it go at Dr. Morrow's lab tonight?"

"Good," she answered in between bites of Frosted Mini-Wheats. "I told them everything I could remember about my pivot point. They'll do whatever it is they do with all the data and be ready to help me dream on Saturday morning."

"Did you talk to Caldwell?"

Meghan nodded. "She's coming with me."

"And you're sure you don't want to back out?" Chase asked. "It's not too late."

"I don't want to back out. I'm very anxious to try the dream therapy."

"And what is it that you hope to gain from this exercise in … fantasy?"

"Closure, I guess," she said. "Peace."

He shook his head. "You're disturbing the peace you've already gained, peeling away years of healing, like ripping off the new skin that's grown over a deep wound."

Chase was not insensitive – just excessively logical. It was perhaps his only negative trait. There was nothing she could do to change what had happened years before so to him it made no sense to agonize over it. She wished that it was possible for her to discard the past and the pain that came with it, but she'd been trying for ten years without success.

"I don't really expect it to work," she admitted. "But if I don't give it a chance, I'll always wonder."

He nodded. "I can't say I understand, but if it's important to you, I won't complain."

She covered his hand with hers. "And after Saturday it will all be over."

***

On Saturday morning, Meghan picked Caldwell up at seven-thirty and they drove together to Dr. Morrow's lab.

"Are you sure you don't want to take my car?" Caldwell offered. "You may not feel like driving after the session."

38

"I'd rather take my car," Meghan replied. "But you can drive home if I'm groggy afterward."

Caldwell settled herself into the passenger seat, tucking her zebra print skirt around her artificially tanned legs. Her tank top was neon pink and a matching scarf was tied around her head like a pirate. Gold stilettos completed the ensemble. Since her father was a negligent multi-millionaire, Caldwell had always had too much money and not enough supervision. She was always on the cutting edge of the latest fashion trends. Based on her attire, apparently 'hooker' was in.

"Are you nervous?" she asked.

"A little," Meghan admitted. "This is going to sound crazy, but I feel like I'm actually going to see Joey again. That's what I'm nervous about. Not the safety of the procedure itself. I have confidence in Dr. Morrow."

Caldwell chewed a pink fingernail, destroying what was certainly an expensive manicure. "It does sound crazy. Most girls would kill to have a husband like Chase and you're risking your marriage over a teenage romance."

"I'm not risking my marriage," Meghan objected. "Chase supports me completely. I just want to work through some feelings I have about the aborted pregnancy – not about Joey."

"You can't have one without the other," Caldwell muttered.

It was different this time when she arrived at the lab. Before she had been an interested observer, a fellow medical professional investigating Dr. Morrow's research. Today she was a patient, a dream-therapy client. She wasn't sure if she was comfortable with this new role, but she knew she could not turn back now. For so many years she'd wondered how her life would have been if she'd made a different choice. And because of Dr. Morrow, soon she would know.

She led Caldwell in through the big wooden door. There was no receptionist at the desk in the lobby, but a bell rang, alerting the staff of their arrival. A beautiful Asian woman dressed in hospital scrubs joined them almost immediately.

"Hello, I'm Heidi," she said. "And I will be your technician today."

"It's nice to meet you, Heidi," Meghan said. "This is my friend, Caldwell St. James."

To Heidi's credit, she didn't react at the sight of Caldwell in her streetwalker attire. "Follow me please." Then she led them into a room similar to the one Meghan had seen during her tour. It looked like a nice hotel room with wood cabinets that housed most of the medical equipment, soft drapes and a couple of Monet prints on the wall. It was uncomfortably cold and for this Heidi apologized.

"The low temperature is necessary for the equipment. Dr. Collins, you will be warm once we get you into the bed. And I can get a blanket for your friend if she'd like one."

"Her friend would definitely like a blanket," Caldwell said.

"Do I need to change into a hospital gown or something?" Meghan asked.

"No, since it's only an hour session you can stay in your street clothes. Just take off your shoes and any jewelry."

After removing her shoes, Meghan handed Caldwell her watch and her wedding rings.

"I hope this isn't this symbolic," Caldwell murmured, staring at the rings.

"Just don't lose them, please." Then she stretched out on the bed and Heidi pulled a blanket up over her. The mattress was the perfect firmness and heated. Meghan snuggled down into it – enjoying the sheer comfort.

Caldwell was rubbing her arms to keep from freezing.

Meghan laughed. "I'm sorry they don't have a heated bed for you too."

"Not as sorry as I am," Caldwell replied.

Heidi pulled a blanket out of the closet and handed it to Caldwell. She immediately draped it over her shivering shoulders.

Then Heidi turned her attention to Meghan. She started the IV, pasted electrodes on her chest. She put a sensor on her finger to monitor temperature and a blood pressure cuff around her upper arm. Meghan watched the procedures with detachment. It was odd to be the patient.

Once Heidi was finished prepping for the session, Dr. Morrow came in. He leaned over Meghan and asked, "Are you ready?"

She took a deep breath and nodded. "I am."

He smiled. "Sweet dreams." Then to Heidi he said, "Start the drip."

Meghan closed her eyes, unsure of what to expect. At first she had to struggle to keep her eyes closed. She heard all the conversation around her – Caldwell talking to Heidi, Heidi talking to Dr. Morrow. She heard the beeping of monitors and the whoosh of the cold air circulating.

Then gradually the sounds lost their distinction and became just a combined clamor. She no longer had to fight to keep her eyes closed. There was a feeling of weightlessness that she attributed to the glove-like, heated bed. She experienced a moment of dizziness – as if she'd stood up too fast. Then she opened her eyes.

Chapter Four

Meghan's arms were resting on the cool marble countertop of the breakfast bar in her parents' kitchen. Her mother was haranguing Joey. For a few seconds she couldn't pay attention to what was being said. She was too busy absorbing the sight of him. Tall and muscular, he was wearing a polo shirt and a pair of khaki pants – his version of dressing up – in honor of the occasion. His dark hair was too long and curling around his ears. His brown eyes were earnest and afraid.

Her mother's voice broke into her reverie. "There is no excuse in this day and age for an unplanned pregnancy! So if you thought you were ready for an adult relationship with my daughter, why didn't you have the sense to use protection?"

Joey flushed with embarrassment. "I know this is going to sound stupid . . ."

"I'm quite sure of that," her mother predicted.

Joey tried again, "Its old fashioned and maybe even unrealistic, but we were planning to wait until we get married. We didn't mean for it to happen. That's why we weren't prepared."

Her mother's smirk eloquently expressed how she felt about this. "Well, there's nothing we can do about that now. At this point a medical miscarriage is the only sensible solution to the problem."

Meghan couldn't see Joey's face – since her father had moved to stand between them – but she could see his fist clenched tight and knew he hated this plan.

"I'm Catholic, Mrs. Dunaway," Joey said, as if this was news. "Abortion is a mortal sin."

"And what about sex before marriage," her mother shot back. "That didn't seem to bother you!"

"It's a sin," Joey admitted. "But not mortal."

"Let's keep religion out of this," her father said.

"My religion is part of who I am," Joey insisted. "I can't leave it out."

"You don't even go to church," her mother dismissed this. "And you're not the one who is pregnant!"

"I'm the baby's father," Joey said with admirable poise.

"There is no baby!" her mother said. "And there won't be – not now."

"But there's another way to handle the situation." Joey stood, so brave, even though she knew her parents intimidated him under the best of circumstances, and this was far from the best.

He held out his closed fist and slowly relaxed his fingers. There in the middle of his calloused palm lay a little gold ring. He stepped to the side so he could look into her eyes. "Marry me, Meg," he said.

Her parents laughed. Not the funny kind of laugh – the cruel, mocking variety. "You can't be serious."

"I am," he said without taking his eyes off of Meghan.

She heard the tremor in his voice. He needed her support to continue his stand against them.

She felt like she might throw up. There was so much tension in the room - so much anger. She wanted to please her parents. She wanted to support Joey. But mostly she wanted to make the right choice for all of them. It was the biggest decision of her life and she didn't feel old enough or qualified in any way.

Her father said, "One of you would have to give up your scholarship."

"I'll give up mine," Joey said. "We'll move to Nashville. I'll take night classes and watch the baby while Meghan goes to school."

"How will you feed your family?" her father asked.

"I'll get a job."

"When are you going to work if you're babysitting and taking classes at night?" her mother demanded.

Joey ran his fingers through his hair. "I'll work on weekends."

Her mother changed tactics. "And you expect Meghan to take on a rigorous class schedule while she's pregnant?"

"I'll help her as much as I can."

"No, no, no!" her mother yelled. Then she turned to face Meghan. "This is the wrong time in your life for motherhood. Someday, after college and careers you can have a child. But not now."

Joey pushed the long dark hair that had fallen onto his forehead back in a nervous gesture. "It's not the best timing, I admit. But I'll figure out something. I'll do whatever I have to."

"You've done quite enough," her mother assured him. "Now I'd like for you to go."

"Meg?" His eyes captured hers.

Her parents turned in unison and fixed Meghan with a stare so strong it seemed to hold her in place.

She tore her eyes from them and focused on the little circle of gold resting on Joey's palm. Then using every ounce of strength she possessed, she walked over to him.

"We'll have our baby. The rest will work out." Afraid she wouldn't be able to stand against another onslaught from her parents, she pulled him to the door.

"No!" her mother cried. "You can't throw your life away!"

"If you walk out of here now, do not expect any help from us, young lady," her father threatened.

Meghan didn't trust her voice so she just nodded and kept walking.

Joey held back, like he thought there was something he could say that would bring her parents onboard with his plan. Meghan knew better. She tugged hard on his hand and finally he went along with her.

"I can't believe you're doing this to us." Her mother's voice followed them, full of anguish.

Meghan wavered with her hand hovering over the knob on the back door. Joey, sensing her uncertainty, turned the knob himself. Then they stepped outside. Birds were singing and a fragrant breeze was blowing – oblivious to the heart-wrenching scene that had taken place inside the house.

Joey led her across the stone patio, past the swimming pool and over to the driveway where his old truck was parked. They walked around to the passenger side and Meghan waited for him to open the door for her. But when the truck was blocking them from the view of anyone watching from the house, Joey dropped down on one knee.

She'd never seen him cry before, even when the football team he quarterbacked lost in the state championship game or when his grandfather died. But as he knelt on the driveway she could see tears glittering in his beautiful brown eyes.

"Your parents were right," he began. "I haven't been looking out for you like I should. I put what I wanted first and didn't think about the consequences for you. I promise I won't do that again."

"Oh Joey." She wiped at the tears that blurred her own vision.

"I don't have much to offer you now. Just my name and my love and my promise that if you'll marry me I'll try hard to keep you from regretting it. So will you, Meg? Will you marry me, please?"

She leaned down and pressed her cheek against his. Their tears mingled as she whispered, "I'm scared."

"Me too." He turned his head so that their lips were touching and kissed her gently. Then he reminded her, "I've asked you a question and I'm waiting for an answer."

"I'll marry you," she said. "I guess I have to -- now that I've walked out on my parents they'll probably never speak to me again." She smiled to pretend like this was funny.

"They would take you back in a second," Joey said seriously. "This is a big decision and you need to be sure. I want us to be married – and not just because of the baby – but because I love you. I didn't think it would be now, but I'm not sorry. I want you, Meg, forever."

New tears flooded her eyes. "I want you too."

He slipped the ring on her finger. "Then we're engaged."

She stared at the ring, simple yet beautiful – much like Joey himself. "Where did you get this?"

"It's my mom's," he said as he opened the truck's door. "She loaned it to me."

Meghan's heart pounded. "Then your parents know?"

He nodded and helped her up onto the seat. "They're at the house, waiting to talk about it."

Meghan stared out the dusty windshield as he started the truck. She dreaded the meeting with Joey's parents. Not that it could be worse than the one with hers – but this time she would be the outsider. The one everybody wanted to blame.

But instead of going straight to his house, he stopped by the old cottage where his grandparents had lived when they were alive. It was where they had stopped after the senior prom. Where they had foolishly and irresponsibly become parents-to-be. She thought he had similar ideas again and shook her head.

"Not now," she said. "Not right before I face your parents for the first time like this." She waved a hand vaguely toward her midsection.

"I just want to talk for a few minutes." He came around and opened the door. Then he lifted her to the ground. He did kiss her, but it was a gentle, reassuring kiss, not a passionate one that might lead them in a direction she was determined not to go.

They walked inside and sat on the wooden chairs arranged around the scarred kitchen table. She kept her eyes averted from the bedrooms.

He took a piece of paper from his pocket and spread it out on the table. Across the top of it he had written *Our Goals*.

She looked up at him, waiting for an explanation.

"We've disappointed both our parents."

This simple confirmation of the facts was not surprising, but even though she was prepared for it, the knowledge that Joey's parents were unhappy with them hurt.

"But starting today we're not going to measure ourselves by anyone else's expectations," he continued. "We're going to set our own goals and nobody is going to make us feel bad about who we are and what we accomplish. Okay?"

She nodded a little uncertainly. "Okay."

He wrote the number 'one' at the top of the page and then looked at her. "So what is our first goal?"

Clutching her hands together in her lap, she said, "We'll be good parents."

He recorded this on the paper in his sloppy, teenage-boy handwriting. Then he added goal number two. "We'll both graduate from college."

She nodded. "What's number 'three'?"

"Someday we'll have a home of our own." He wrote this down. "I'm not promising anything as nice as what your parents have – but a place where we can be comfortable."

"What about playing college football?" she asked. "That's important to you so it should be on the list."

He shook his head. "Whether I play football or not won't decide if our lives are a success."

They were quiet for a few minutes, thinking.

Finally he said, "Once you graduate from college you can go on to medical school and become a doctor."

She shook her head. "That's like you playing football. It isn't something that will determine success or failure."

His eyes grew warm. "You're right."

"I think our last goal should be that we stick together – no matter what."

His hand trembled a little as he wrote this down. Then he rummaged in the kitchen drawers until he found a nail and affixed their list to the wall over the fireplace. "Now it's official," he said. "If we can accomplish these four things – we'll consider our lives a success – even if nobody else thinks so."

She walked over to stand beside him. He put his arm around her shoulders and they looked at their list of goals together. "It won't be easy."

"But we can do it." He turned and pulled her close. After a few kisses he asked breathlessly, "Are you sure you don't want to stay here for awhile instead of going to see my parents?"

Gently she pushed him away. "I'm sure. Everything is serious from now on, Joey."

He sighed. "I know."

As they walked out of the house she felt a little better, a little more confident. They weren't just two kids anymore. They were future parents and they had goals.

***

It was almost lunchtime when they pulled up at his parents' house. The Patrones' house was not in a carefully laid out subdivision. It was surrounded by acres of tall grass. Heavy construction equipment was parked haphazardly in the front yard beside stacks of wood and pipe and cinderblocks.

The interior of the house was nice but always a little cluttered. Joey's mom, Paula, wasn't a bad housekeeper but she wasn't obsessively neat like Meghan's mother. And the differences between Paula Patrone and Meghan's mother, Suzanne, didn't end there. Suzanne was thin and stylish. Paula was pudgy and always wore jeans and a t-shirt. Suzanne had a reputation as a wonderful hostess, but she always hired a caterer. Paula was a great cook, but was loud and boisterous like her sons.

Although Paula was different from Suzanne, she had always been kind to Meghan. However, Meghan was afraid that might be about to change. Jocy was the Patrones' oldest child – their pride and joy. Paula had particularly high hopes for him – including a college education and a chance to play football for Georgia State – both of which were now in jeopardy.

The walked up the sidewalk and across the front porch strewn with sports equipment to the Patrones' front door. No one came running when the door opened, which was unusual and ominous. Worse, the house was silent.

Meghan clutched Joey's hand and they walked together into the large kitchen where his parents were seated at the table. Paula was wearing a dress – which meant she'd been to Mass – something that only happened at Christmas and Easter. The Patrone family was proud of their Catholic heritage but not devout. Apparently in moments of extreme stress, Paula became more religious.

Joey and Meghan sat down across from them. Once they were settled, he said, "So, we're getting married."

Paula closed her eyes briefly and then nodded. "When?"

"As soon as possible," Joey replied. "We'll go this afternoon and see about getting a license. I don't know how long that takes – but maybe we could do it on Friday."

"Friday?" his mother repeated. "That is not enough time to notify the family and plan a little reception."

Joey shook his head. "We don't want any of that. It will just be the priest, us, you and Dad -- and Meghan's parents," he added as an optimistic afterthought. "We just want to be married and start planning our future."

Troy asked, "What kind of plans do you have?"

Joey seemed to relax a little. His parents were on board – if reluctantly- with the marriage. But the next topic of conversation would not go over as well. "I'm going to give up my football scholarship so we can move to Nashville where Meghan will go to school."

Paula couldn't control a little whimper. "But that's your chance for an education!"

"I'll get my education, eventually," Joey assured her.

"Son, I don't see any reason for you to give up your scholarship," Troy agreed with his wife.

Paula leaned closer to her son. "You're the one who has to support your family so your education is the most important. Meghan can give up *her* scholarship and go to Georgia State."

Joey shook his head stubbornly. "Meghan is not giving up her scholarship. Like I told you earlier, this is my fault and I'm going to pay the price – not her."

Paula showed she could be stubborn too. "But if you keep your scholarship – the two of you could live here and I can help with the baby. It will make things so much easier for both of you."

Joey shook his head. "This is not negotiable."

Meghan saw the distress on his parents' faces and thought about what they had said. In Nashville, she and Joey had no support system. Joey would keep the baby while she went to school and work at night. They would rarely even see each other and his education would be put on hold indefinitely. It would take them twice as long to get through school – to accomplish their goals.

She reached out and put her hand over his. "I think your parents are right. It makes more sense for you to keep your scholarship so we can stay here where we have family to help us."

Joey turned to face her. "I won't let you make that kind of sacrifice for me."

"It's a sacrifice that needs to be made for our future and the baby's," she told him. "We'll both be making a lot of sacrifices from now on. And if your mom is willing to babysit for us – well I think that's what we need to do."

Paula and Troy turned hopeful eyes to their oldest son.

"Your parents won't like it," Joey told her.

She shrugged. "There's only one thing we could do that would make them happy and we've agreed that's not a possibility."

"After the wedding you two can live here with us," Paula said.

Meghan tried to imagine herself in this household full of rambunctious boys. No peace, no privacy, living in Joey's childhood bedroom, sharing a bathroom with his brothers. She shuddered.

"We'll talk about that later," she said. "Right now we need to go see about a marriage license. And I need to call Vanderbilt to decline my scholarship."

"Don't you want to wait a couple of days in case you change your mind?" Joey suggested.

She shook her head. "I won't change my mind and they need to know they have a scholarship opening up so they can give it someone else."

Joey looked unhappy, but he nodded. "If you're sure."

"I'm sure," Meghan said with more confidence than she felt.

Paula gave them a shaky smile as she stood. "I'll make lunch while you two go to the courthouse. We'll eat when you get back."

"Hurry," Troy told them. "I'm starving."

So it seemed that things were returning to normal – a new normal – but the crisis had passed.

During the drive to the courthouse Meghan called Vanderbilt and declined her scholarship. Letting it go wasn't as hard as she thought it would be. Then the marriage license process was equally painless. After filling out the paperwork they got blood tests at the Health Department and were told they could come back to get the license the next day.

When they arrived at the Patrones' house, lunch was ready as Paula had promised. Joey's brothers – who had been missing earlier – had returned so things were back to the customary chaos.

They all settled around the table, said a quick grace, and then started passing plates of food.

"This looks delicious, Mrs. Patrone," Meghan said politely.

"You should call me Paula now that you're joining our family," she offered. "I told the boys that you and Joey are getting married on Friday."

The older two boys, Matt and Ben, looked embarrassed, so Meghan guessed that Paula had also told them the reason for the impromptu marriage. Michael, who was eight, was just curious.

51

"Don't you have to wait until you're twenty to get married?" he asked.

"No." Joey kept his eyes on his food.

"I thought you were going to college to play football," Michael added.

"I am," Joey said. "I can be married and play football."

"Oh." Michael considered this. "I guess Meghan can be like your cheerleader or something."

Joey reached over and ruffled the boy's hair. "Or something."

When the meal was over Meghan helped Paula clear the table and load the dishwasher. While they worked Paula said something else about Meghan and Joey moving in with them after the wedding. "I know it's crowded here – not like what you're used to," she acknowledged. "But we'll do our best to make you comfortable."

"I appreciate your offer," Meghan replied carefully. "But especially with the baby coming, we'd like to get a place of our own. Something small and cheap and nearby since you're going to babysit for us."

"There aren't many apartments around here," Paula said doubtfully. "But we can look into it." She dried a pot and put it in the cupboard. "I don't guess there's any chance you and Joey could move in with your parents?"

Meghan shook her head. "No."

"Why don't they live in Grandma and Grandpa's house?"

They turned to see fifteen-year-old Matt standing in the doorway that separated the kitchen from the family room.

Meghan's heart pounded. The cottage was nearby. It was cheap. And they had already made it their own.

"It's a wreck!" Paula objected.

"We could fix it up," Matt insisted. "The uncles would help. We could make that old place good as new. It's close and they wouldn't have to pay rent."

Paula considered this for a few seconds. Then she put a hand to her mouth and yelled toward the family room. "Troy! Joey! Come in here! Matt has an idea."

***

Joey called the admissions office at Georgia State and found out that once they were married, Meghan could apply for the upcoming school year even though they were past the deadlines. Meghan was relieved to hear this since she knew her parents would take the news about Vanderbilt better if she was enrolled in another college.

Then that evening Troy came home from a meeting with his brothers and announced that they had agreed to help renovate the cottage for Joey and Meghan.

After Matt was congratulated by everyone for having such a great idea, they sat around and discussed what needed to be done to make it livable. The list was long and Meghan was feeling guilty by the time the family meeting broke up.

Joey led Meghan out onto the front porch and said, "Even after my dad and my uncles fix up the cottage, it still won't be half as nice as your parents' house." He sounded nervous and a little unsure.

It was her turn to comfort him. She wrapped her arms around his waist and pressed her cheek against his chest. "I will love it because it will be our first home together."

He held her close and she knew she'd said the right thing.

After a few minutes he told her, "You're going to have to do something about clothes and a toothbrush. I guess we should go shopping."

She shook her head. "It doesn't make sense to buy new stuff when I have plenty of everything at home. I mean, at my parents' house," she corrected quickly.

"But they pretty much kicked you out. I don't think they are going to let you come by and take whatever you need."

"Actually, I think they will," Meghan said. "They disagreed with the decision I made but they love me and they want me to have clothes to wear. So I'm going to go back and talk to them again."

"What if they are still mad and tell you to get out?"

"Then we'll go shopping," she told him with a smile.

He didn't return her smile. "I don't like the idea of you groveling to them."

"They might not be able to accept me on our terms, but I want to give them the opportunity."

"Do you want me to come?" he offered.

"No. It will be better if I go alone."

"Good," he said with obvious relief. "I don't really want to face your parents again until we're legally married."

"I guess I'll invite them to the wedding while I'm there."

"My advice is – get your stuff first." This time he did give her a little smile.

She drove his truck to her parents' house. She parked in front and walked up to the door, like a guest. Her mother answered the door. When she saw Meghan she stood in the entryway, frozen for a few seconds.

Meghan said, "Mama?"

Her mother stepped out and embraced her daughter. "Keegan!" she called to her husband. "Meghan is here!"

"I haven't changed my mind," Meghan said when her father joined them. "Joey and I are getting married on Friday at the Catholic church in Old Mountain. It's going to be a private ceremony – just his parents and the two of you – if you'll come."

Her mother wiped tears from her eyes. "We believe with all our hearts that it is a mistake."

"I know."

Her father sighed. "But it's your choice and we'll be there to support you – of course."

Meghan was surprised that happiness could make her heart hurt almost as much as sadness. "Thank you."

They drew her into the living room and sat on the couch – Meghan in the middle and one of her parents on each side.

"We said some things earlier that we're not proud of," her father said.

"We're sorry," her mother added.

Meghan shook her head. "It's okay. You were upset. I understand."

Her mother pasted on a bright smile. "What are your plans for after the wedding?"

"I'll be going to Georgia State. I declined my scholarship at Vanderbilt so we could live near the Patrones. Paula is going to babysit for us."

Her mother looked away but didn't comment.

"Georgia State is a good school," her father said.

No one said *not as good as Vanderbilt*, but Meghan knew they were thinking it.

"Where will you live?" her mother moved on.

"There's a little house a few blocks away from the Patrones that belonged to his grandparents. They are going to fix it up for us. Our lives won't be easy, but we'll make it work."

Her mother nodded, in acceptance – not agreement. "We wanted a very different life for you."

"I know," Meghan said. "But this is what I've chosen and I really believe I can be happy – as long as I am with the ones I love."

Her mother smiled with a trace of bitterness. "That is because you are very young."

"Your mother and I will support you in whatever life you choose," her father said.

"I will support you," her mother agreed, "but don't expect me to enjoy watching you turn into Paula Patrone – overweight, unkempt, with a passel of unruly children."

"They will be *your* unruly grandchildren," she reminded her mother. "And they will love you – just like I do."

Her mother raised sad eyes. "And I will love them just like I love you."

"Are you going to stay here until Friday?" her father asked.

"I just came back to pack up some clothes, but if you don't mind, I'd like to stay until the wedding."

"It's the most sensible thing," her mother said. "The Patrones don't have room for you."

Meghan was relieved. "I'll ask Joey."

Her mother seemed to relax a little. "We can start packing up your things for your move into the grandparents' place."

Meghan smiled. "I'd appreciate the help."

As they walked upstairs, Meghan saw her childhood home more critically than she had before. The huge expanses and high ceilings seemed wasteful instead of spacious. Her father brought some boxes from the garage and they started packing.

"You can take your bedroom furniture if you want," her mother offered. "And anything else you need for your house. We want to help fix it up too. We can't let the Patrones have all the glory."

"Thanks, Mom." There was no way her furniture would fit in the small bedroom at the cottage, but she didn't tell that to her mother.

Once they had a couple of boxes packed, her mother said, "Let's take a break and go find you a wedding dress."

And for the first time Meghan felt like a real bride.

Chapter Five

They went to a fancy little boutique in Meadowbrook and purchased a dress that was simple and elegant and probably expensive. Her mother was careful not to let Meghan see the price tag and she didn't really try. She loved the dress and wanted to be beautiful on her wedding day.

When they got home Meghan told her parents she was going to take Joey's truck back to him. "And while I'm over there I'll ask him how he feels about me staying here until Friday."

"Invite Joey to come over for dinner," her mother suggested politely if not sincerely.

"Thanks, Mom," Meghan replied as she climbed out of the car. "But not tonight."

"You'll be back soon?"

"If I'm not coming back I'll call," Meghan promised. Then with a wave, she got in Joey's truck and drove toward Old Mountain.

Joey must have been watching for her because he walked out onto the driveway as she pulled up. He gave her a kiss and asked, "So, how did it go?"

"Fine," Meghan told him. "My parents apologized and suggested that I stay with them until Friday. That way you won't have to sleep in your brother's room."

"I hate the idea of you staying with them," he said. "I'm afraid they'll change your mind about marrying me."

"They won't," she assured him.

He didn't look happy, but he didn't argue. "Let's go inside. Mom made dinner."

The food at the Patrones' was good but prepared with no apparent consideration for nutrition or heart-health. It was hard to follow the conversation since everyone was talking at once and the television was still blaring in the family room. The men occasionally got up from the table and walked into the other room to check on the scores to various games.

After the meal the men took their dessert into the family room while Paula began clearing the table. Meghan really wanted to go with Joey, but she knew she couldn't leave Paula to clean up alone. So she helped Paula with the dishes.

Then she sat by Joey while he watched TV with his family until it was time for her to go home. When he dropped her off at her parents' house, he looked anxious.

"Don't worry," she said. "Everything will be fine."

"You promise me that we'll get married on Friday."

She nodded. "I promise."

Her parents were waiting up and she talked with them for a few minutes. Then, exhausted, she went upstairs.

It was so strange to stare at the same ceiling that had been over her head for years knowing that everything had changed. She was going to be a wife. She was going to be a mother. Scared but determined, she fell asleep.

On Thursday Joey picked her up and took her to the cottage. He showed her the improvements his father and uncles were planning to make.

"My parents want to give us the furniture from my bedroom," she told him. "I know it won't all fit, but we can take the bed and the dresser at least. And they have an old couch in the attic that I know they'd let us have for the living room."

"I don't want to take their stuff."

"We're accepting help from your parents."

"Yeah but that's different. They don't hate me."

"My parents don't hate you," she said. "They hate the situation and they disagree with our decision to get married. And I'm not sure your parents are that crazy about me either."

"If they don't like you they are smart enough not to show it."

Meghan sighed. "It will hurt my parents' feelings if we refuse their help. We have to try to get along with them – not just for our sake but for the baby's. We're a package deal – when you marry me you get them too."

He frowned. "Maybe I need to think about this a little more."

"Joey!"

"Just kidding." He pulled her into his arms. "You know I am."

"I know."

"And I guess we can take some furniture from your parents."

She kissed him. "Thank you. It will make them feel better and it will save us money."

He didn't respond to this, just kissed her back.

When he to took her to her parents' house, he declined when she invited him to come in. He did walk her to the front door, though.

"By this time tomorrow you will be my wife." He shook his head. "I can't believe I just said that."

She laughed. "You'll get used to it."

"It's not that late," he pointed out. "We could go to a movie or something."

She shook her head. "Let's just stay with our own families tonight – one last time. Then I'll ride with my parents to the wedding."

"You won't leave me standing at the altar?"

"No," she promised. "We'll be there."

That evening she played chess with her father. Then she went to bed in her childhood room for the last time. It was a sad and yet exciting time. She would miss the familiar – but longed for Joey and their future together.

The next day her mother offered to take her to a hair salon, but Meghan wanted to keep things simple. She fixed her shoulder-length blond hair the same as always and then put on her makeup. To minimize wrinkles she waited until the last minute to slip the dress on. Once she had it zipped up she studied herself in the full-length mirror. The dress fit perfectly and the cream color contrasted nicely with her tanned skin. Her blue eyes looked huge in the mirror. She wasn't afraid exactly – but definitely a little apprehensive. This wasn't how she thought she'd feel on her wedding day.

She reminded herself that Joey was waiting. That cheered her up a little.

Then she left her room, pulling a suitcase behind her. When she reached the top of the stairs she saw her parents waiting on the landing below. Her father was wearing a black suit and her mother a gray-silk suit. Their attire and solemn expressions were more appropriate for a funeral than a wedding.

She gave them a brave smile as she descended the stairs. Her mother's lips trembled. Her father took the suitcase from her hand and led the way out to the car. They were quiet during the drive to the church.

When they arrived at the church, her father pushed open the door and they stepped into a small room with marble floors and stained-glass windows. Through another set of open doors they could see the chapel area with rows and rows of empty benches. Joey was standing at the front of the room with his parents and a priest in white robes. He was wearing a new suit and his hair was neatly combed.

They walked down the long aisle toward Joey and his family. The chapel was dimly lit with flickering candles and smelled a little musty. Meghan felt like a stranger there, and not particularly welcome. She knew her parents felt the same, maybe more so.

Joey looked relieved to see her and took Meghan by the hand. The Patrones greeted her parents with handshakes. Her parents were polite but obviously uncomfortable. Joey had a bouquet of pink roses for her. She noticed when he passed them to her that his hands were shaking.

The ceremony was oddly impersonal but blessedly short. When it came time for them to exchange rings Meghan felt bad that she didn't have one for Joey. She felt even worse when he pulled a new ring for her out of his pocket.

"Do you like it?" he whispered as he slipped it on her finger. "My mom needed hers back so I used the money I had saved to put tires on my truck to buy you a ring of your own."

"Oh Joey, you really need new tires."

"Those tires will last a while longer," he said. "What I really needed was for you to have my ring on your finger."

Meghan admired her hand with the simple gold band. "I love it."

"Someday you'll have a diamond to go with it."

"For now, I'm just glad to have you."

The priest told Joey he could kiss his bride. Then they turned to face their parents as husband and wife. Both mothers were crying. Both fathers looked grim.

Her father offered to take everyone out to lunch, but the Patrones declined. "If I leave my younger boys alone any longer there will be bloodshed," Paula said.

Her parents smiled politely, assuming this was a joke.

"Thank you, though," Troy added.

"Meghan and Joey, would you like to get something to eat?" her mother asked.

"I'd like to Mrs. Dunaway, but my parents got us a room in Savannah," Joey told them. "We'd better get driving if we want to make it before dark."

"Troy's brother had some hotel points," Paula explained. "It might not be the best honeymoon in the world, but it's the best we could do on short notice." Then she turned to Joey, "I want you to take my car because I don't trust your old truck, especially with those slick tires."

"It's not necessary for you to give up your car," Suzanne said. "They can take Meghan's Honda." When she saw her daughter's surprised look she added, "What did you think your father and I were going to do with it? Sell it on Craigslist?"

That was pretty much what Meghan had thought, but she smiled. "Thanks Mom and Dad!"

Joey didn't look grateful or even happy. "Meghan does need a car to get to school, but we'll pay you for it," he said. "Fair market value."

Her father shook his head. "Consider it a wedding gift."

Joey looked even more unhappy.

"We can take your mother's car if you want to," she whispered to him.

"We don't even have to go on a honeymoon right now," Joey said. "We could just stay here and help with the cottage."

Paula shook her head. "You're going on a honeymoon! And while you're gone to the beach maybe we can get that cottage livable. And you're going in Meghan's car. You're in no position to turn down a generous gift like that. Now tell Mr. Dunaway thank you."

"Thank you," Joey said.

"We're glad for you to have it," Suzanne told them.

There were awkward hugs all around and then they left the church. Meghan and Joey rode home with her parents to get Meghan's car. Meghan and her mother made small talk while the men maintained an uncomfortable silence.

At the house Joey stood by her car while Meghan changed clothes and said goodbye to her parents. When she rejoined him outside he was sitting in the passenger seat.

She opened the car door and asked, "Don't you want to drive?"

"Naw," he said. "It's your car. You drive."

She slid under the wheel and started the car. "If you don't feel right about taking this as a gift, we can pay my parents a little each month until we've given them a fair price."

His entire demeanor changed. "That *would* make me feel better. I want your parents to respect me. It may take me my whole life, but eventually I'll convince them that I'm not a bum. And paying for this car is the first step."

She smiled. "So, now that we're buying this car, do you want to drive?"

He laughed. "You can drive halfway and then we'll switch."

When they got close enough to the beach to smell the ocean, Joey said, "I didn't like this idea at first, but I think my mom was right. We need to celebrate this moment in our lives."

She nodded. "It will be nice to have some time alone together before we have to go back and start school and everything."

"It's hard to believe we're married."

She held up her hand so he could see the ring gleaming on her finger. "Here's proof."

When they got to their room Joey insisted on carrying Meghan across the threshold.

"That's just supposed to be when we walk into our new home for the first time."

"I'll do it again. I like carrying you – you're light as a feather."

"Just wait a few months," she muttered.

He laughed. "I'm pretty strong, you know."

She caressed his straining biceps. "I know."

"Are you hungry?" he asked as he lowered her feet to the floor. "We could go out to eat."

She shook her head and wrapped her arms around him. "I don't want to go anywhere."

Their eyes met, their lips touched, and all their troubles seemed to disappear.

***

Later that evening they walked hand in hand along the beach.

Looking up at the stars Joey said, "Hello, I'd like to introduce you to my wife, Meghan Patrone."

"That sounds like someone else besides me," she said. "A totally different person."

"A new person," Joey told her softly. "We are married to each other. Tonight we're going to sleep beside each other and tomorrow we'll wake up together."

She smiled at him. "That does sound nice. What are we going to do tomorrow?"

"We can go to a souvenir shop and buy some silly tourist T-shirts."

"Ones that say bride and groom?"

"Maybe not that silly."

They sat on the beach and watched the waves crashing onto the shore by moonlight. After a while he asked, "So how do you like being married so far?"

"So far – it's great."

He leaned forward and wrapped his arms around his knees – staring at the water. "When we have hard times we need to remember how we feel right now. Then we can make it through."

She smiled. "Maybe when we have hard times we can just come back to the beach."

He grinned. "Maybe." Then he stood and brushed the sand from his clothes. "Now let's get back to our room. We don't want to waste my uncle's hotel points."

***

The next day they bought T-shirts and tanned in the sun and ate seafood at a restaurant they couldn't afford.

63

The weekend was wonderful, but it quickly came to an end. Driving back to Atlanta with the windows down, the wind blowing her hair, her nose sunburned, and grains of sand in her shoes – Meghan couldn't imagine being happier. She was anxious to see the cottage and the progress that had been made while they were gone. She was even anxious to start school.

"Our honeymoon has been like a dream. I know real life won't be so perfect but at this moment I'm looking forward to it."

"As long as I'm with you I'll be happy." He put a hand over her stomach. "I wonder if it's a boy or a girl."

"One thing is for sure," she said. "It's cute!"

Joey laughed and started singing at the top of his lungs. She joined in and they sang until they were both hoarse.

They were only an hour from home when her eyes got so heavy she couldn't keep them open. "I think I'll take a little nap," she told him. And then she was sound asleep.

***

"Meghan," the voice calling her was gentle but insistent. "Meghan."

She opened her eyes, expecting to see Joey sitting beside her in the car on the ride home from the beach. Instead she saw a stranger wearing a lab coat.

"Welcome back," the woman said. "Did you enjoy your dream?"

Meghan's mind skidded, searching for a point of reference. The room was cold, not warm like the car on a summer day with the windows down. It was also dark. There was no bright sunshine. No singing. No Joey. She was Meghan Collins, 28 years old, a pediatrician, and wife of Chase.

"Are you okay?" the technician asked. She was very beautiful and Meghan remembered that her name was Heidi.

"I'm fine, thank you," she said, but she didn't feel fine. She felt off-balance, out of sync, in the wrong time.

"How long before she'll be ready to leave?" Caldwell asked. "I have a lunch date."

Meghan glanced over at her friend. The hot pink scarf around Caldwell's head was enough to shock her into total consciousness.

"She should be fully awake in just a few minutes," Heidi said. "Then she'll have a short post-dream session with Dr. Morrow. After that she'll be ready to go. Would you like to wait in the lobby where it's a little warmer?"

"Is that okay with you, honey?" Caldwell asked.

Meghan nodded. "Sure."

She saw Caldwell go out of the room. Heidi walked around adjusting monitors, writing down information. Finally she came over and removed the electrodes. "Time to get up."

Meghan sat on the edge of the bed, trying to get her bearings.

"It takes some patients a few seconds to find their land legs so be prepared."

Heidi took Meghan's arm for support as she slid off the bed and onto the floor. Her legs did feel a little jelly-ish, but the sensation passed quickly.

"Have you ever done the dream therapy?" Meghan asked.

Heidi shook her head. "No. Now if you'll put on your shoes, I'll take you to Dr. Morrow's office for your PDS."

"Post-Dream Session," Meghan guessed.

"Yes."

Meghan slipped her feet into her shoes and followed the technician out of the room. Even though her feet were firmly on the ground – her mind seemed still in the clouds. She didn't feel completely at home in her own body.

Heidi rapped her knuckles on Dr. Morrow's office door and he called for them to come in.

"Meghan!" he said with a smiled. "So, how was it?"

She sat down and turned somewhat dazed eyes to him. "I'm not sure what to say. The dream was so vivid – so real. It seems more like a memory than a dream."

He nodded. "That's the way it is for most people. Only those with no imagination or brain damage say the dreams didn't seem real. Was there anything about it that you didn't like?"

"The transition from dream to reality is jarring," she told him. "I still feel a little . . . lost."

He nodded. "That is an issue we are trying to resolve. We've tried allowing the client to wake up more gradually. Given this extra time most clients will have other, undirected, dreams. That cushion of space between the dream life and real life seems to help."

"That might be an improvement." Meghan didn't want to dismiss the idea outright, but she didn't have much confidence in it. No matter how much cushion she was given between the dream and waking up – she felt sure she'd still be shocked by the return to reality.

Dr. Morrow continued, "But not all clients want to invest this extra time in their session and some want to keep their dream memories as vivid as possible – which requires the abrupt ending."

Meghan was sure she didn't want to sacrifice any of her dream's vividness, so perhaps the jarring return to real life was unavoidable.

"Did you feel like the experience was helpful to you?" Dr. Morrow asked.

"Yes," Meghan said. "I got a sense of how things would be if I had chosen a different path, but it was just too short. I only dreamed about one week."

"That means you're a detailed dreamer – like me. I know it's frustrating if you're trying to get to a specific point in your dream-life, but really we are the lucky ones. Our dreams are the most realistic."

She couldn't be unhappy about that. "I understand."

"Any questions?"

"Just one – when can I have my next session?"

He smiled. "That's what I was hoping you would ask. You can come again next Saturday if that's convenient."

"Saturday is good for me. And this time I'd like to dream for the maximum 24 hours."

His smile widened. "Come on Saturday at eight AM and you'll be ready to go on Sunday morning at the same time."

She stood and extended her hand. "Thank you, Doctor. This experience has been more than I ever dreamed." She smiled. "No pun intended."

She met Caldwell in the lobby and they walked out to the car. Caldwell was chatting about pedicures and a new clothing line at her favorite boutique and her lunch date and her upcoming cruise. It was all just background noise to Meghan. She couldn't make herself care about any of it. She could think only about Joey and their cottage – and how it would look once the renovations were done.

***

"Honey, you look exhausted," Caldwell said when Meghan dropped her off. "And you've barely said a single word. Do you want me to drive you home? I can bring your car back to you tomorrow."

"No," Meghan declined this offer. "I'll be okay. But thanks, for everything."

"You're my best friend!" Caldwell reminded her unnecessarily. "I'll sit in a freezing cold room for you any day!"

Meghan smiled and waved. Then she drove away. It was a relief to be alone with her thoughts and memories of her dream.

When she pulled up to the condo she tried to clear her mind, somewhat, and shift her thoughts away from Joey and their dream life. Chase was already nervous about the therapy sessions and if he knew how she was feeling after dreaming for an hour – he'd be more so.

When she walked inside he was sitting at the kitchen table, working on his laptop. She walked over and gave him a hug.

He pulled her onto his lap and asked, "So, how was it?"

"Amazing," she told him. "As Dr. Morrow promised, it was like watching a movie starring myself."

"And Joey Patrone," Chase muttered. "I presume you chose to marry him and have the baby."

Chase was a good lawyer and experienced at reading witnesses. So she didn't meet his eyes when she answered. "Yes."

"Did it give you the peace or closure or whatever you were hoping for?"

"It was a start," she said carefully, still keeping her eyes averted. "But because I am a detailed dreamer – it only took me through about a week of dream-life. I want to go on until I have the baby."

He lifted her off of his lap and stood. Putting his hands on her shoulders he said, "You know how crazy that sounds."

She had no choice but to meet his eyes now. "I just want to see if it's a girl or a boy."

"You didn't have a baby, Meghan."

"You know what I mean."

"No, actually I don't." He dropped his hands from her shoulders and put them on his hips. "I can't understand any of this. I thought that once you tried the therapy you would be satisfied, but I don't know if I can go along with another dream session."

Meghan was annoyed by this remark but tried not to let that show when she said, "I'm not asking for your permission, Chase. I'm just trying to explain how I feel."

"And I'm telling you how I feel too."

"It's my past, not yours."

He nodded. "But it affects us both."

"Just have a little patience," she requested. "I'll work through it and we'll be back to normal."

"If I believed that, I'd have more patience," he said. "But you're not trying to work through your past. You're trying to *return* to it. Where does that leave me, Meghan? Where does that leave us?"

"I'm not going back permanently – I can't," she said. "I just want to pursue the dream a little further. It's like opening up a memory – not changing our reality. And it will only take probably two more Saturdays to get to the point I want to reach. That's all the patience I'm asking for."

"Like you said, you don't need my permission." He reached over and closed his laptop. "I think I'll go into the office and work for awhile."

She knew she should stop him. She should kiss him and reassure him and suggest that they go out for lunch like they usually did on Saturdays. But honestly she was glad he was leaving. She needed some time to herself and she didn't want to encourage any physical contact with Chase. Because she wasn't only caught between two worlds – she was caught between two men.

*** *

Meghan slept off and on for the rest of the day. She dreamed and sometimes she even dreamed about Joey. But they were not the vivid, intensely realistic dreams like the one at Dr. Morrow's lab. They were disjointed, disorganized and unfulfilling.

That evening she heard the television in the living room so she knew Chase was home. She went into the living room and curled up on the couch beside him. He put his arm around her shoulders and she savored his warmth. She loved her husband. She really did.

When she woke up on Sunday morning, Chase was gone to the gym. He texted later and said he was going to the country club to play a round of golf with his father and then eat lunch there with his parents. He invited her to join them but she couldn't bear the thought of Chase's parents grilling her about dream-therapy. So she used rounds at the hospital as an excuse.

***

She had completed her rounds and was at the nurses' station, signing off on the patient charts when Dr. Hahn, one of the staff physicians, found her.

"I have a case I'd like you to consult on," she said. "It would be pro bono."

"Of course it would be," Meghan replied. She liked Dr. Hahn and didn't mind taking on patients who couldn't pay. In fact she enjoyed the challenge of unusual cases. "What do you have?"

"A three year old male with Rheumatic Fever as a result of untreated strep."

Meghan frowned. "That will be a short consult. A round of antibiotics and an anti-inflammatory and he should be good as new."

Dr. Hahn smiled. "It's his teenage parent that I thought you might find interesting. And he has a three-month old sibling."

Meghan was always looking for candidates for the *Mom*entum clinic. And as Dr. Hahn knew, she was particularly interested in teenage mothers with more than one child since the statistics were significantly worse for girls with multiple teenage births. Intervention and support was their best hope. And if Dr. Hahn was making a referral, she must think that this girl both needed and deserved some help.

Meghan nodded. "What room is the patient in?"

Dr. Hahn had a funny look in her eyes as she put a chart in Meghan's hand. "Room 346."

When Meghan pushed open the door to room 346 she saw a small boy with light brown skin and an intricate network of braids asleep in the hospital bed. An infant who bore a strong resemblance to the patient, including a mini version of the older boy's braids, was also asleep, still strapped into a car seat. Meghan's eyes moved to the chair beside the bed where a young man was sitting. He looked just like both the children, braids and all.

Meghan was startled. She worked with teenage mothers, not fathers.

"You Sedrick's doctor too?" the boy asked. She judged him to be late teens, maybe eighteen. He looked tired and worried.

"Dr. Hahn asked me to consult on your son's case," Meghan confirmed. She walked a little closer to the hospital bed. "How is he doing?"

The young man stood and joined her. "Good now. His fever was bad when we got here and he had that rash. I know it seems like I wasn't taking good care of him, but he never said his throat hurt, I swear!"

Meghan smiled. "That is very common and I have no doubt that you take good care of your children. They are both clean and healthy and those braids take time and patience." The most endearing thing about the braids was that they were just like the father's – his way of saying, these boys are mine.

The young man relaxed a little. "If he gets strep throat again will it the same?"

"Probably. I can show you how to look at his throat for signs of strep, but my best advice is if he runs a fever for more than twenty-four hours, bring him in and get him checked for strep."

"Okay," he said. "I'll do that."

Meghan held out a hand. "I'm Dr. Collins."

The young father hesitated for a second, obviously a little suspicious of her friendly overture. But finally he put his hand in hers for a brief, but firm, shake. "Quentin Jackson."

"Where is the boys' mom?" she asked casually.

"Don't know," Quentin said. "We broke up last year. I didn't even know she was pregnant with Little Ty." He pointed at the sleeping baby. "She dropped him off three months ago and I haven't seen her since."

"Do you have anyone to help you with them?"

"I live with my mother and she helps me some," Quentin said. "But she has bad nerves and the kids make her worse. So I can't leave them with her too long."

"Have you finished high school?"

He shook his head. "I'm going to finish." His tone was defensive. "But right now I have to work extra hours to pay for daycare."

"I have a clinic near the hospital called *Mom*entum. You might have heard of it?"

He shook his head. "Naw."

"Well, it's a place where we help teenage parents. I think we might be able to make things easier for you."

Quentin shook his head. "If DHR gets the idea that I can't handle the boys on my own, they might take them away from me."

"We have a good relationship with DHR and they consider enrollment in our program a very positive thing," Meghan assured him. "We don't try to assume any of your parental responsibilities, we just support you and help you to be the best parent you can be."

Quentin seemed slightly less suspicious and mildly interested. "What kind of help?"

"We have a GED class and administer the test once a month. You could take care of that in no time and move on to college or a trade school or whatever you want to do with your life."

His eyes brightened. "You help with that too, getting into college?"

She nodded. "We have advisors who help you pick a career course and then walk you through the application process. They help you apply for Federal financial aid and we also have scholarships provided by local donors to help with expenses."

"Wow," Quentin said.

"And we have a daycare that is staffed by volunteers from the hospital and pediatrician offices. It's free to program participants."

"Free?" Quentin whispered in awe.

"We also do well check-ups and immunizations at the clinic," Meghan told him. "There is a room full of clothes donated by local stores. And once a week you'd get a box of groceries, also donated."

"Why do people give all this stuff to your clinic?"

"Because they really want to see teenage parents like you succeed," Meghan told him.

Quentin held up a hand. "And how do I join?"

"You have to have a referral from a member of the clinic's staff. That's me," she said with a smile. "If you're interested, I can start that process today."

"I'm interested," Quentin said. "Even without all that other stuff, just the free daycare and the help with school – that's what I need."

"There's only one catch."

His face fell and she regretted her phraseology.

"I figured," he muttered.

"It's nothing big," she rushed to reassure him. "But up to this point, all of our clients have been teenage mothers."

"There's no men there you mean?"

"No. But it was short-sighed of us not to realize that there are teenage fathers who need our help too."

"I don't mind being the only guy," Quentin said. "As long as I don't have to wear pink or anything."

Meghan laughed. "I promise we won't make you wear pink." She pulled a card from the pocket of her lab coat. "I'll enter your name into the computer so the clinic will be expecting you. Here is the number, just call and set up a time to come in."

Quentin took the card from her with near reverence. "Thank you."

She wanted to hug him, but knew he wouldn't appreciate her treating him like the child he was. So she shook his hand again, giving him the respect of the adult he was trying to be. "I look forward to seeing you and your boys at the clinic."

Meghan slipped out of the hospital room and walked back to the nurses' station. Dr. Hahn was waiting there with a smirk on her face.

"You could have warned me that you were referring a father instead of a mother," Meghan told her.

"What's the fun in that?" Dr. Hahn asked. "So, is he going to join the program?"

"I think so," Meghan said. "Of course now I've got to think of another name for the clinic."

"Serves you right for picking something sexist to begin with," Dr. Hahn teased over her shoulder as she walked down the hall.

Meghan was smiling as she returned to her patient charts.

***

It was almost dark by the time she got home. Chase was watching a ballgame and she leaned over the couch to kiss his cheek. This tepid greeting was intended to indicate that while she didn't want them to be at odds with him, she also was not ready to pick up their relationship where it had been before the dream session.

He kept his eyes on the television neither accepting nor rejecting her half-hearted overture. Meghan was perfectly satisfied with this stalemate.

She took a shower, changed into her pajamas, and went to bed. There she dreamed of the past that could have been.

Chapter Six

The week went by slowly for Meghan. She threw herself into her work, but didn't find her medical practice or even the *Mom*entum clinic as distracting as usual. She found it difficult to concentrate on her patients and almost impossible to handle all the administrative duties associated with a large medical practice. Penelope asked her several times if she was sick.

"I might be coming down with something," she said, grateful to have an excuse.

"Goodness knows you come in contact with enough germs on a daily basis," Penelope replied. "Doctor, you should go to the *doctor*."

Meghan smiled at the little joke. "I will if I don't get feeling better."

The one bright spot of her week was Quentin Jackson and his two sons, Sedrick and Tyrone. Meghan got an email that they had an appointment for their initial interview at the *Mom*entum clinic on Thursday night, so she made a point to be there.

Quentin looked the same as he had at the hospital – tired. Little Ty was awake and cute in a toothless, slobbery way. But it was Sedrick who commanded her attention. He was fully recovered from Rheumatic Fever and was a bundle of three-year-old energy.

"My dad said you came to see me when I was in the hospital. I'm not sick anymore!" He held out his hands to showcase his return to health.

Meghan bent down so she could address him on eye-level. "I'm glad to hear that."

"My dad said that I might come to a new daycare here," Sedrick continued. "My old daycare has toys and ice cream. Do you have that stuff here?"

"We definitely have toys and I'm sure we can round up some ice cream." Meghan told him. Then she turned to the receptionist. "Will you call one of the daycare workers up to show Sedrick around?"

The receptionist made the call and a few seconds later a nursing student volunteer came out of the daycare room. Introductions were made and then Meghan suggested that Sedrick and Little Ty go with the future nurse – a girl named Jaci.

"Jaci will show you where the toys are and maybe even get you some ice cream."

Jaci took the baby from Quentin and held out her hand to Sedrick. "I think I can handle that," she said.

Sedrick frowned at Meghan. "I wanted to stay with you."

"But I need to talk to your dad for awhile," Meghan said.

"Are you going to help him get a better job?" Sedrick asked. "He told me you are."

Quentin groaned with embarrassment. "Sed, you talk too much."

Meghan patted the boy's braided hair. "Yes, I'm going to help your father."

Sedrick grinned and reached for Jaci's extended hand. "I like chocolate ice cream but Little Ty can't eat any. He's too little," they heard him say as the boys left with Jaci.

Meghan was smiling as she turned back to Quentin, who was still standing near the door. He looked embarrassed and uncomfortable and like he might bolt at any minute.

"Let's go back and find your advisor," Meghan suggested, pointing to a hallway lined with cubicles.

"He's been assigned to Seresta," the receptionist provided helpfully.

"Oh, you're one of the lucky ones." Meghan started down the hallway and Quentin hurried to catch up.

"What will I have to do?" he wanted to know.

"Nothing right now, except talk." Meghan was used to defensiveness.

They reached the cubicle where Seresta was waiting for them. A tall, athletic woman she looked like a female Wilt Chamberlain. "It's nice to meet you," she told Quentin. "Have a seat."

Once they were sitting across from Seresta's desk, the advisor continued, "I like to tell the people I work with a little about myself. I'm an accountant for Georgia Power and I volunteer here one night a week. I was raised by a single mother and never thought I'd have a chance to go to college. But then I started playing basketball and through hours and hours of hard work and a lot of luck, I got a scholarship to the University of Georgia. My degree helped me get a great job and now I help others. That's what you will do too."

"I'd like to help others," Quentin said. His tone was wistful, as if he'd never considered the possibility.

Seresta pointed at an award on the wall. It was for Most Valuable Player in the NCAA Women's Basketball Championship. Right below it was a picture of the championship team. "You know why I have this picture and my award hanging here in my little cubicle at *Mom*entum?"

"So people will know you were a good basketball player when you were young?" Quentin guessed.

She narrowed her eyes at him. "No, that is not the reason. I keep it here to remind myself that I didn't make it to where I am alone. I had a lot of help along the way. Most people who are successful do have help. Now, what can *Mom*entum do for you?"

Quentin looked confused. "You're asking me? I thought that was why I came here, for you to tell me what I need to do."

Meghan always enjoyed the initial interviews. These kids had rarely been asked for their opinion or been given the chance to make any decisions for themselves. That was the first thing they tried to give back. Control.

"It's your life," Meghan said. "You get to choose the path you want to take. We're just here to help you along the way."

Quentin considered this for a few seconds. Then he stared down at his hands. "I work for a tire company, but I always thought I'd like to be a doctor. I know that sounds crazy."

"I've heard a lot of crazy things," Seresta assured him, "but that's not one of them. You can be a doctor if you want to, but it's going to take a lot of hard work. A lot."

Quentin nodded. "I know how to work hard."

Seresta made some notes. "First we'll work on getting your GED. Then we'll apply to college."

77

Meghan sat quietly while Seresta helped Quentin fill out all the paperwork to get him started on the path to a good education.

When they were through Seresta said, "This clinic has many other resources that are available to you. We have classes about nutrition and making healthy meals. We'll even teach you how to grow your own vegetables. We have tutors to help you with your college courses, a free clothing store and weekly grocery supplements."

"And if there's anything else you need, specific to your circumstances, all you have to do is ask," Meghan told him. "We'll do anything we can to help you achieve success."

"Thank you." Quentin looked a little overwhelmed as he stood, collected his college paperwork, and headed for the door.

"I'll see you next Thursday at the same time!" Seresta called after him. "Don't be late!"

Meghan winked at the young father. "Don't worry about Seresta. Her bark is worse than her bite. Now, let's go find your kids."

***

Finally Saturday morning came. Twenty-four hours was too long to ask Caldwell to stay with her, so Meghan drove herself to Dr. Morrow's lab. Instead of the anxiety she'd experienced the week before, all she felt was anticipation.

Because of the extended length of the dream session, Heidi had her change into a hospital gown before reclining on the soft, warm bed. It seemed to take the technician forever to get the IV started, the electrodes in place, and the monitors hooked up.

"This time we'll be giving you some nutrients while you sleep to keep you from feeling hungry and so your blood sugar stays level," Heidi explained.

Meghan resisted the urge to tell the woman to hurry.

When all was ready Dr. Morrow came in to see her off.

"It will pick up just where I left off last week, right?" she asked.

He nodded. "Sweet dreams."

She closed her eyes and waited for the dizziness that let her know she was moving into her dream-state. When it came, she smiled, welcoming the feeling. She drifted weightlessly for a few seconds. And then she opened her eyes.

***

She was back in her old car, driving home from Savannah. She sat up and stretched. "How long until we get back to Atlanta?"

"About thirty minutes. Mom said they've gotten a lot done on the house. Uncle Jim had some almost new appliances he took out of a renovation so he installed them in the kitchen."

She smiled. "I can hardly wait to see it. It doesn't seem real to me yet. I can't believe we are going to walk in that cottage and stay there with nobody telling us we have to go home."

"I know what you mean. These past few days have been great – but almost like a dream."

She nodded. "That's exactly what I mean."

They drove in companionable silence for a few minutes. Then Meghan said, "Once our house gets finished we can have our parents over for dinner."

"Do you know how to cook?"

She shook her head. "I know how to order pizza."

He gave her a gorgeous smile. "Oh, we're good then."

When they got back to Old Mountain they drove straight to the cottage. It looked like a mess to Meghan – with construction materials scattered everywhere. But Joey explained the progress.

"We have a new roof that doesn't leak and new wood on the porch floor so we won't fall through. We have new plumbing and almost-new kitchen appliances!"

She rubbed her hand along the stove. "The appliances are my favorite part!"

He continued through the house. "The bathtub, sink, and tile have been re-glazed so instead of pink – they're now sparkling white. And we have a new toilet." He glanced back at her. "I told them we can only take recycling so far."

"I agree completely."

There was a knock on the open front door and Joey's father called out, "Anyone home?"

Joey rushed into the living room. Meghan stood a little apart and watched as father and son embraced briefly.

"This place looks great!" Joey enthused.

Meghan couldn't go that far, but she said, "We really appreciate all your hard work!"

Troy smiled. "It is coming along. We still need to paint inside and out, refinish the old hardwood floors, and replace some broken window glass. Then this old house should be good as new!"

"Heck, better than it was when it was new!" Joey corrected. "Where's Mom?"

"She's making your curtains." Troy opened one of the newly painted kitchen cabinets. Inside they could see a neat stack of dishes. "The aunts contributed pots and pans and dishes to stock the kitchen. So you should have everything you need."

Meghan was overwhelmed by their generosity. "That was so nice of them."

"They are pretty great!" Joey said. "Now I guess I'll go get our stuff out of the car so we can get settled in."

Troy frowned. "But the cottage won't be ready to move into until this weekend."

Joey shrugged. "We've got to stay here whether it's ready or not. It's too crowded at our house, I won't stay with Meg's parents, and we can't afford a hotel. So we'll camp out until it's finished."

"You don't even have any furniture," Troy pointed out. "Except that table and you can't sleep on it."

Joey laughed. "Meghan's parents are giving us some furniture, but we can't move it in until Saturday when the place is finished. I figured we'd borrow a couple of sleeping bags from you and Mom."

Troy said, "You're really going to camp out here until Saturday?"

Meghan toed a pile of construction debris. "Apparently."

Troy shook his head. "I'll bring you a couple of sleeping bags and some sandwiches."

Meghan smiled. "That would make camping out here much more comfortable."

So they spent the first night in their house on the floor in what would eventually be their master bedroom.

Joey pulled her close and whispered, "Are you sorry we didn't go to a hotel?"

"No." Meghan shifted her weight to keep her hipbone from digging into the old hardwoods. "I'm glad we're here."

He nuzzled her neck. "Welcome home, Mrs. Patrone."

She wrapped her arms around him and forgot all about the hardness of the floor.

***

When Troy and his brothers arrived the next day to work on the cottage, Joey asked what they could do to help.

"We can certainly use you for unskilled labor – like picking up trash and hauling it to the dumpster," Troy teased his son. "But it's not healthy for Meghan to be exposed to fumes or dust so that pretty much eliminates everything here. I guess she could go to the house and help your mother with curtains."

Meghan shook her head and took Joey's hand. "I want to stay here."

Troy gave the question more consideration. "Maybe you two could work on refinishing that old kitchen table. If you do it outside there shouldn't be any danger to the baby."

This project was appealing to both Joey and Meghan. She helped him sand and prepare the old table. But when it was time to stain he asked her to sit on a lawn chair several yards away.

As she settled on the old chair she said, "I know this sounds crazy, but sometimes I forget about the baby – even though it's the reason for all of this."

He grinned. "Wait until you get fat. Then you'll remember."

She made a face. "Quit teasing me and stain that table."

"But speaking of the baby," Joey said as he wiped brown goo on the freshly sanded wood. "Shouldn't you go to a doctor soon – just to be sure everything is okay?"

She closed her eyes and stretched her legs out to get some sun. "I'll make an appointment tomorrow."

"That's good." He dipped his rag back into the can of stain. Then he looked over at her. "Meg?"

"Yes?" she responded without opening her eyes.

"I guess this is all because of the baby, but the baby happened because we love each other."

She opened her eyes and saw him there, leaned over the old table, brown stain on his hands, hair hanging in his sweaty face, and thought he was the most beautiful thing she had ever seen. "I know. Thank you for reminding me."

He gave her a goofy grin and went back to staining. She smiled and reclosed her eyes.

***

Meghan was able to get an appointment at the doctor the next day. He declared her to be in perfect health and gave her a due date right after Thanksgiving. It was exciting to have an actual day to look toward. It was also a little scary because now the baby seemed more real.

Despite Meghan's doubts, the house was finished on schedule and they moved in officially on Saturday. Paula and her mother worked side-by-side helping to clean up the mess left by days of frantic renovation. They didn't talk much, but Meghan didn't sense any hostility between them. They were dedicated to a common goal – getting their children settled in a comfortable home. And that seemed to be enough for the moment.

When the moms reached the fireplace they saw the list of goals nailed above it.

"What's this?" her mother asked.

"And can it be thrown away?" Paula added.

"It's a list of our goals," Meghan explained. "Its how we are going to judge the success or failure of our lives. So no, it can't be thrown away."

"Can we frame it at least?" her mother suggested.

Paula frowned. "It will still look terrible, even in a frame."

"But it will look better," Suzanne replied. Then she reached up and took down the list of goals and the nail that held it to the wall. "I'll take care of it."

Meghan gave her a thankful smile.

Once the cottage was clean they started unloading the rental truck full of furniture. Joey's dad and uncles helped move everything in. The little house filled up quickly and some items had to be returned to the truck. But the furniture made the house look more like a home and Meghan could tell her parents were pleased with their contribution.

Paula's curtains were perfect – simple and white and non-style specific they covered the windows and gave the house a cozy feel. Suzanne had purchased new bedding and helped Meghan put it on her childhood bed.

"I got something less feminine," Suzanne explained. "It seemed best if it didn't belong to either of you before."

"That was very thoughtful," Meghan said. "I'm sure Joey will appreciate it."

When her mother saw that some of her bedroom furniture would not fit in their small room she said, "It's a shame to break up a matching suite. Maybe you could keep the things that won't fit in your extra bedroom."

"That's the baby's room," Meghan said.

"I know, but the baby doesn't need it yet."

"I don't want it to be a storage room," Meghan said. "I want to go ahead and fix it up so everything will be ready when the baby comes."

"Do you have any ideas about how you want it to look?" Paula asked.

Meghan walked into the room that would become her nursery. "No. I haven't got a clue."

The mothers joined her there.

"I like this light green color," Paula said.

"Joey picked it," Meghan told her. "He said we needed something neutral that would work for either a boy or a girl."

"It's a small room," Suzanne pointed out and it was true. The three of them could barely turn around.

"There's just enough space for a crib and a little dresser," Paula said.

"I can have your father get your baby furniture out of the attic if you want to use it," her mother offered.

Meghan was so thankful she hadn't offered to buy them new stuff – emphasizing the economic gap between the two families.

"It's nice to pass things like that down," Paula said. "Kind of like connecting the generations. I'd offer you Joey's crib but after four boys it was destroyed so I threw it away when Michael was old enough for a twin bed."

Meghan laughed. "I can just imagine." Then she turned to her mother. "Thanks, Mom. I'd like to use my crib and chest."

Paula walked over to the far wall. "You could put the crib here," she suggested.

"And you could get a wallpaper border," Suzanne added.

"I could make some special curtains for the baby."

Suzanne looked at her daughter. "All subject to Meghan's approval, of course."

"Of course," Paula agreed quickly. "We're not trying to take over your nursery."

Meghan saw the beginnings of a friendship developing between the mothers and she wanted to encourage it. "I'm going to be so busy with school and learning how to be a wife and all. Maybe the two of you could decorate the nursery and then surprise me."

Paula's eyes lit up. "You don't mind?"

"Not at all," Meghan assured her. "I don't know anything about nurseries, but you two do."

The mothers smiled at each other.

"We'll be delighted to take care of it," Suzanne said.

"Call me some day next week and we can go shopping," Paula said. "I'm free any day except Wednesday."

"I'll call you," Suzanne promised.

Meghan watched them with wonder. Who would have ever thought Paula and Suzanne could be friends?

The little house was crowded with people all day. Joey's aunts and uncles came to admire the renovations and deliver additional house warming gifts. Meghan had never said 'thank you' so many times before in her life. She was grateful, but she longed for peace and quiet. So it was a relief when everyone finally left and they were alone. Joey took her hand and they walked through each room of their new home.

"Isn't this great?" he asked as they toured.

"It is amazing," she agreed. "More than I could ever have expected."

When they reached the baby's room, Meghan said, "My parents are donating my old baby furniture to our cause and our mothers are going to work together to decorate this room."

Joey raised an eyebrow. "They are going to work together?"

She nodded. "More than that, I think they are going to be friends."

"Your mom and my mom?" he clarified.

"Yes."

"Wow," he said. "I never would have predicted that."

For dinner they heated up some of the refrigerator full of food Paula had left for them and ate them at their newly refinished table. Then they sat on their front porch swing and stared at the stars.

"Football practice starts tomorrow," Joey told her.

"So I won't see much of you anymore?"

"Not as much anyway. Will you be okay here alone?"

"I'll be fine, but I don't want to just sit around. I think I'll go to the mall and see if I can find a part-time job – at least until school starts. The extra money would be nice."

"As long as you're feeling okay," Joey agreed conditionally.

"I won't get anything too demanding," she promised.

"So how are we going to celebrate our last day before football practice?"

"I don't know," she said. "Do you have any ideas?"

He stood and held out his hand to her. "I've got one."

She laughed as he led her inside.

***

The next day after Joey left for practice Meghan went to the mall. While talking to the manager of a candle shop, her best friend since kindergarten, Caldwell St. James, walked in.

When Caldwell found out that Meghan was trying to get a job, she told the manager, "If you hire her, I promise to come in every week and spend tons of money."

The manager, who obviously knew Caldwell and her deep pockets well, agreed immediately. She gave Meghan the new-employee paperwork to fill out.

"As soon as you bring these back I can put you on the schedule," the manger said.

Meghan thanked her profusely and promised to return the forms the next day. Then Caldwell hauled her out of the candle shop and into the food court. Once they were settled at a table, Caldwell pointed at the ring on her finger and said, "What's up? Did Patrone give you a promise ring or something?"

Meghan took a deep breath and made the announcement for the first time. "I'm married to Joey now."

Caldwell looked aghast. "Shut up."

"It's true."

Now Caldwell was angry. "And why wasn't I invited to the wedding? I am your best friend after all."

"It was just a small family ceremony," Meghan explained vaguely. "We're living in his grandparents' little cottage."

"That rundown old shack where kids go to drink after football games?"

"It used to be a rundown shack," Meghan confirmed. "But Joey's family fixed it up for us. You should come visit me sometime."

"How about right now?" Caldwell stood. "This I've got to see."

When they reached the cottage, Caldwell walked in and looked around. She didn't rave about the improvements, but she didn't criticize them either.

"So I guess living here with Patrone is kind of like playing house?"

"Kind of," Meghan agreed. "It doesn't quite feel real yet."

"And I guess you're pregnant."

"Yes." Meghan wasn't surprised by the question. Caldwell was known for her brutal honesty. But admitting that they had married for something other than love made her feel a little sad. "We wanted to get married anyway."

"Sure you did," Caldwell said with typical cynicism. "When will the baby come?"

"Around Thanksgiving."

"So what about college?"

"I'm going to Georgia State."

Caldwell frowned. "You must be disappointed that you're not going to Vandy like your dad – since that was always like your number one goal in life. And I know your parents are devastated."

"I'm not disappointed," Meghan claimed. "And my parents have been great. I love Joey. We didn't plan to get married this soon or to have a baby now – but it's going to be fine."

"What about going to medical school?"

"I can still go. It just might take me a little longer to get there."

Caldwell made a face, indicating that she didn't have much confidence in this. "I feel like I let you down."

This remark took Meghan by surprise. "What do you mean?"

"I've got years of experience in the romance department. I could have told you how to avoid all this." She waved a hand to encompass the ring on Meghan's finger and the small house.

Meghan could see how the cottage must look to Caldwell – shabby rather than cute, small rather than cozy. "Believe me my mother told me everything there is to know about avoiding pregnancy so you don't have to feel responsible."

"If you knew how to prevent it, then how did it happen?"

"We had decided to wait," Meghan explained. "But then one night – well, we changed our minds. And we didn't even think about the risks."

Caldwell shook her head. "Amateurs."

Meghan laughed. "Caldwell – you are the least romantic person I know."

Caldwell sighed. "Somebody's got to keep their head on straight around here."

***

The next week Meghan started her job at the mall. The candle shop smelled wonderful, her coworkers were pleasant, and interacting with the public was more fun than she expected.

After work she would stop by the practice field and watch Joey and the rest of the football team. When he saw her sitting in the bleachers he'd wave and this usually got him yelled at by the coaches. But he didn't seem to mind – even when he had to run as punishment.

Once school started their weekdays were filled with attending classes, writing papers, and studying for tests. On Saturdays Joey played football and the Patrones attended en masse whether it was home or away. Meghan enjoyed the games – especially since Joey was red-shirted and just stood on the sidelines looking handsome. But she cringed when her in-laws screamed at the referees and opposing players.

On Sundays they ate breakfast with the Patrones and then Joey worked for his father while Meghan worked at the candle shop. The money they made went into jar marked 'new truck tires'. On Sunday evenings they ate dinner with Meghan's parents. Their lives had taken on a busy, pleasant rhythm.

One Sunday night after dinner Suzanne gave them a gift. It was their list of goals, neatly matted and framed.

"It's beautiful, Mom. Thank you!" Meghan said.

Even Joey was impressed. "Yes, Mrs. Dunaway, it looks great."

When they got home they hung it over the fireplace.

"I'm glad to have it back," Meghan said. "It's good for us to look at it regularly and think about the future."

Joey put his arm across her shoulders. "And remember the things we want to accomplish."

In late September Joey came in after a game one Saturday evening and while they were eating dinner he told her that he had invited some of his teammates over to his parents' house to watch a pro football game the next afternoon.

Meghan was surprised. "Why didn't you invite them to come here?"

Joey looked uncomfortable with the question. "It's just that we don't have much room and I figured you wouldn't want a bunch of rude guys burping and hollering and drinking beer in your house. Besides they eat a lot and my mom is used to cooking for the guys. I wouldn't want you to go to all that trouble."

"It's not because you're ashamed of me?" She looked down at her little baby bump.

"No!" he insisted, and he did look horrified.

"It's okay," she said, although it wasn't. "None of the other guys have wives, let alone a pregnant one. It's a little embarrassing. I understand."

He pulled her into his arms and held her tight. "I'm not ashamed of you! If you want me to call them right now and tell them to come here instead, I will."

"No, don't change your plans," she said, but the feelings of hurt and inadequacy lingered.

That night when they were lying in bed Joey told her, "I meant it about the guys. I don't care if I never see any of them again. You're all that's important to me now."

Snuggled against him, she felt reassured. "I don't mind if you host the party at your mom's house," she said and this time she meant it.

She listened as the rhythm of Joey's breathing changed to the soft cadence of sleep. And then she felt the baby move. It was so slight at first she wasn't sure – but then she felt it again and she knew. Her baby was alive and growing and moving. She didn't wake Joey. She wanted to savor the news herself for just a little while.

***

The next week they went to the doctor to have her ultrasound. Meghan had been looking forward to this day and was excited to find out if the baby was a girl or a boy. But while they were in the waiting room Joey told her that he'd rather wait and find out when the baby was born. She was a little disappointed.

"Are you sure?" she whispered. "Our moms are trying to decorate the nursery."

"They can pick stuff that will work either way," he said. "I want it to be a surprise."

So they told the technician not give them any details except if the baby was healthy. Joey was fascinated when he saw the 3-D picture on the ultrasound monitor. He asked the technician all kinds of questions and when they walked out, he had a dazed expression.

"It seems so much more real to me now," he explained. "Seeing the baby moving with a beating heart and everything."

Meghan held up the printout the ultrasound technician had given them. "Our baby's first picture."

Joey glanced down at it. "Let's hope it gets cuter before it's born."

Meghan shook her head. "You're hopeless."

The parents were a little disappointed when they learned that they would have to wait until the baby was born to find out whether they were having a grandson or granddaughter. But the mothers started enthusiastically decorating a non-gender-specific nursery.

By the time the weather turned cooler and fall was in the air – Meghan felt huge. The baby moved all the time. Joey would sit beside her with his hand on her belly and sing at the top of his lungs.

"I hope tone-deafness isn't hereditary," she teased him.

"If it is we'll make unbeautiful music together," he replied.

Once the nursery was finished Meghan liked to sit there in the early mornings and watch the first rays of sunlight stream through the curtains Paula had made. She loved the baby so much already. She couldn't imagine how she would feel when they actually met.

In October they took mid-terms. Meghan did very well, but Joey barely passed. She suggested that he stop working with his dad on Sundays so he could study more. He said they needed the money for tires on his truck and that once football season was over he would have more time to dedicate to his studies.

On Halloween they decorated their house and passed out candy to trick-or-treaters.

In November they started taking childbirth classes and their classmates made fun of Joey since he was a big tough football player but nearly fainted at least once during every class.

The football season ended in mid-November and Joey turned his attention to his grades. He studied harder and stayed up late into the night completing his assignments. Meghan knew he was feeling stressed and discouraged because he never sang anymore. To cheer him up she made him discuss baby names. Most of his suggestions were awful, but at least it made him laugh.

The week before Thanksgiving Meghan went into labor and Joey went into panic mode.

"But the baby isn't due until after Thanksgiving!" he told her.

"The due date is just an estimate," she said. "Babies come when they are ready and this baby is definitely ready." She put a hand to her stomach and breathed through a contraction. "My suitcase is by the front door. Now let's go."

On the way to the hospital Joey called both moms. Then he missed the entrance to the Women's and Children's Center at the hospital and had to drive around the block and try it again.

"I've never felt so nervous," he told her as he opened the car door for her.

"Take a few deep breaths," Meghan suggested. "I can't be worrying about you. I have to concentrate on delivering this baby!"

They went into the emergency room and Joey explained to the security guard that his wife was in labor. He took them to the admissions desk. While Joey filled out paperwork, Meghan was taken in a wheelchair up to the labor and delivery floor.

By the time Joey joined her she was wearing a hospital gown and being hooked up to various monitors.

"My parents are in the waiting room and yours are on their way," he reported. "How are you doing?"

"Fine," she replied.

"She's doing great," the nurse told Joey. "You'll have a baby soon."

He sat down heavily, looking very pale.

"Keep an eye on him for me please," Meghan requested between contractions. "He's a fainter."

The nurse leveled a stern look in his direction. "If you faint on me I'll just have to kick you aside and keep going. My job is to make sure your wife has this baby safely. You understand?"

Joey sat up a little straighter. "Yes, ma'am."

"Good." The nurse turned to Meghan. "I'll be back in a few minutes. Push the call button if you need me before that."

After the nurse left, Joey said, "Mom wants to come in and see you. Are you okay with that?"

"As long as she doesn't stay long," Meghan agreed. "These contractions are getting pretty bad and I don't want to scream in front of her."

A few minutes later Paula rushed in. Troy hovered near the door, obviously uncomfortable. Paula marched up to the bed and handed Meghan a box of chocolates. "These are for afterwards. Trust me, you'll need them."

"Thank you. Where are the boys?"

Paula sighed. "I told them they'd have to wait until the baby is actually born before they come to the hospital. Wherever they go property damage usually follows. The less time they are here – the less opportunity for disaster."

Meghan started to laugh but then a contraction started and she grabbed her stomach.

"Let's go back to the waiting room and stop bothering Meghan," Troy said.

"You can do it!" Paula called over her shoulder as she left. "We'll be praying for you!"

Meghan's parents arrived a few minutes later. They were emotional – excited about the baby but worried about the ordeal she was going to have to endure. Her father talked to the obstetrician and seemed reassured afterward. Her mother still looked anxious when she left to join the Patrones in the waiting room.

Labor was painful but not more than Meghan could bear. Joey was right beside her still looking pale but in control. He gave her ice chips whenever she needed them. Then the doctor said she was ready to push. This process took longer than she expected but every time she got discouraged Joey reminded her of how cute the baby was sure to be.

Finally the doctor said, "Here's the head! Your baby has a lot of dark hair."

Joey took his eyes off Meghan's for just long enough to look. When he returned his gaze to hers he was white as a sheet.

"Cute?" Meghan managed between pushes.

"I didn't see the face and I'm sorry, but I can't look again."

"Don't make me laugh during labor!" she gasped as another contraction engulfed her.

"One more push and we'll have a baby," the doctor said.

Meghan closed her eyes and pushed with all her might. The pain disappeared and she thought the baby had been born. But when she opened her eyes the delivery room was gone. She was in the session room at Dr. Morrow's laboratory.

"Send me back!" she begged. "Just for a few more minutes!"

"I'm sorry, Dr. Collins," Heidi said in her cool, clinical voice. "Once we bring you out we can't send you back."

Meghan turned her face into the pillow and sobbed.

Chapter Seven

Meghan had mostly composed herself by the time she was ushered into Dr. Morrow's office for her Post Dream Session. She sat in the chair and faced him, shaken.

"You didn't enjoy your dream this time?' he asked with obvious concern.

"It ended just as I was about to give birth," she told him. "When can I go back? I want to see the baby at least."

"It might be better to leave the dream behind now – before you see the baby," Dr. Morrow said. "Are you sure you want to continue?"

She nodded. "I have to."

"You know we have a one week minimum between sessions."

"I'll be back next Saturday," she told him, wondering how she would ever survive so much time until she could be with Joey again and meet their baby.

***

Chase was not home when she got back to the condo on Sunday morning. Meghan was glad. She needed time to compose herself. She took a shower and as she ran a washcloth over her flat stomach she wanted to weep. It felt like she was in someone else's body – someone else's life.

She went to the hospital and did her rounds. When she got home Chase was on the deck, watching the sun sink behind the skyline.

"How was your session with the witchdoctor?" he asked.

"Fine," she replied carefully.

"So you're done now?"

She licked her lips. "I'm going to do one more." She knew this was a lie when the words left her mouth. She could not imagine living without her dreams.

"One more," he repeated.

She nodded.

"Why?"

"The dream ended before the baby was born. I want to see if it's a boy or a girl."

"I'm starting to worry about you, Meghan. I think those dreams are playing with your mind."

"You have to understand," she told him. "It's like reading a good book and when you finish with one – you want to read the next in the series."

"Except that this book is about you and another man."

"It's fiction," Meghan said. "I know that." But she couldn't meet his eyes. "I love you," she added, as much to convince herself as him.

He stood and took her into his arms. "I love you, too."

***

The week was grueling for Meghan. She couldn't sleep, she couldn't eat, she couldn't concentrate on her work. Every little thing she did seemed to take so much thought and energy. And she wanted to devote all her time to thinking about her dream life and her baby. Even the hours she spent at the *Mom*entum clinic were hollow and unsatisfying.

Finally Saturday arrived and she got to Dr. Morrow's lab an hour early.

"Anxious aren't you?" Heidi teased.

Since Meghan was used to the routine now she was able to facilitate the set-up process and it went quickly. Dr. Morrow came in to wish her happy dreams. She thought he looked a little smug as he gave permission for her session to begin, but she didn't care. She closed her eyes and waited for the dizzy feeling that would usher her into her dream.

***

Meghan held her eyes tightly closed.

"Push!" the doctor commanded.

She bore down with all her might and felt a lightening – a relief.

"Oh my gosh . . ." Joey was pale as a ghost.

"Don't faint!" she begged him.

He whispered. "We have a baby!"

"It's a girl," the doctor informed them. "Have you picked out a name?"

They looked at each other and she nodded.

"Sophie," Joey said.

Then a nurse placed the squirming little bundle on Meghan's chest.

She pulled back the blanket and looked at her daughter's face. Two round blue eyes, a small mashed nose, a tiny rosebud mouth. Meghan's heart was overwhelmed with emotion. Speechless, she widened her gaze to include Joey. His expression was something between wonder and terror. It would have been funny if it hadn't been so sweet.

He reached out with a finger to touch one of Sophie's tiny fists. "How can we love her so much when we just met her?"

"I don't know." Tears splashed onto Meghan's cheeks. "But what I do know is that a few months ago in my parents' kitchen – we made the right decision."

He nodded. "Thank you for having the courage to go through with it."

"Thank *you* for convincing me to try."

The nurse interrupted the moment. "We've got to get this young lady measured and weighed and cleaned up." She scooped Sophie from Meghan's chest and took her across the room to table. Meghan watched the nurse with her baby. Sophie was perfect with clenched fists, rosy skin, and an angry cry.

Later when the grandparents were allowed to come in, it was love at first sight for them, too. They took turns holding the baby and admiring her. Even Joey's brothers were almost reverent with Sophie. The baby looked around at everyone, like a tiny queen holding court.

They left the hospital the next day and drove straight to their cottage. Both mothers had offered to let the new little family stay with them for the first week or so, but Meghan wanted to be home. Sophie was a good baby, eating vigorously, sleeping peacefully. They made a brief appearance at each of their parents' homes for Thanksgiving and then spent the rest of the holiday weekend secluded, falling more in love with the baby every day.

In early December Caldwell dropped by, without calling first, to see the baby. When Joey looked out the front window and saw her standing on the porch he groaned. "Of all your snobby friends at Meadowbrook I hated her the most," he whispered.

"Caldwell has been my friend since we were in pre-school."

"Then I say it's time to cut her loose."

"Open the door," Meghan hissed.

"I brought your offspring a gift!" Caldwell proclaimed when she walked in carrying the world's largest teddy bear.

"He's going to need his own room," Joey remarked as he eyed the bear.

"The lady at the toy store told me every baby should have one."

"Every giant baby, maybe," Joey conceded.

Meghan sent Joey a disapproving look. "We appreciate it very much, but it must have cost a fortune."

Caldwell shrugged. "I used my dad's charge card."

Meghan lifted the baby out of her bassinet. "Do you want to hold her?"

"She won't wet on me or throw up or anything – will she?"

"No guarantees," Joey said.

Meghan frowned at him again as she settled Sophie in Caldwell's arms. "Sophie is very well-behaved."

"I can't believe this huge baby came out of you!" Caldwell cried. "It must have hurt like the devil."

"It doesn't seem that bad now," Meghan said, smiling down at her daughter. "It was well worth it anyway."

Caldwell passed the baby back. "I don't think I'll ever have kids. I have a low pain tolerance and I don't like smelly things. Besides I don't think I could go a whole nine months without a drink."

Joey frowned. "If you can't give up drinking, you definitely shouldn't be a parent."

"Don't judge me lover-boy," Caldwell said. "I'm not the one who had to get married at eighteen because I didn't pay attention in health class."

Joey's face turned red and Meghan decided she'd better intervene. "Caldwell, I appreciate you coming by, but it's time for me to feed Sophie and put her to bed."

Caldwell looked between them. "Well, I know when I've worn out my welcome."

"If you knew that you wouldn't have walked through the door," Joey muttered.

"Funny." She flashed him a fake smile.

"Thanks for the gigantic teddy bear," Meghan told her friend. "And say hi to the girls at the candle shop for me."

Joey opened the door. "We know you're busy so don't feel like you have to rush back anytime soon."

Caldwell sailed through the door. "Patrone, you're a riot."

Sophie was only three weeks old when Meghan had to take her first final. Joey helped her pack everything up before he left for school. Then Meghan drove to the Patrones' house, checking the baby constantly in the rearview mirror. When the moment came for her to actually leave without her daughter – she wasn't sure she could do it.

"Go on, now," Paula said, propping the baby on her shoulder. "I need a little grandma-time with Sophie."

Meghan forced herself to walk out to her car and cried all the way to school. Fortunately the final was not difficult and she finished quickly. When she returned to the Patrones' house – Sophie was sleeping.

"Did she cry?" Meghan asked, worried that the baby had refused to take a bottle.

"Not a whimper," Paula said. "You don't know how fortunate you are to have an angel for a baby. Your next child will probably scream all day and night."

It was impossible for Meghan to think about her 'next' child. So far she only thought it terms of Sophie. And although she was glad the baby had been happy in her absence, it made her feel a little non-essential.

She picked up her sleeping daughter – earning a frown from Paula who had already warned her about the ills of waking a baby. Then she carried her to the couch and nursed her. Sophie's eyes looked up into hers intensely as she ate.

"I think her eyes are going to stay blue, like mine," Meghan remarked.

"You can't be sure for a few more months," Paula said. "How was it?"

"I survived the separation," Meghan replied. Then she realized her mother-in-law meant her exam at school – not the trauma of leaving Sophie for the first time. So she added, "The test wasn't hard. I'm sure I did fine."

And when the grades were posted she found out that she did better than fine. She had A's in all her classes. Joey had passed all his, but barely scraped by in a couple. Once finals were over Meghan tried to forget about school and turned her attention to Christmas. She made Joey cut down a pine tree and set it up in their tiny living room.

"This room isn't big enough for the tree and that blimp-sized Teddy bear. One of them has to go," he decreed once he had the tree in front of the window.

"The Teddy bear," Meghan chose. "Can you take it to your mother's house?"

"Why not your mother's house?" he asked.

Meghan wrinkled her nose. "She'd think it was tacky."

"It is tacky," Joey assured her. "But I'll take it to my mother. Maybe the boys can use it for target practice."

"You know that Teddy bear was very expensive?"

"I know it came from Caldwell – so I don't care how much it cost or what happens to it."

The bear was removed – to parts unknown – and they decorated their tree with ornaments they found in the attic. "These are probably antiques," Meghan said as they put the delicate glass ornaments on the tree.

"I'm sure they are," Joey agreed. "I remember seeing them on my grandparents' tree when I was little. It seems crazy that I live here now, with a family of my own, and we're decorating our tree with the same ornaments."

Once their tree was done it felt like the holiday season began in earnest. Sophie was the star of the show at all Christmas gatherings. On Christmas Eve they ate with the Patrones and then went to Mass as a family. When they got back to the cottage, Meghan fed Sophie and put her to bed in her little Christmas pajamas. Then Joey helped her play Santa Claus. While filling Sophie's stocking and laying out her little gifts, Meghan felt like the happiest woman in the world.

On Christmas Day they ate dinner with Meghan's parents. They had several nice gifts for Sophie – including a savings bond. For Meghan and Joey, they had wrapped up the title to her car.

"But we haven't paid you for it yet," Meghan said.

"Please let us do this." Suzanne's plea was directed toward Joey. "You're both working so hard. We just want to make things a little easier."

Meghan knew Joey felt very strongly about paying her parents for the car – no matter how long it took – so she braced herself to hear him decline, and ruin her parents' Christmas gift.

But he surprised her. Instead he swallowed his pride and thanked them graciously. "We appreciate this very much."

Meghan's heart swelled with love for him.

He leaned close to her and whispered, "Merry Christmas."

***

Meghan and Joey received invitations to several New Years' Eve parties, but they decided to celebrate quietly at home with Sophie. While the baby slept, Joey put in a sentimental movie. They sat on the couch, holding hands and watched it until midnight. When the fireworks started outside, Joey turned off the movie. He put a CD in and asked her to dance. As they swayed together in front of the fireplace Meghan's eyes were drawn to their list of goals. They were making progress, becoming the people they wanted to be.

"This is the nicest New Year's party I've ever been to," she told him. And she meant it.

The winter semester started and Meghan found it considerably more difficult to attend classes than she had in the fall. She hated taking Sophie out into the cold, damp weather every morning so Paula could babysit. When Sophie got a cold, Meghan told Joey she was going to drop her classes and sit out the semester.

Joey laughed. "You can't quit school. Babies just get colds – even babies who don't have to get out in the winter weather."

"I just think it would be better if I could stay home with Sophie."

Joey pointed at their list of goals. "You see there where it says *graduate from college?*"

"It also says *be good parents.*"

"You can be a good parent and a student at the same time. Sophie is fine. She has a little cold."

"I don't know if I can keep doing it – taking her out every day."

"Then we'll ask Mom to come here," Joey said.

"Here?" Meghan repeated.

"That way you won't have to get Sophie out in bad weather."

She threw her arms around his neck and hugged him tight. "You're the best person in the whole world."

He nuzzled her neck. "Well, in Georgia anyway."

***

On Valentine's Day Meghan skipped her afternoon class and came home early. After Paula left, she baked Joey a heart shaped cake. It turned out terrible, burned on the edges and shaped more like a Mickey Mouse head than a heart. When she tried to spread on the frosting, the cake kept peeling up until it was a hideous, lumpy, pink Mickey-mess.

She was about to dump the cake in the garbage when he walked in with a dozen roses they couldn't afford. She accepted the bouquet and brought the fragrant blossoms to her nose. "They are beautiful – thank you."

He kissed her. "Happy Valentine's day."

She waved at the cake on the table. "I made you a cake but you can see how that turned out."

He picked up a spoon and scooped out a bite. "I'd say it turned out great."

She felt better immediately. "Really?"

He nodded. "Where's Sophie?"

"Sleeping. You want some more cake?"

He pulled her toward the bedroom. "Naw, I've got something else in mind."

***

Slowly but surely winter gave way to spring. Joey was at school all day and worked late hours with his father in the evenings and on weekends, trying to make as much money as possible before spring football began.

One warm Saturday while Joey was at work, Meghan went to the local home improvement store and bought some flowers. Then, with Sophie watching from her stroller, Meghan planted them in the beds that ran along the front of the cottage.

She was admiring her new little flowerbed when Caldwell drove up in a flashy silver sports car. Meghan just had time to be glad that Joey was at work before Caldwell climbed out and minced up the sidewalk wearing high heels, skin-tight jeans and a halter-top. She looked fabulous in a sleazy sort of way.

"You need to start making some trips to the gym if you ever plan to get rid of that baby-fat," she told Meghan instead of saying something more traditional like – hello.

"I'll get it off," Meghan replied. As long as Joey wasn't complaining about the few extra pounds – she wasn't going to worry about it.

"So, are you going to the beach with your parents for spring break?"

"No, Joey has an opportunity to work for his father and make some extra money," Meghan replied. "He wanted me to take Sophie and go but it doesn't seem right to leave him here working while we have fun. How about you?"

"I was hoping you'd ask," Caldwell said. She sat on the bottom step so she'd be as close to Meghan as possible. "I'm going to Kuwait!"

"Kuwait?' Meghan repeated.

"Yes! I met an international student at school and he's a sheik. Well a junior-sheik – kind of like a prince."

Meghan put down her trowel. "You met a sheik in Georgia? No way."

"Right there in my Western Civ class!" Caldwell confirmed. "He invited me to come home with him for spring break and spend the week on his father's yacht. He bought me a first class plane ticket and I leave on Friday!"

"Wow." Meghan smiled. "You are a lucky girl."

"I know! He said for me to keep in kind of quiet so he won't have a bunch of other people wanting to go. But I had to tell someone and I figured an old married woman like you could keep a secret."

"I won't tell a soul," Meghan promised. "But you be careful. I don't to see you on a television show about Americans who went missing while vacationing in the Middle East."

Caldwell laughed. "I'll be careful. And if you see me on TV – it will be on *Lifestyles of the Rich and Famous.*"

Caldwell was leaving as Joey came home for lunch. She blew her horn at him and waved. He ignored her.

"What did that psycho want?" he asked Meghan when he walked up to the house.

"Just to chat," she said. "Do you like my flowers?"

"I love them." He picked up Sophie and carried her inside.

As they walked through the door she asked, "Do you think I'm fat?"

***

The semester ended and they embraced summer – enjoying the Georgia sunshine as much as possible. And they really enjoyed Sophie.

She was crawling and could say a few words – including *Mama* and *Dada*. When she called to Meghan by name, she thought her heart would melt. Both sets of grandparents doted on her. And even her rambunctious uncles turned into baby-talking fools when she was around. It was amazing that one little person could generate so much emotion in so many people.

On Memorial Day weekend they were eating Sunday dinner at the Patrones' when Joey's brother, Matt, said he had something he wanted to discuss with the family. Meghan put down her fork and gave Matt her full attention. Paula did the same. The rest of the Patrones continued eating.

"This past week one of Michael's friends named Seth said he needed a ride home from school so we've been taking him," was Matt's inauspicious beginning.

Paula nodded encouragingly. "Michael told me. That was very kind of you."

Matt shook his head. "That was nothing. But when Seth said he needed a ride 'home' he meant a ride to his mother's car. She works on a road construction crew and he has to sit in the car alone until she gets off."

Paula was disapproving of this. "If she thinks he's too young to stay home alone, she should arrange afternoon daycare."

"That's just it, Mom," Matt explained. "The car *is* their home."

This remark got everyone's attention.

"He lives in his car?" Paula demanded.

"No way!" Ben added in disbelief.

"It's true," Matt insisted.

"Seth's mom didn't have a job for a long time and they got kicked out of their apartment," Michael contributed, obviously pleased that his friend was the focus of the conversation. "Now she's got a job but she doesn't have enough money to get another apartment, so they have to sleep in their car. Then every morning they go to the Flying J because it has showers."

"Is that even legal?" Joey demanded. "Living in a car?"

"I'm sure DHR would object to a child living in a car," Troy said.

Paula was aghast. "It's a shame that we have all these government programs to help people and there's a woman right here in our own community living with her son in a car."

Michael said, "His mom is afraid if she asks anyone for help they'll take Seth away from her."

Paula put a hand on her ample hip. "And put him where? What's a better place than with a loving mother?"

"Any place besides a car," Joey muttered.

Paula hit him on the back. "This is not funny."

Joey looked offended. "I'm not laughing! The kid can't live in a car. If his mother doesn't have a place to live then he's going to have to stay with someone else until she does."

"I talked to the priest about helping her find a place to live," Matt surprised them all by saying.

"You talked to the priest?" Troy said.

Matt shrugged. "I figured someone needed to."

Paula leaned down and kissed his cheek. "You did the right thing."

"What did he say?" Ben wanted to know.

"He told me he'd check on it and for me to come back this afternoon. So I did."

"Does the priest have a solution?" Troy asked.

"He called around and found man who is willing to donate a house to the Church and they'll let Seth and his mother live there."

Paula beamed at him. "Look what you did, Matt! You got them a home."

"Well, that's the thing," Matt said. "The house is in pretty bad shape."

"It's got to be better than a car," Paula pointed out.

Matt pressed on. "I was thinking we could fix it up a little. Maybe the uncles would help."

"Goodness knows we've got plenty of leftover construction supplies lying around," Paula muttered.

"I guess we could fix it up a little," Troy agreed.

"We're so blessed," Matt added. "We should help other people if we can."

"We can call it *The Patrone Project*," Ben suggested. "And maybe we'll get our own show on that how-to-do-it-yourself channel."

"We're going to be famous!" Michael cried.

Joey winked at Meghan. "We're philanthropists!"

"We're crazy," was Troy's opinion. "But I guess you can tell the priest that we'll repair the house."

Matt grinned. "I already did."

Troy got his brothers involved again. They all spent a solid month of their spare time turning the dilapidated structure into a two-bedroom home. Seth and his mother put in as many hours as anyone and by the time the house was finished, she was more than grateful for the chance to live there – she was invested in the project.

Meghan had no construction skills and she had Sophie to care for – so she wasn't very involved in the project. But she took the baby to the house almost every day to watch the progress and offer encouragement. When the project was completed she planted some flowers along the front, with Sophie watching from her stroller.

"That was the perfect finishing touch," Troy told her.

Meghan was unaccountably pleased by this small compliment.

Dana and Seth were supposed to move in on Saturday so church members rounded up spare furniture and bedding and towels and dishes. Meghan and Joey were happy to be contributors this time, instead of recipients. People bought Seth clothes and toys. They filled their refrigerator and cupboards with food.

The final result was nothing like the shows on TV where everything is state-of-the-art. But when Seth and his mother saw the house completed and furnished for the first time – it seemed like they were moving in to the most beautiful home in the world. There were tears all around.

And the Patrone family considered the project a success.

In August Joey started practicing football so he was gone all the time. Meghan lounged around the house – feeling lethargic. Sophie was cutting teeth and didn't sleep well at night so she blamed her exhaustion on lack of rest.

One day Caldwell dropped by for a visit. She looked wonderful – so vital and carefree. Meghan felt a little jealous as she listened to her friend report on her new boyfriend – a linguist from New York.

"What happened to the sheik?"

"Oh, he was two boyfriends ago. You know how I like to try new things. So I decided to date a smart guy. His name is Nigel and he is so cultured."

Meghan couldn't help wondering what someone like Nigel saw in Caldwell. But she kept that to herself.

"He speaks four languages fluently and three more well enough to be understood. Isn't that amazing?"

Meghan agreed that it was.

"I love it when he speaks to me in a foreign language. It's so exotic," she said. "And he can do huge math equations in his mind."

Meghan rolled her eyes. "I'm sure that comes in handy."

Caldwell smiled. "Now tell me all about being married to Joey Patrone. I want to know every intimate detail."

Suddenly Meghan felt very ill. She clutched her stomach and ran for the bathroom. When she came out, Caldwell was frowning.

"If you don't want me to tell you about my love-life – all you have to do is say so. There was no need to run off."

"I'm not feeling very well," Meghan said weakly. "In fact, I haven't felt very well for several weeks. I called they doctor and they can see me in an hour. Will you drive me?"

"It won't take long, will it?" Caldwell asked. "I've got a date with Nigel at seven tonight."

"Caldwell!"

"I'm sorry! Of course I'll take you to the doctor."

"You'll have to drive my car so we'll have Sophie's car seat base."

"I'm not sure what bothers me more," Caldwell muttered, "driving a dull Honda or knowing that there's a car seat in it."

Meghan got the baby and carried her outside. Caldwell stood by and watched as she secured the car seat. Then they drove to doctor's office in Atlanta.

"Maybe you have food poisoning," Caldwell suggested as they rode along.

"If I'd had food poisoning for weeks I'd be dead by now."

Caldwell chewed her lower lip. "I hope it's not something really bad like stomach cancer."

Meghan cut her eyes over at her friend. "Are you trying to depress me?"

"No!" Caldwell laughed. "I'm sure it's not a big deal."

Meghan was afraid she knew exactly what it was and if she was right – it was going to be a huge deal.

They arrived at the doctor's office and once again Caldwell stood by and watched Meghan handle everything. Meghan unloaded the stroller, pulled Sophie out of the car seat, and then threw the diaper bag over her shoulder. As she pushed the stroller into the office she reminded herself that Caldwell had driven them there. Apparently that was going to be her only contribution.

When Meghan was called back to an examination room she turned to Caldwell. "Can you watch Sophie for me?" she asked, pointing to the sleeping baby.

Caldwell looked a little panicked. "What if she wakes up or cries or something?"

"Then ask one of the nurses to come and get me," Meghan said impatiently. "I'll be back in a few minutes."

As she walked away Caldwell was staring at Sophie like the baby was a time-bomb.

After a blood test and a short wait the doctor came in to deliver the news.

"You're eight weeks pregnant, Meghan."

She was glad she was sitting down because her knees went weak. "Oh gosh. How could this have happened?"

The doctor didn't smile. "I think you know the answer to that."

"I just mean, well, obviously we weren't planning to have another baby so soon. Sophie is only eight months old and she's still nursing . . ." At this point Meghan burst into tears.

The doctor handed her a box of tissues and waited patiently until she got herself under control.

"Maybe you weren't planning on another baby so soon," he said finally, "But your plans have changed. You're due the first of March." He gave her some instructions and a prescription for prenatal vitamins. Then he told her to set up an appointment to come back in one month.

Somehow his unsympathetic attitude helped Meghan get control of her emotions. Once he left she blotted her tears and got dressed. Then she went out to the waiting room to collect her baby and give Caldwell the news.

Caldwell was predictably horrified. "What is the matter with you two? You're multiplying like rabbits – except rabbits have an excuse! They don't know any better!"

"Please," Meghan begged. "Don't lecture me. I feel foolish enough and Joey is going to be . . . well, more overwhelmed than he already is."

"Why weren't you taking birth control pills?"

"I can't while I'm nursing Sophie."

"Well, this is just terrible." Caldwell seemed at a loss. "What are you going to do?"

Meghan sighed. "I'm going to have a baby. But first I've got to make an appointment with the doctor for next month. Then I've got to figure out how to break the news to Joey."

Meghan walked up to the counter to make her follow-up appointment.

"Mrs. Patrone?" the nurse at the desk asked.

Meghan nodded.

"I set you up an appointment with the oncologist on Friday. We emailed your mammogram to him so he can be prepared to discuss the various treatment options. Since you will have to make some important decisions, we recommend that you bring your husband with you."

Meghan stared back blankly. "Oncologist? I have *cancer*? The doctor only told me I was pregnant!"

The nurse glanced back down at the file in her hand. "Paula Patrone?"

"I'm Meghan Patrone."

The nurse paled. "Oh I made a mistake. I'm so sorry."

A familiar voice spoke from behind her. "I'm Paula."

Meghan turned and came face to face with her mother-in-law. Then the full meaning of the nurse's mistake became clear. "Oh Paula!"

"It's going to be okay, sweetie," Paula said. Then she drew Meghan into her arms and comforted her instead of the other way around.

Meghan closed her eyes and wept.

Chapter Eight

When she opened her eyes and saw the room at Dr. Morrow's lab, Meghan thought her heart would break. Even though this grief-filled gap between dream sessions was becoming routine, she still hated it. And this time she was not only sorry that her session had ended, she was dealing with the news that Paula had cancer without any of the details. Intellectually she knew it was just a dream. But it felt very real.

Once she had composed herself she went into Dr. Morrow's office for her PDS.

"I'd like to set up my session for next Saturday," she told him. "In fact I'd like to just schedule that time indefinitely."

Dr. Morrow looked worried. "Your husband called me this morning. He says you're having trouble separating the dreams from reality. He thinks it's time for you to stop."

She was furious with Chase for interfering. "I'm not having any trouble distinguishing what is real." This was completely true. It was easy to tell the difference between the dreams and reality. She was happy in her dreams. "My husband is just a little jealous of my dream-life since he can't be a part of it."

Dr. Morrow nodded but he still seemed uneasy. "It can be hard for the non-dreaming spouse. They feel left out. Perhaps you can discuss your dreams with him?"

She wanted to discuss her dreams with someone. It would be such a relief to talk about Paula and her cancer and maybe get some reassurance. But she knew she couldn't discuss it with Chase. So she shook her head. "Talking to Chase about my dreams would make things worse instead of better."

"I don't want your dream-therapy sessions to damage your marriage relationship."

Even at the risk of her marriage, Meghan knew she had to go on. "I appreciate your concern, but I am your client, not Chase. And from now on I'd rather that you didn't discuss me or my dream sessions with him."

"Very well," Dr. Morrow said slowly. "I'll set you up for a 24-hour session next Saturday."

Meghan was relieved. She didn't know what she would have done if she'd been cut off from her dream-life, from her dream-family. She stood and shook Dr. Morrow's hand. "Thank you. I'll see you next week."

When she got home Chase was packing for a business trip.

"I've been assigned to a consult on a case in Omaha," he told her. "I'll be gone at least a week."

Meghan was inappropriately relieved. She had been planning to confront him about calling Dr. Morrow, but under the circumstances she decided to let it go.

When he was ready to leave she followed him to the door and kissed him goodbye. He seemed pleased by this.

"See you in a week," he said with a wave.

She watched out the window until she saw him drive off. Then she climbed into bed and closed her eyes so she could worry about Paula and dream about her life with Joey and Sophie.

***

On Monday Meghan got up and drove to the hospital for rounds. Then she moved on to the office to see patients. She went through the motions of her day, detached and not really interested in anything. It was as if her real life had become a background. She was just biding her time until she could get back to the dream.

The *Mom*entum clinic called as she finished with her last patient.

"The young man you referred, Quentin Jackson, passed his GED," the receptionist told her. "He's meeting with his advisor this evening and he'd like you to be there to help him plan his future."

It took Meghan a few seconds to remember the details about Quentin. "He has two sons, Sedrick and Little Something."

"Little Ty," the receptionist confirmed.

"And he's our first teenage father."

"Right," the receptionist confirmed. "So can you come to the meeting?"

Meghan wanted badly to say no. The only comfort she had during the long days between dreams was reliving the previous one. She'd been looking forward to getting home, putting on her pajamas, climbing into bed, and dreaming. But if she didn't go Quentin and his boys might not get all the help they needed. So Meghan told the receptionist she would be there.

When she arrived at the Momentum clinic, Quentin and the boys were waiting. Quentin still looked tired. The boys were perfectly groomed with neat braids and clean clothes. Meghan's respect for the teenage dad rose even higher.

When Sedrick saw Meghan he gave her a big hug. "I go to daycare here now," he told her. "They have good toys and they read us stories and when it's not raining we go to the park and play. And sometimes we get ice cream!"

Meghan smiled. "I'm so glad you're enjoying it!"

"And my dad passed his test so he can go to college and wear a tie to work instead of getting greasy hands!"

Meghan glanced at Quentin, who looked embarrassed.

"That's not exactly what I told him," Quentin said.

"But that was the gist of it," Meghan said. "You're on the road to a career you can enjoy while providing for your family."

Quentin nodded. "Yeah, that's it."

They dropped the boys off in the daycare room and then walked back to Seresta's cubicle. The former basketball player greeted them with a smile. "So here's our one and only Momentum father," she said. "You haven't had to take your kids back to the hospital this week have you?"

Quentin shook his head and then said to Meghan. "She's hard on me."

"Not as hard as the world will be if you let it have a chance!" Seresta assured him. "And I'm mostly kidding - except about the hospital part. You've got to take care of those little boys."

"You're lucky to have Seresta," Meghan told him. "She's our most successful advisor."

"That's just because they give me all the best patrons!" she claimed.

Now it was Quentin's turn to smile.

Once they were seated, Seresta explained her reason for wanting Meghan to be present at the meeting.

111

"Quentin here thinks he wants to be a doctor, but he's never had much exposure to the medical field – unless you count taking his kids to the hospital."

Quentin rolled his eyes.

"And I know a lot of people who thought they wanted to be doctors until they found out medicine involves blood and needles and sometimes worse." She made a disgusted face. "So I'm hoping you can set him up a medical internship. That way if he hates medicine he'll find out before he spends thousands of donor dollars."

"I'm sure I can do that," Meghan agreed.

"Preferably one that pays what he's making now at the tire shop," Seresta continued her list of demands. "They'll have to be willing to work around his college class schedule and he wants to wear a tie."

"The tie part is the only thing I'm worried about," Meghan said dryly. Paid medical internships for kids with Quentin's complete lack of experience were non-existent – as Seresta knew well. But Meghan would find someone to take Quentin as an intern and she would pay his salary herself. "I'll go work out the details and let you know."

With a wave to Quentin she walked down to an empty cubicle and started making phone calls.

It was late when Meghan left the clinic and she was tired. But knowing that Quentin would be starting his new job in a week and that his new life was on track gave her some sense of satisfaction.

At home she intended to eat a bowl of cereal but the milk in the refrigerator had expired. Staring at the old milk she couldn't remember the last time she'd been to the store. Chase always took care of the buying groceries.

Meghan poured the cereal from her bowl back into the box and went to bed.

On Tuesday night when she finished up at the clinic, she went to the grocery store. None of the food there appealed to her but she knew she had to eat, so she got some milk and a bag of salad. Surely she could live off of that until Saturday. And she couldn't force herself to think beyond her next dream session.

Each day seemed to take forever, but at long last Saturday came. As she drove to Dr. Morrow's lab she wanted to weep with joy. Soon she would be reunited with the people she loved. Soon she would be back in her dream-life.

The preparation process was tedious, but almost tantalizing. It helped the anticipation to build until Meghan wasn't sure she could bear it. Finally the moment came and she closed her eyes, surrendering to the power of her dream.

When Meghan opened her eyes she was still standing in the doctor's office with Paula's arms around her. Meghan pulled away and wiped the tears from her eyes.

"Why don't we go somewhere for lunch and talk about it," Paula suggested. She looked at Caldwell. "Your friend is welcome to come too."

Caldwell sent Meghan a panicked look. The last thing she wanted to do was be involved in a conversation about death and cancer.

"My friend already has a lunch date," Meghan said. "Caldwell, you can take my car. I'll ride with Paula. Then after your date you can come to my house and we'll switch vehicles."

"I hope my date doesn't lose interest in me when he sees that I'm driving a Honda – with a *car seat*, in the back" Caldwell muttered.

Meghan ignored this and started to push the stroller toward the exit, but Paula took it from her.

"I've got Miss Sophie."

"Are you sure it's okay?" Meghan asked and fresh tears threatened. "I mean pushing her won't hurt you?"

Paula shook her head. "I'm not in any pain."

When they got to the parking deck Caldwell drove off in Meghan's boring car while Paula secured the baby into the car seat she kept in her station wagon. Then she drove them to a small deli. They sat at a table by the window and ordered sandwiches that neither of them wanted while Sophie slept peacefully in her stroller.

After their sandwiches were delivered to the table, Meghan asked, "How long have you known?"

Paula pushed potato salad around with her fork. "About a week."

"Have you told anyone?"

"Just Troy. I'm sorry you had to find out that way."

"I guess there isn't a good way to find out," Meghan said. "But everything will be okay – right?"

"It's in the Lord's hands," Paula replied. "But my doctor was very positive about my chances. We caught it early which improves the survival rate."

"When are you going to tell the boys?"

"Tonight after dinner. I want you and Joey to be there and I'd appreciate it if you'd go ahead and tell him before you come. If he's over the shock he can help the younger boys deal with it better."

"I'll tell him," Meghan said, although she didn't want to. "And then we'll do whatever else you need us to. We're a family."

Paula clutched Meghan's hands. "Yes we are. I didn't want Joey to marry you," she added slowly. "Because of the baby we knew it was for the best, but you were not what I wanted for him."

This hurt, even though Paula was using the past tense.

"I wanted a Catholic girl, or at least a religious one. I wanted someone who could cook and clean and live on a budget. I thought that wasn't you – but I was wrong. You've become the wife he needs. I'm sorry that you had to give up some of your youth but I'm so proud of the way you're living your life and caring for Sophie. And I'm thankful to have your support over the next few weeks. I'm a proud woman, but I will need help."

Meghan nodded. "You can count on me."

They left the deli and Paula took Meghan home. She fed Sophie and then called Georgia State. She explained about Paula and arranged to withdraw from her classes for the semester.

Joey got home just as she ended her call.

"Who was that?" he asked as he greeted Meghan with a kiss.

"School," she replied vaguely.

He picked up Sophie and swung her over his head while she giggled. "What's Caldwell's car doing here?"

"She stopped by to visit and while she was here I started feeling sick, so she drove me to the doctor. I ran into your mother there."

He raised his eyebrows. "Really? What are the odds of that?"

"It was quite a coincidence," Meghan agreed.

"Are you feeling better?"

She nodded.

"And why does Caldwell have your car?"

"She had a lunch date so when we finished at the doctor she took my car and I rode home with your mother."

Joey made a face. "The downside of that is that Caldwell has to come back to switch cars."

Meghan gave him her best impression of a smile. "That's true."

He got a Coke out of the refrigerator and told her about football practice, talking animatedly to make Sophie laugh. He was in such a good mood Meghan hated to spoil it. But she'd promised Paula.

So she took Sophie from Joey and put her in the walker. Then she held his hands and drew him toward the couch. Once they were settled she said, "You know how I've been tired a lot lately?"

He kissed her forehead. "When Sophie starts sleeping at night you won't be so tired during the day."

She looked into his beautiful brown eyes. He looked back, unaware that a dark cloud of trouble hung over them.

"My fatigue is more than lack of sleep," she said. "I'm pregnant again, Joey."

"You're pregnant." He wasn't questioning her. It was more like he just had to say it out loud to be sure he had heard her right.

She nodded. "We seem to keep making the same mistakes over and over."

He was a little pale as he looked at Sophie playing in her walker. "I wouldn't call Sophie a mistake."

"No," Meghan agreed. "I wanted to have more children eventually, but it's going to be hard to have another one now. Even harder than when we had Sophie since we'll have two babies at once."

He nodded. There was no denying this.

"So I withdrew from all my classes this fall. I can pick up classes again when I'm ready."

He shook his head. "I don't want you to postpone school. We'll manage. Mom will help us."

She took a deep breath and continued with the worst news. "The reason I ran into your mother at the doctor today is because she's having some health issues."

She felt him tense and rushed on to get it over with. "I'm sorry, Joey. Your mother has breast cancer."

He reeled back, as if he could escape from her words. "My mom? *Cancer?*"

She held his hands tightly. "She said her doctor is very optimistic. They caught it early." She decided not to mention survival rates and finished up with, "She has another appointment on Friday and she'll know more about her treatment plan then."

He shuddered. "Cancer."

"She'll be a survivor," Meghan told him. "We'll make sure of it. But she's going to need some help and she can't babysit for awhile."

"That's the real reason you're sitting out this semester."

Meghan nodded. "Yes, although the pregnancy would have made classes difficult even without your mother's illness."

He glanced up at the goals on the fireplace. "At this rate we'll never make it."

"We'll accomplish our goals," she insisted. "But we have to keep things in perspective. Right now the babies and your mom come first."

He nodded. "Is Mom upset?"

"At lunch she seemed very calm. Of course she's known for a week so she's had time to get used to it. They're telling your brothers after dinner tonight and she wants us to be there – but she wanted you warned in advance so you can help reassure the younger boys."

Joey put his head in his hands. "Hopefully by tonight I'll be able to put on a good face."

"It's what your mother needs from you," Meghan reminded him. "You can do it."

***

The meeting with the Patrones went better than Meghan expected. The boys were scared, but they had the confidence of youth. They didn't think anything could really rock their world, so of course their mother would be okay.

116

The next day Meghan went to see her mother. While Suzanne was holding Sophie she told her about Paula. Suzanne was upset by the news. The moms were not exactly friends, but they had developed a good working relationship.

"I'm sorry that Paula is facing such an ordeal," she said. "But if they caught it early her chances are very good."

Meghan nodded. "That's what her doctor said. Of course that means that she can't babysit for us anymore – at least not for awhile. Especially since I found out today that I'm expecting another baby."

She saw the shock register on her mother's face, but she controlled it quickly.

"We weren't planning to have another child so soon, but, well it seems like we're prone to surprises in this area."

Her mother smiled. "Compared to Paula's news, another baby isn't much of a problem."

"No," Meghan agreed.

"If you're going to have another baby you might as well do it now so they can grow up together."

"They'll be friends," Meghan said. "I always thought it would be nice to have a sister."

"Your father and I discussed it, but we never could find the right time."

"Maybe that's why I keep getting pregnant by mistake – God doesn't trust me to find the right time."

Her mother smiled.

"I'm going to defer this semester at school, since Paula won't be able to babysit."

Suzanne didn't argue about this. "If Paula needs surgery, I can take a few days off work to keep Sophie so you can be with the rest of her family at the hospital. Just let me know when."

Meghan hugged her mother. "Thanks Mom."

***

On Friday the oncologist told Paula that she would need to have a radical mastectomy and chemotherapy. The surgery was set up for a week from Monday.

Meghan and Joey spent most of the week at the Patrone's house. They didn't discuss the cancer or Paula's surgery, but things were different. Troy wouldn't let Paula cook. For meals they ordered pizza and made sandwiches. He insisted that she sit in his recliner and let them wait on her.

On the Sunday before the surgery they all went to Mass as a family. The priest met with them afterwards and said a special prayer for Paula. Then they went out to eat at their favorite restaurant. The boys teased Paula, telling her to eat as much as she wanted since it might be awhile before she could enjoy a good Italian meal again. Paula laughed along with them but Meghan noticed that Troy was not amused. He sat quietly during the meal and didn't each much of the food on his plate. She wanted to comfort him, but didn't have that kind of relationship with her tough-guy father-in-law.

When it was time for Meghan and Joey to leave on Sunday evening, Paula walked them to the door. Meghan knew it would be hard to say goodbye since they wouldn't see Paula until after the surgery the next day.

"Now Meghan, while I'm recovering you'll be the woman of the house."

Meghan considered it a great honor to be given charge of the family, but Paula's shoes would be impossible to fill. "I hope that doesn't mean I have to cook. That's not my strong point. Ask Joey."

"There's a freezer full of food," Paula assured her. "And you can always order out. Now give me a hug."

Meghan embraced her mother-in-law. Then she watched as Paula kissed Sophie. Joey was last and when he stepped away from his mother his eyes were damp.

Paula frowned at their serious expressions. "I'm going to be fine!" she promised. "Now go on home and get some rest. Tomorrow is going to be a long day."

On Monday Meghan dropped Sophie off at her parents' house and then rushed to the hospital to wait with the Patrone men while Paula was in surgery. The wait was long and tedious, but finally they saw the doctor coming down the hallway toward them.

Everyone stood and watched the surgeon approach. Meghan closed her eyes, praying for good news. And when she opened them, she was in the dream session room at Dr. Morrow's lab. Heidi, the technician was leaning over her bed.

118

"My mother-in-law has cancer," she told Heidi. "I didn't get to find out how the surgery went."

Heidi gave her a tight smile. "You can always come back next week."

"I can't wait until next Saturday!" Meghan felt panicked. "I need to go back now."

"You know the rules, Dr. Collins," Heidi reminded her. "And next Saturday will be here before you know it."

During her PDS in Dr. Morrow's office she told him she wanted to set up a session for the next Saturday as usual.

Dr. Morrow looked concerned. "You've had enough sessions to see how the therapy works and to form an opinion. I think that it's time to stop, or at least suspend, your dreams."

"Oh no," she told him. "I can't do that. Not yet."

"As I told you at the beginning, Meghan, these sessions are very expensive. I offered to let you participate because I wanted your feedback – and hopefully your endorsement. But I really can't let you continue."

"I'll pay," she offered. "I won't be a part of your clinical tests anymore. I'll be your first paying client."

"I'm planning to charge $100 per hour for the full 24-hour session."

She wrote him a check for $2,400. "I'll see you at nine o'clock next Saturday."

Chapter Nine

When Meghan left the lab on Sunday morning, she checked her phone and saw that there was a missed call from Chase. She called him back and apologized for not answering.

"I was in my dream session."

He completely ignored the subject of her dreams and said, "I'm going to be in Omaha for another week. Why don't you fly out here and join me?"

She was stunned. "You want me to fly to Omaha?"

He laughed. "We haven't had much time together lately and the College World Series is being played here. I could get us some tickets and we could take in a few games."

"I can't miss work," she used as an excuse.

"Then fly out Friday night after you get off. I'll pick you up at the airport and we can fly home together on Sunday."

"That's a lot of flying for a few hours in Omaha," she said.

"But at least we'd be together." There was hope and longing in his voice.

"We'll be together when you get home," she said. "And besides, I have my dream session on Saturday."

There was an ominous pause. "I thought you were finished with that."

"No," she said. "Not yet."

"And you can't skip one to be with me?"

"I'm sorry, Chase." And she really was sorry. She hated that what now meant most to her was causing him pain. "But it's already set up."

"At this rate you and Joey Patrone will be middle-aged soon. Maybe then you won't find him as interesting and you can give it up."

She forced a laugh. "Probably." But she knew that wasn't true. She wanted to see them grow old, watch their children grow up, meet their grandchildren. And when she finally did get to the end of their dream-lives together, she planned to start over. She couldn't imagine a Saturday without Joey and Sophie.

"So you're not coming?" Chase confirmed.

"No, maybe another time."

"Okay."

She heard the hurt in his voice and she wanted to try an explain – but she couldn't. If she said more, it would only make things worse.

"I'll see you next Sunday," she said and they ended the call.

She stopped by the hospital and did her rounds in record time. Then she went home. The condo was peaceful and quiet and she was grateful to have time to herself. She stretched out on her bed and relived the latest installment of her dream life.

At one o'clock she got a call from her parents inviting her to dinner. She politely declined.

Her mother laughed. "Well, it's a little too late for that. We're standing outside your door."

Reluctantly, Meghan let them in. They had a vegetarian pizza from her favorite restaurant.

"We brought this just for you!" her father announced as he held up the box.

She tried to smile. "What a nice surprise."

"Meghan!" her mother cried. "You've lost weight since the last time we saw you. And you look exhausted."

"Did Chase call you?" she asked.

They both looked guilty so she had her answer even before her father admitted, "We did talk to him and he mentioned that he was a little worried."

They sat down in the living room and she waited for the inquisition.

"He feels like the dream sessions are unhealthy," her mother said. "And based on your appearance, I can't disagree."

"He also thinks it's affecting your marriage," her father added. "He feels you're in love with another man. Is that true?"

"In my dreams it's not me exactly," she skirted the question. "It's a 19-year-old version of myself. I tried to explain to Chase. It's like watching movie. It's harmless entertainment."

"But you can't stop," her mother said. "You're addicted to it."

Meghan laughed. "That's ridiculous. I can stop. I just don't want to."

"How long do you plan to keep doing this? Until one of you dies in your dream?"

"I don't know. Maybe." She didn't like being pressed about it.

"And Dr. Morrow just lets you come every week and use his technology for free?"

"It has been free up until today," Meghan said. "But I don't think that's fair to Dr. Morrow so I insisted on paying from now on."

"How much?" her father asked.

"A hundred dollars an hour."

Her parents did the math and then her mother gasped. "That's $2,400 a week!"

"Almost $10,000 a month!" her father added. "You can't intend to pay that for very long."

She didn't care if it cost her every dime she had, but she shook her head to appease them. "Oh no."

"So will next Saturday be your last session?" Her mother was an expert at exerting subtle pressure.

"Maybe," she hedged. "I'll have to wait and see."

"Meghan," her mother began, preparing for a second assault.

"I don't want to talk about that anymore," Meghan interrupted. "Let's eat pizza."

The food tasted like dust in her mouth but she forced herself to eat a few bites while her parents talked. She couldn't help thinking about the way her parents interacted with Sophie in her dream She wanted to tell them how much they would have loved grandparenthood if they'd given it a chance.

Then her mother said, "I wish you'd reconsider and go meet Chase in Omaha. He sounded so disappointed that you wouldn't come."

"You work too hard," her father added. "It would be a nice little mini-vacation."

"*Mini* is the right word," she said. "I'd spend more time on an airplane than I would in Omaha. I've made my decision and I'm not going to change my mind. Chase and I can go somewhere else, later."

Her mother frowned. "When you get through with your dreaming hobby?"

She nodded.

"Which will be?"

"I can stop whenever I want to."

"That's what all addicts say, but it's not true," her father said. "Most can't stop themselves. Maybe we should talk to Dr. Morrow about it or, better yet, someone who isn't involved with the lab - like a psychiatrist."

Meghan put down her piece of pizza and stood. "Thank you for your concern and the pizza, but I'm not addicted to anything and I don't need a psychiatrist. And the next time Chase calls you complaining about me – maybe you could take my side instead of his."

"We're on your side!" her mother exclaimed.

"He's worried about you," her father defended Chase's disloyal actions – and theirs. "We're worried too."

"Well don't be. I'm fine."

Her parents exchanged a glance and then stood in unison. "Okay, I guess we'll go. But call if you need us."

"I will," Meghan promised.

After they left she went back to her bedroom and her daydreams.

At four o'clock she got up and tried to eat another piece of the pizza her parents had left for her, but she couldn't manage more than a couple of bites. Even though she enjoyed the peace that Chase's absence provided, the total silence made her feel restless.

Finally she got in her car and drove to Meadowbrook High School. It looked pretty much the same as it had nearly ten years before when she and Joey graduated. She parked for a few minutes by the football field where she'd watched Joey play. She still felt eighteen in her heart – like any minute the team would come running out for practice and Joey would wave.

When she left the high school she passed the lot Troy Patrone had purchased for the back taxes. The house that had been fixed up so nicely in her dream was falling in on itself. No little boy and his single mother lived there. It was a ruin.

Next she drove to Old Mountain where Joey and his family lived. She found the Patrone's house. It needed a paint job, the grass needed to be cut, and the construction equipment needed to be isolated in one part of the large yard instead of scattered around helter-skelter. But it was achingly familiar – almost like home.

She parked across the street, hoping to get a glimpse of Paula. She didn't know how accurate her dream was, but it was possible that Paula really had a scare with cancer. After a fruitless hour she was afraid the neighbors would call and report her as a prowler. So she pulled back on to the road and headed to the last place on her mental list. The cottage.

Her hands started shaking when she turned onto the road. This house had been significant in both her real life and her dream life. She didn't know what to hope for. It would be sad to see it fallen to ruin like the house by the high school. But it might be worse to see someone else living there – treating her space like their own.

Then the cottage came into view and the reality was somewhere between her two fears. It had not fallen in and there was evidence of some repairs over the past ten years. But it did not appear to be occupied either. The cottage was in limbo – much like Meghan herself.

Since it was a quiet road and darkness had fallen she felt safe sitting there for a long time, looking at the cottage. It made daydreaming easier when she was actually there.

Finally, when it was too dark to see the cottage, she drove home and spent another sleepless night alone.

On Monday when she got to the office Penelope met her at the elevator. "The partners want to see you," she said. "Now."

Meghan frowned. "But I have patients coming soon and I need to review their charts."

"The partners have patients too. But they need to talk to you first. Dr. Lamb's office." Penelope wouldn't quite meet her eyes, which made Meghan think the assistant knew the reason for this impromptu meeting and that it wasn't good.

125

Frowning, Meghan turned the opposite direction from her office and walked up to the more luxurious part of the building reserved for the founding partners of the pediatric practice.

When she reached Dr. Lamb's office his secretary nodded. "Go right in."

Nervous now, Meghan smoothed her hair with her hands and wished that she'd taken the time to put on some makeup before she left the condo. She pushed the door open and found all four partners sitting in a tight, unified little group by the desk. She walked up to stand in front of them.

"Dr. Collins!" Dr. Lamb greeted. But he didn't stand or extend a hand to her as would seem normal.

"Penelope said you wanted to see me," she said.

"Yes, well, we're worried about you, Meghan."

"Worried, sir?"

"Over the past couple of weeks your appearance has become alarming – you've lost weight and your grooming habits are, well, not professional. There have been complaints from patients and from the nursing staff."

Meghan was stunned. She didn't think that anyone would notice her weight loss or whether she was wearing makeup or how often she showered. And she thought she had been able to cover her distraction well enough to provide adequate care for her patients.

"I'm sorry," she told them stiffly. "I'll do better."

"We are not here as disciplinarians, Meghan," Dr. Freeman told her. "We are your partners, your friends. We want to help you."

Dr. Lamb picked up the tag-team type presentation. "It's been suggested that you might have some undiagnosed health problems and we recommend that you see a doctor."

It was Dr. Wilde's turn. "It is not uncommon for medical professionals, especially in the early years of establishing their careers, to ignore their own health."

"You have a very promising future," Dr. Aranov assured her. "We are delighted to have you on board. But we can't risk our patients or the firm's reputation if you're not at your best."

Meghan was nearly dizzy after looking from one partner to another as they tossed out comments. "What are you saying?"

"We're suggesting that you take some vacation time," Dr. Freeman clarified. "Just a few weeks."

"Get some rest," Dr. Wilde encouraged. "Go get a check-up."

"We'll cover your patient load until you feel ready to return," Dr. Aranov offered.

"And if you need more time, we can hire an interim physician to cover your patients until you're ready to come back."

"A leave of absence?" she asked – her mind immediately began calculating the extra time she'd have to concentrate on her dream life if she wasn't obligated to come see patients every day.

"Unofficially," Dr. Lamb confirmed. "Really you'd just be taking some of your well-earned vacation time."

Meghan was less than thrilled by the partners' invasion into her private life, but she embraced the idea of a leave. It would give her more time to dream. "Thank you for your consideration, doctors. I'll plan on just a few weeks, but I'll let you know when I'm feeling well enough to . . . return."

Dr. Lamb's eyes were hopeful. "We will look forward to hearing from you. Now if you'll give me your keys you can go and start relaxing."

"You want me to leave now? Without even seeing today's patients?"

Dr. Freeman smiled. "We've got things covered, Meghan. Go, enjoy life for a couple of weeks."

Unnerved, she pulled her keys out of her pocket and put them on the desk. "Thank you," she said. Then she shook hands with each man before leaving the office. She walked down the hallway and back onto the elevator that had brought her up a few minutes before. She did not take time to talk to Penelope or any of the nursing staff since some or all of them had tattled to the partners instead of bringing any complaints or concerns they had directly to her.

Since she was already dressed for work instead of going home Meghan walked across to the *Momentum* Clinic. She met Quentin and his boys in the parking lot.

Sedrick waved to her vigorously.

"Well, good morning," she said. "Are you coming to daycare?"

"Yep," Quentin replied.

"And today we're having ice cream!" Sedrick informed her.

"I start my new job today," Quentin told her. "I work in the afternoons since my college classes will be in the morning."

Meghan was well aware of this since she had arranged his schedule and his salary personally. But she just said, "I hope you plan to wear a tie to your new job because that was one of the conditions of your employment."

"Oh, I got a tie!" Quentin assured her.

"We bought it at Wal-Mart yesterday," Sedrick added.

Quentin rolled his eyes and Meghan laughed.

They walked together into the *Mom*entum offices.

Quentin signed in at the desk and told the receptionist and then walked the boys back to the daycare room.

"Let me know how you like the medical field," Meghan called after him.

"I will," he promised.

After they were gone Meghan walked up to the desk and smiled at the receptionist. "I had some extra time today so I thought I'd come in early. I can see patients, talk to new patrons, whatever you need me to do."

The girl stared back at her. "We were told that you had taken a leave."

Meghan smiled. "I have taken a leave from the pediatric practice, but that just means I'll have more time to volunteer here."

The girl picked up the phone. "I'll have to ask someone about that." After a brief pause she turned away and spoke into the phone. "Dr. Collins is here. What am I supposed to do?"

Meghan was concerned by her tone and her question. But before she could question the receptionist, a door opened down the hall and Barrie Wilhelm, *Mom*entum's director, came rushing toward them.

Meghan expected her to round on the receptionist and inform the girl that Dr. Collins had built *Mom*entum into what it was today and could come whenever she wanted and do whatever she wanted.

Instead Barrie addressed Meghan. "I'm sorry, but we can't let you volunteer at the clinic while you're on leave. It's a liability issue."

"I can't be here?" Meghan repeated.

"You helped draw up the requirements for volunteers," Barrie reminded her. "This particular clause saves us thousands of dollars in malpractice insurance."

Meghan nodded. "I remember the clause, I just didn't think it applied to me since I'm still employed – just taking some vacation."

Barrie pulled her aside, away from the receptionist. In lowered tones she said, "There are rumors going around that you have cancer or may even a drug addiction."

Meghan was appalled. "Both of those rumors are completely false!"

"I believe you," Barrie rushed to assure her. "But until you return to work, I think it's best for all concerned, including you, if you don't volunteer at the clinic."

Meghan's world was crumbling around her, but she couldn't make herself care. All she could think was that maybe Dr. Morrow would allow her to have more than one dream session a week.

So she nodded. "Okay." Then without saying goodbye to Barrie or the receptionist, she turned and walked outside. She got into her car and drove to Dr. Morrow's lab.

The receptionist there looked surprised to see her. "Dr. Collins, your session isn't until Saturday."

"I know, but I've taken a few weeks off work and so I was hoping that we could move it up to maybe – now?"

"I don't remember Dr. Morrow ever doing a session so soon after the last one, but I'll ask." The receptionist reached for the phone.

Meghan paced around the waiting room, organizing her thoughts into the compelling argument she would use to convince Dr. Morrow. She was so deep in thought that when he walked up behind her she was startled.

"Meghan?"

"Oh!" She pressed a hand to her pounding heart. The she pasted on what she hoped was a cheerful, mentally-balanced smile. "Dr. Morrow – you sneaked up on me."

"What can I do for you?"

Succinctly she pled her case, stating her temporary lack of employment and his need to generate capital as her two best rationales. And she tried not to sound like she was begging, although she was.

"I'm sorry, Meghan, but it would be irresponsible of me to let you have another sleep session so soon."

"You've never let anyone have sessions twice in one week?"

"Well, once I did but there were still several days separating the sessions."

"How about Wednesday, then?" she asked. She thought she could make it that long. Maybe.

He looked very hesitant, but finally he nodded. "Wednesday at nine o'clock."

"Thank you!" She grabbed his arm. "Thank you so much."

"This time I think you need to bring a friend or family member with you."

She was happy to agree to anything. "I will."

"Go home and rest, Meghan. You aren't looking good."

***

Time crawled. Each hour was an eternity. Meghan had to fight the almost uncontrollable urge to pick up the phone and beg Dr. Morrow to move the session up a day. The only thing that prevented her from making that call was the fear that if she did he would cancel her session on Wednesday. She missed Joey and Sophie and her dream-life.

Finally Wednesday came and she forced herself to wait until eight o'clock before knocking on Caldwell's door. Her friend yanked it open and muttered, "I thought you said eight-thirty."

Meghan tapped her toe impatiently. "I like to be early."

Caldwell squinted at her. "Meghan," she breathed. "You look like a ghost."

"I feel like a ghost," she replied. "Now let's go."

Chapter Ten

Meghan held her breath as the doctor approached Troy.

"Mr. Patrone?" the doctor said in a serious tone.

Troy nodded, apparently speechless with fear.

"Your wife came through the surgery very well," the doctor told him.

Meghan exhaled as Joey grabbed her for a celebratory hug.

"We will give her a couple of weeks to heal up and then start the chemotherapy."

"But that's just a precaution, right?" Joey asked. "Because the surgery got all the cancer."

The doctor turned his solemn eyes to Joey. "The surgery is one step in the fight against your mother's cancer. Chemotherapy is the second step. If necessary, we'll use radiation treatments as well. Think of it as a war and we've won the first battle."

The Patrones were a little more subdued after being reminded that there was still a long road ahead before Paula could be considered 'healthy'.

"When can we see her?" Troy asked.

"She'll be in recovery for at least another hour," the doctor said. "The nurses will let you know when she's ready for visitors – but keep it short. She needs to rest."

It was almost two hours before a nurse told them Paula was in her room and they could see her. "But no more than two guests at a time," she warned.

Troy told the family that he was going in and would stay with Paula while the rest of them took turns filling the other 'guest' spot.

When it was her turn to visit, Meghan felt a little awkward. Paula looked uncomfortable and Troy looked helpless. Meghan made a few inane remarks and then escaped back out to the waiting room. None of the sons stayed long either – except Matt. He seemed better able to deal with Paula's pain and fear than the rest of them.

Paula's sister came from Knoxville and stayed with her for awhile. Meghan and Joey brought Sophie by to visit regularly but Paula always looked tired so they never stayed long.

Meghan felt a little guilty that she wasn't over at the Patrone's house helping in some way. After all, Paula had named her temporary woman of the house. But the sister was cooking and cleaning and keeping Paula company. So Meghan didn't know what else she could do.

She also felt guilty about putting her education on hold – even though there was no choice. A college degree was a very important goal that she was determined to achieve. But she treasured the time she was able to spend with Sophie.

The day after the sister left, Paula called and asked Meghan if she could bring the baby over. When Meghan arrived she was shocked by the change in Paula's appearance. She had lost weight but instead of making her look better – she looked haggard and old. Her clothes had always looked a little sloppy, but now they hung off of her thin frame. And because Paula hadn't had the time or the energy to color her hair, she now had gray roots.

Meghan tried to keep the horror she felt from showing on her face, but apparently she failed.

"I know I look terrible," Paula said as she took Sophie and held her close. "Grandma has missed her precious girl," she whispered into the baby's ear and Meghan felt guilty again. She should have come more often during the past few weeks.

Sophie started to squirm, unhappy about the confinement. So Paula put her down and let her crawl around the family room. She sat on the couch and Meghan sat beside her.

"Are you okay?" Meghan asked, concerned.

Paula ran her fingers through her uncombed hair. "Not really. I'm tired and old and ugly."

Meghan's concern turned to alarm. Paula needed help. She needed encouragement. She needed someone besides the daughter-in-law she never wanted. But Meghan was the only one there. So she cleared her throat and said, "You're recovering from surgery and taking chemotherapy, so of course you feel tired. You're not old and you're certainly not ugly. I think you are beautiful."

Paula gave her a sad smile. "You haven't seen my scars. I know you probably think at my age something like that wouldn't matter, but it does. I can't stand for Troy to look at me. I can't stand to look at myself."

Meghan glanced toward the door, willing someone to come in and take over this uncomfortable conversation. But the door remained closed.

"You'll get reconstruction surgery," she said. "That will help."

Paula nodded but she didn't look convinced.

Meghan sought desperately for a way to cheer Paula up and finally inspiration struck. "You know what I think we should do right now?"

"What?"

"I think I should take you to a salon. Once you're hair is back to normal you'll feel a hundred times better."

"What if I fall asleep in the chair?"

"What if you do?" Meghan replied, encouraged that Paula hadn't refused outright.

Paula smiled. "Then I guess we can go if you're not ashamed to be seen with me."

"I could never be ashamed of you."

Since Paula colored her own hair she didn't have a regular salon. When she needed a haircut she went to whatever place she had a coupon for. Meghan still got her hair cut at a salon near her parents' house in Meadowbrook – nearly an hour away. She knew that would be too much for Paula. So she looked in the phone book and found a salon in Old Mountain. Then she called ahead and explained Paula's situation so the wait could be minimized.

When they arrived they were met at the entrance by all them employees of the small shop. None of them knew Paula personally but all of them had some association with the Patrone family and they all wanted to help.

"We're giving you the works!" a tall girl with unnaturally red hair named Vivienne informed her.

"I'm not sure if I have the energy for the works," Paula said. "I'm exhausted just from the drive over here."

Vivienne smiled. "The works won't take any longer that just getting your hair colored. We'll do your nails and your hair at the same time. We're multi-taskers!""

Vivienne introduced the other stylist and the manicurist.

"First you have to pick out the polish you want," Vivienne told Paula.

Paula reviewed the hundreds of choices, obviously overwhelmed.

"Maybe you could make a suggestion," Meghan said finally.

The manicurist recommended a hot pink nail polish. "This is our most popular color."

Paula looked at Meghan, "Do you think it's too flashy?"

"I think it's fabulous," Meghan said.

Paula shrugged. "You only live once, right?"

Meghan nodded and tried to keep her lips from trembling.

Vivienne led Paula to her station and got her settled in the chair. The manicurist pulled her tray over and went to work on one hand while the other stylist started soaking Paula's feet.

Vivienne lifted a clump of hair. "Have you ever thought of going blond?"

"It never crossed my mind," Paula replied.

Meghan felt mildly alarmed. "Change is good, but we might not want to throw caution completely to the wind."

Vivienne rethought her suggestion. "Well if we went with a little lighter shade of brown overall and then put in some blond highlights – you'd get the look of blond without such a drastic change."

Meghan was relieved. "I love that idea."

"That's tempting," Paula admitted. "I'm sick of looking like an old woman."

Vivienne leaned in close and whispered. "Like you said, honey, you only live once!"

"Why not!" Paula declared bravely. Her eyes met Meghan's in the mirror. "And it's not like she could make me look worse."

"You're going to be a beautiful almost-blond," Vivienne said as she went to work.

Meghan felt responsible for the outcome of Paula's transformation so she watched Vivienne and her co-workers nervously. Sophie was easy to entertain since she was fascinated by all the new sights and smells.

Vivienne reclined the chair and let Paula lean back on the headrest. Paula kept her eyes closed throughout the foiling process. Meghan wasn't sure if she was sleeping or just afraid to look.

The manicurists finished Paula's nails and they moved to her feet. Meghan's eyes moved from one to the other as she bounced Sophie on her knee.

The manicurist finished with Paula's toes about the time the foils were in. Vivienne wrapped plastic around Paula's head and set a timer – which seemed to take forever. When the timer finally went off Meghan watched with her heart in her throat as Vivienne rinsed Paula's hair and styled it.

But as the hair dried Meghan could tell that Vivienne had done a beautiful job. The chestnut brown color was softer than the harsh almost black shade Paula had been purchasing at the drug store for a decade. The blond highlights were subtle and looked like the natural result of spending time in the sun.

When Vivienne spun the chair around so Paula could see herself in the mirror, Paula stared for a few seconds and then she cried, "I love it!"

Meghan was relieved. "I love it too!"

Paula stood and embraced Vivienne. "Next month if I have any hair left I'll come back and let you give my roots a touch-up."

Vivienne smiled. "Come back anyway. If your hair is gone we'll order you a cute, blond wig."

While Meghan was paying the bill, Vivienne whispered that there was a shop a few blocks away that specialized in clothing for women with cancer. Meghan got the address and decided that would be their next stop.

The boutique was called *Pretty in Pink* and had the breast cancer bow with a dot under it forming an exclamation point at the end. When Meghan parked in front of the store and announced her intention of buying Paula an outfit – her mother-in-law objected.

"You've already spent way too much on me!"

"Let's just go in and see what they have," Meghan suggested. "Then if you find something you like we can argue over whether or not I should buy it."

Paula shrugged. "How can I say no to that?"

The store was bigger than it looked from the outside. It was full of every type of clothing from underwear to outerwear. There was a huge section of hats and wigs. They even had shoes. A helpful sales woman met them at the door and took Paula into the bowels of the store. Sophie was tired and fussy so Meghan found a quiet corner and fed her.

The baby had dozed off by the time Paula returned. She was wearing a cheerful floral print blouse. It had several rows of small ruffles starting at the neck that hid her flat chest. Elastic at the waist gave it some body. It was flattering and perfectly styled for someone in Paula's stage of cancer recovery. The black pants were tailored to fit Paula's newly thin legs. And a pair of gold sandals showcased her hot pink toenails.

"I'm buying that whole outfit," Meghan said. "No matter what you say!"

Paula twirled around for her to see it from all directions. "I definitely want it, but I'll pay."

Meghan knew the medical bills had made finances tight at the Patrone's house. Besides she couldn't allow Paula to pay when she had suggested the whole thing.

"No, it's my treat." She handed the sales woman her debit card. "Maybe next week you can come back and buy another one."

Paula shook her head. "We won't have to do that. I like this outfit well enough to wear it everyday. Now take me home. I can hardly wait for Troy to see me."

And at that moment Meghan knew the day had been a success – no matter what the cost.

All the Patrone men were pleased with Paula's appearance and her more optimistic attitude. They credited Meghan with the transformation and each thanked her in their own way. Troy was too emotional to speak, so he just gave her a hug. Matt gave her a look of respect. Joey said she was the best wife in the world.

To which she whispered, "I basically cleaned out our saving account."

He smiled. "It was worth it. And hopefully my old tires will last until we can save up some more."

Paula continued to take her chemotherapy sessions and Meghan made a point to go by her house at least once a day. Paula enjoyed the time with Sophie and the attention. And Meghan was able to live almost guilt-free.

After the chemotherapy sessions, Paula's doctor declared that her cancer was in remission and radiation would not be necessary. She had retained most of her blond-kissed, chestnut colored hair and Vivienne had a new regular customer. The reconstructive surgery was another painful ordeal, but Paula faced it with courage and enthusiasm. And she was pleased with the final results.

Meghan was still uncomfortable with some of the personal things that Paula told her – like how happy she was with her reconstructed chest. But she realized that Paula had no daughter or sister nearby to share such things with. So she overcame her discomfort and learned to be a good listener, no matter how delicate the subject.

Paula's brush with death left her very health conscious and meals changed around the Patrone household. No more fat-laden pastas or sugary desserts. Instead there were salads and lean meats and fresh fruits. Exercise became a regular part of Paula's day and soon she was fit and trim instead of just thin. She still wore jeans and T-shirts most of the time, but there was a look of health and vitality about her that had been missing before.

Meghan had her ultrasound and this time Joey agreed that they could find out what they were having. When the technician told them it was a girl, Meghan watched his face for any signs of disappointment. But he seemed happy with the news.

"I thought you would want a boy," she told him as they walked out to his truck.

"I love girls," he said, pressing a kiss to her forehead. "I'll admit that I hope we have a boy eventually. Maybe next year."

She swatted at him. "We're not going to have a baby every year."

He raised an eyebrow. "You're sure about that?"

She couldn't think of a clever comeback.

137

Football season ended and Meghan was relieved. With Paula's illness the family hadn't been able to attend all the games so it wasn't as much fun as the year before. And there was always the worry that Joey might get hurt.

In November they participated in a walk for breast cancer. The entire Patrone clan was there – dressed in matching pink T-shirts that said "We walk for Paula". Paula cried when she saw them – manly men willing to wear pink in her honor. She had just gotten her tears under control when she saw Sophie wearing her tiny shirt. And the tears began again.

The group walked slowly to accommodate Meghan's pregnant-gait and they took turns pushing Sophie in the stroller.

"We're going to make this walk an annual tradition," Matt told his mother.

"Matt, please don't make me cry again," she said as she gave him a side-hug. "I'll dehydrate."

Sophie's first birthday was celebrated with a big party at the cottage. The weather was nice so they were able to eat outside. Joey grilled hamburgers and hot dogs. Meghan made a cake that was only marginally better than the one she'd made for Joey at Valentines. His family came en masse. Her parents dropped by long enough to give Sophie a kiss and a present. Then they claimed to have a pressing engagement, but Meghan knew that they just felt out of place around so many Patrones.

Thanksgiving felt special that year. They were all so grateful for Paula's return to health and were looking forward to the arrival of the new baby.

After eating dinner on Thanksgiving Day they were sitting around the table when their priest called. He had heard about the *Patrone Project* and the home they had provided for Michael's friend from school. He knew of a family in need of housing and wondered if they had another house to rent.

So they started looking for a property they could buy and renovate.

The next Sunday after dinner they had a *Patrone Project* meeting with the uncles and aunts included. Troy announced that he had found a lot for sale cheap – only $3,000.

"Is there a house on it?" Uncle Jim asked.

"No."

"Then we'd have to build from scratch," Uncle Cliff stated the obvious.

"Sometimes that's easier," Troy pointed out. "We could use one of those pre-fab kits. They include the frame, exterior and interior walls, roof, windows, doors, all the basics. The plumbing and electrical is already in, it just has to be hooked up."

"I like the idea of a pre-fab since it's quick and easy," Uncle Jim said. "But even if we all donate our time, you're looking at $20,000 for the lot and the prefab. Where would we get that kind of money?"

Since she had no construction skills, up until this point Meghan had been just listening with nothing to contribute. But when the subject of money arose, all that changed. She smiled and said, "I think I might know."

That evening when they went to eat dinner with her parents, Meghan explained the *Patrone Project* and asked them if they would like to finance the house.

"How would that work?" her father asked.

"We will register the *Patrone Project* as a charity so that your contribution will be tax deductible. You'll give Troy a check. He'll put it in the project's account and use it to purchase the property and the pre-fabricated house. Then the Patrones will build the house and rent it to a low-income family for a reasonable amount."

"What happens to the rent?"

"It's collected in a project's account along with rent from the first property we renovated," Joey said.

"Eventually we hope that the fund will have enough income to finance the purchase of new properties," Meghan added. "But for now we need a generous sponsor."

Her father nodded. "That sounds like something we'd like to be a part of." He gave her a check and she took it back to the Patrones.

Troy smiled when he saw it. "Looks like we're in business."

For the first time Meghan felt like she was a real part of the *Patrone Project* – and a real part of the family.

That night after they put Sophie to bed, Joey and Meghan sat by each other on the couch in their little house and watched a sentimental, love-laden movie. When it was over they discussed names. He wanted to name the baby for Paula in honor of his mother, but they both hated the name and didn't want to offend Suzanne.

"Maybe we could take the letters from both our mothers' names and rearrange them into a new name," Joey suggested.

"We're going to give our baby a made-up name with twelve letters?" Meghan was appalled.

He laughed. "We don't have to use *all* the letters."

She was relieved. And that was how they came up with Anna.

Meghan leaned her head on his shoulder and whispered the name. "Anna." Then she dozed off to sleep.

***

When Meghan opened her eyes and found herself back in the session room at Dr. Morrow's lab, the familiar grief and loneliness settled over her. This time the break in her dream had come at a moment that was not hugely suspenseful. It seemed like that would make it easier to leave her dream-life. But it didn't.

She tried to hide her feelings during her PDS, afraid that if Dr. Morrow knew how the dreams affected her that he wouldn't let her continue. As she was writing her check, she asked Dr. Morrow if she could keep her appointment on Saturday. "In fact, I'd like to continue having two sessions a week."

"For how long?"

"I don't know," she admitted honestly. "Do you have an end date in mind for the sessions with your wife?"

"No," he admitted. "But I only have a one hour session each month. I know that I have to keep my dream-life in perspective. I'm afraid you have lost sight of that."

"I know it's not real," Meghan responded a little annoyed. "But I just really enjoy it. I think that once I get past the early years where babies are being born, I'll get to a point where I want to quit. But why should I stop now, while I'm still enjoying them? Isn't that the whole point of commercializing your technology?"

He shrugged. "I guess I won't object." He took the check. "As long as your money holds out." He smiled when he said it but Meghan wasn't sure he was kidding.

"Now let's discuss the schedule. I want you to be healthy and happy. So I'd like to propose two twelve hour sessions a week, one on Wednesday and one on Saturday. It would be the same amount of money and the same amount of dream time but you wouldn't have so long to wait in between sessions."

She wanted two 24 hour sessions, but could tell that he wasn't going to agree to that so there really was no choice to be made. She would agree to any terms to continue her dream sessions.

For the next two days she stayed at her condo, sleeping and daydreaming. But instead of finding satisfaction, she found only frustration. Both her regular dreams and her mental reenactments seemed bland and one-dimensional. She longed to be back in her dream-life.

On Saturday Meghan returned to the lab and dreamed about Sophie's second Christmas. She returned to school at Georgia State for the winter semester. On Valentine's Day Joey brought home a bouquet of flowers for each of his girls.

The pre-fabricated house was finished on the lot Troy bought for the *Patrone Project* and the family recommended by the priest moved in at the end of February. One of Joey's uncles found another property and her parents agreed to donate half of the purchase price. They mortgaged the rest, the payment to be made from rents collected. Spring arrived and all the flowers she had planted at the cottage were once again in bloom. She was just a few weeks from her due date when she woke up.

During the PDS, Dr. Morrow made her promise to eat three meals a day and gave her some sleeping pills to help her rest. He told her to go outside occasionally and get some sun. He even threatened that if she wasn't the picture of health when she came back the next week he'd be forced to cut her off.

When she got home Chase was back from Omaha. He stared at her like she was a stranger.

"Have you looked in a mirror?" he whispered.

She put a hand to her hair self-consciously. "I know I look a sight. But I've been busy."

"Too busy to bathe? To brush your teeth? To comb your hair?"

She sighed. "I'll go take a bath right now."

"No," he said with surprising firmness. "Right now we're going to talk about this dream therapy thing. I called your office yesterday and they told me you were on leave. Was it voluntary?"

"The partners suggested it," she admitted. "But I was glad to take some time off. I've worked so hard for so long. I think I deserve it!"

"*Mom*entum too?" he asked. "That was your pet project. You raised it from nothing. And now you're just going to walk away?"

"I wanted to keep volunteering there, but since I'm on leave from the practice – I can't. It's a legal clause we used to save money and now, well, it's working against me."

"You're going to get fired, Meghan," he said. "You're going to lose everything you've worked for."

She looked away. "I can go back whenever I want and I will, soon. Dr. Morrow and I discussed today breaking my weekly dream into two twelve hour sessions, one on Wednesday and one on Saturday. That will make it easier for me to fit the dreams into my normal schedule."

"How are you going to dream on Wednesday and work at the same time?"

"Well, obviously I'll have to take Wednesdays off. But I can work the other four days. I'll clean up and make an effort to concentrate. I can do it."

He walked over and put his hands on her shoulders, forcing her to look at him. "You can't live suspended between two worlds – especially since only one of them is real. You have to choose, Meghan."

"Don't make me choose," she begged. She didn't want to hurt him. She just wanted things to go on they way they were. She was sure she could make it work.

He sighed. "So I guess your choice is made. You're picking a fantasy over me and our life together."

"No," she shook her head, but she felt no real conviction.

"I've been patient, hoping you would outgrow this or get bored with it or whatever. But I'm done. It's got to stop."

She thought about the new baby and the house they were building with the *Patrone Project*. She thought about the upcoming summer and their plans to take their little girls on a trip to the beach. Finally she shook her head. "I can't."

Chase said, "And I can't stay here and watch you destroy yourself. If you won't listen to me, I have no choice. I'll move to my parents' lake house."

She frowned. "That will increase your commute by twenty minutes each way."

He gave her an incredulous look. "I just told you I'm moving out and all you can say is that it's going to increase my commute?"

She wrung her hands. "I'm not crazy if that's what you mean."

He stared for a few seconds and she had to turn away, unable to meet his gaze. "Well, whatever you are you weren't like this before you volunteered to be a guinea pig for Dr. Morrow."

She *was* different, so she couldn't argue that point. Wrapping her arms around him she said, "I'm so sorry. I never meant to hurt you."

He was quiet for a few minutes, and then he asked, "So, during these dreams do you sleep with Joey Patrone?"

"I guess," she tried to sound casual. "When you dream you don't see everything – it's just a series of scenes."

"Love scenes?" he persisted.

"It's just a dream, Chase. I'm not actually *doing* anything." But that was a lie too. She loved Joey and her feelings for him were no less physical because they originated in a dream.

He stepped away from her and moved to the bedroom. She heard him packing a bag. She had plenty of time to stop him. She even wondered if he dragged out the packing process to make sure of that. But she was too conflicted. She couldn't disagree with anything he'd said. And the thought of sleeping with him seemed like it would be cheating on Joey. Maybe she had gone crazy. But in any case, it was probably best that Chase stay somewhere else until she sorted it out.

He came back into the living room holding his suitcase and stared at her for a few seconds.

"I'm sorry," she said. "The last thing I wanted to do was hurt you."

He gave her a half-hearted nod. "When you're ready to stop the dream and live in the real world, call me." Then he walked outside and closed the door firmly behind him.

Meghan stood in the entryway, unsure of what to do next. Then she caught a glimpse of herself in the mirror. She took a step closer, shocked by her haggard appearance. Not eating. Not sleeping. Not working. Not interacting with people. It had taken its toll.

She looked like the junky Chase accused her of being. Maybe he was right. Maybe she did have to give up her dream sessions in order to survive. But she wasn't sure she could survive *without* them. Maybe there was no hope for her either way. She rubbed her hands up and down her arms, wondering how this had happened. How had she gone from a perfectly happy, capable, successful woman to this wreck in just a few weeks – all because of dreams?

While staring in the mirror, she started to cry. She was lonely and afraid. She longed for a life that didn't exist. Her husband had never been anything but good to her and she was breaking his heart. And the worst part was she didn't know how to fix any of it.

Finally she thought about the list Joey had suggested they make in her dream – right after they decided to get married. That's what she needed. Goals.

She found a piece of paper. For number 1 she wrote '*shower each day*'. Number 2 was '*get dressed*'. Number 3 was '*get out of the condo for an hour even if she didn't actually have anywhere to go*'. Number 4 was '*eat three meals every day*'. And the last item on her list was '*get in bed only at night and sleep for eight hours*'. It was simple. But it was a start.

She taped the list to the mirror by the front door where she'd have to see it regularly. Then she walked into the bathroom. After a long shower she felt somewhat refreshed. So she went into the kitchen and thawed a frozen dinner. She ate every bite even though she didn't want to.

Next she went to the grocery store and stocked up on food. She went to the salon and got her hair cut. She got a pedicure and a manicure. She sat by the pool at their gated community for an hour every day and by Saturday she looked more like her normal self.

When she walked into the lab, Dr. Morrow smiled. "Well, don't you look nice?"

"I spent this week putting things into perspective. I was allowing the dreams to overtake my life. I've regained control."

He nodded although she wasn't sure he was completely convinced. But she didn't care, as long as he would let her dream.

Chapter Eleven

Joey came into the house all excited.

"What is it?" Meghan asked.

"We ended up with a credit at the pre-fab factory where we purchased the house for the *Patrone Project*. Dad used it to buy a room addition for the cottage."

"They're going to add a room on here?"

He nodded. "Dad said they'll have to put it on the back of the house behind Sophie's room, which is not ideal since we'll have to walk through one room to get to the other. But Anna will have her own room."

"Joey, you realize that the baby's due, essentially *now*!" Meghan reminded him. She didn't relish the thought of bringing a baby home to construction mess.

He was unconcerned. "That's the beauty of the pre-fab room. They just have to attach it, make a door, extend the roof, connect it to the electrical and heat and . . ."

"Stop!" she pleaded. "I don't even want to know all that is involved."

"I thought you'd be excited."

"I love the idea of another room," she assured him. "Sophie's room is so tiny I didn't know how we'd get two girls in there. It's the timing that I'm questioning."

"They are starting tomorrow and Dad says they can have it done in a week – maybe two. So hold on to that baby!"

"Joey!" she scolded him half-heartedly.

"Next time they have a credit with the pre-fab place I told them to get us an extension for our bedroom and a master bath."

Meghan's eyes widened. "You can buy something like that prefabricated?"

"Oh yeah," he assured her. "Just think, Meg. You've got a soaker tub in your future."

She smiled. "Now that is something to look forward to!"

During dinner she told him that she had decided to change her major from pre-med to nursing. "I still think that medicine is the right field for me, but I can't see putting myself or our family through all the schooling required to be a doctor. I can't bear the thought of being away from the girls that much. So, are you okay with that?"

He looked worried. "I don't know. It feels like we're giving up on a goal."

"We're not giving up, just changing one a little. And if you think about it, being a nurse would come in handy. I would know how to take care of our kids through childhood illnesses and accidents. I could get a job with flexible hours – like just a couple of weekends a month or something like that – so I don't have to be away from our family too much."

"You really have thought this through," he said.

She nodded. "I really have and I think it's the right thing for all of us."

He sighed. "I'm okay with it, then. But I don't want you to give up on a dream just because you think it will be too hard on the girls and me. We can handle whatever you need us to."

She kissed him. "I'm really sure this is what I want."

His eyes strayed to the goals over the fireplace.

"We'll get there," she told him.

He nodded. "We will."

The next Sunday at dinner Matt said he had a proposal. "It's really for the uncles and aunts too, since it's about the *Patrone Project*. But I thought I'd try it out on you guys first and see what you think."

Paula beamed at him. "Go ahead, sweetie. Tell us your idea."

"Well, there's an old house on the corner of Mentone and Riverview near the post office. And it's for sale. Cheap."

"Isn't that a crack-house?" Joey asked

"It doesn't have to be a crack-house," Matt replied.

"But it's not in a very nice area, is what I'm saying."

"It's actually not that bad," Matt said. "No worse than that house we renovated near the high school. And the police station is close by so that is a good thing."

"I guess it is if you live in a bad area," Ben sort of agreed.

"But we don't have a homeless friend at the moment," Paula reminded him gently.

"And we don't want to become just regular landlords," Troy said, "Buying a house and then looking for someone to rent it."

"But what if we bought the house and flipped it like they do on TV," Matt suggested. "Then we could sell it to a lower-income family for not a huge profit – just enough to build the funds in our *Patrone Project* account. If we do that a couple of times we might have enough so that we won't have to borrow money or get a donation from Meghan's parents to finance the houses we do for people in need."

Troy considered this. "So we're still doing it to help people, but instead of renting the houses we'll sell them outright – for a modest profit – to people who don't mind living in kind of rough areas."

"And if we flip enough houses in the rough areas, the area might improve." Matt was a true optimist.

"When you say it's for sale cheap," Troy said. "How cheap?"

"It's listed for $40,000 but I think we can get it for $35,000."

"That's still a lot of money," Troy pointed out.

"It's a good idea," Paula gave her endorsement. "And you can get a mortgage for a couple of months until you sell it."

"I'll talk to the uncles," Troy said.

"But build the baby's room first," Paula pleaded.

"Yes please!" Meghan added.

The baby's room was finished the next weekend and painted yellow. They transferred the furniture the grandmothers had purchased for Anna into the new room. Then the aunts surprised Meghan with a little baby shower. It was a whirlwind day, but exciting. And afterward they had plenty of diapers and other baby essentials.

Meghan was ready to have the baby but worried about having enough time, attention, and energy for two children.

When she expressed this concern to the grandmothers, they both encouraged her.

"You'll do what you have to do," her mother said. "And you have us to help you if you need it."

"Do you think Sophie will be jealous?" Meghan asked. As an only child she didn't know if sibling rivalry was avoidable.

"Sophie won't ever remember a time when Anna wasn't here," Paula said.

"You mean she won't ever know what she missed?" Meghan asked, still feeling guilty for their lack of family planning.

"I mean that they will always have each other," Paula corrected. "They will be best friends. Every girl needs a sister."

Meghan hugged Paula and her mother. "I feel much better now."

It was a warm day in early March when Meghan went into labor. Joey was at spring football practice so Meghan called Paula to take her to the hospital. Suzanne met them there and the grandmothers entertained Sophie while a nurse took Meghan to a room.

Meghan tried to be brave, but she needed Joey. She needed his calming influence and his encouragement. She needed to see the look in his eyes when he saw his daughter for the first time.

As her labor progressed and he didn't come, she accepted the very real possibility that he wasn't going to make it. She told herself that it wouldn't be the end of the world. She'd been through delivery before and knew what to expect. She trusted her doctor and the nurses. But she couldn't give up hope.

"You're going to have a baby soon," an overly-cheerful nurse told her.

"You're doing great," another said.

Meghan wanted to watch the door for Joey but she had to keep her eyes shut tight to manage the pain.

"Time to push!" the cheerful nurse said.

"Oh no!" Meghan sobbed, thinking of how hard it would be to walk that path alone. And then she felt Joey's hand slip in to hers. She opened her eyes just enough to see him there, swathed in a blue paper hospital suit, his cap askew.

"I need you," she gasped as another contraction began.

He squeezed her hand, "I know."

Then he coached her through the last part of labor. The baby was born and she was perfect. Meghan got to see that look of wonder on Joey's face and share the moment when they held her for the first time.

"She looks more like me," he said as he cradled his new daughter.

Meghan looked into the muddy blue eyes that would probably turn brown eventually. She stroked the sparse dark hair that topped Anna's head, unlike Sophie's blond curls. "It's funny how they look so different but the feelings we have are still the same."

Joey nodded. "The only time you can ever be completely in love with a total stranger is when you have a baby."

Meghan laughed. "Exactly."

They were able to spend some time with Anna before the nurses took her to the newborn nursery for a bath and a thorough examination by her pediatrician. Meghan was tired but for some reason she was afraid to go to sleep. So she just looked out the window at the Atlanta skyline while Joey went to get Sophie.

But as much as she tried to fight her exhaustion, it eventually overwhelmed her. Meghan's eyes closed and she fell asleep.

***

Meghan was not pleased when she woke up in the dream session room, but she was less traumatized than she'd been before. Dr. Morrow's idea of two twelve-hour sessions per week was a good one. This way she knew when she woke up that she only had a couple of days to wait before she could go back.

She drove home and ate some cereal. Then she went to bed and remembered what she could about her dream and her babies.

When Meghan woke up on Sunday morning Chase was there.

"I hope I didn't startle you," he said when she walked into the kitchen. "I just needed to come by and get a few things. I guess I should have called."

"It's your home," she said. "You can come anytime and you don't have to call."

His shoulders relaxed a little. "You look better."

She gave him a little smirk. "Thanks, I guess."

"You know what I mean, healthier. You were beautiful to me even when you hadn't bathed in days."

"Do you call that a compliment?" she teased.

He smiled. "I've missed you." He kept his distance, waiting for her reaction.

"I know it's been hard for you and I appreciate you allowing me some space, some room to figure it all out."

He looked disappointed and she knew that wasn't what he had hoped she'd say. "Have you talked to the partners about going back to work?"

She shook her head. "Not yet, but I will soon."

"I hope so. It would be a shame to throw away such a promising career – everything you've worked for. Especially *Mom*entum since it was always so important for you to help other people."

"I still help people in my dream. We, the Patrone family, have started a project where we flip houses and rent them to people who otherwise would have nowhere to live. It's very satisfying. I wish we did something like that."

"I help people," he said a little defensively.

"It's not a competition," she told him.

"Well, it sure feels like one," he replied.

He walked over and put his arms around her. She allowed the contact because she loved Chase - just not the same way she loved Joey.

He kissed her gently. She accepted the kiss but didn't kiss him back. She couldn't.

Finally he pulled away and looked into her eyes. "You know that the Joey in your dream isn't real. He's been created by your mind and Dr. Morrow's voodoo to be exactly what you want him to be. It's hard for a human to live up to that."

"My feelings for Joey are in no way a criticism of you or our relationship."

"It's like you're having an affair, only worse because your lover isn't a real person."

"I'm not having an affair," she said. "I just dream."

"About an eighteen-year-old Joey Patrone."

In her dreams Joey had actually turned twenty, but she didn't think it would be helpful to point this out. So she remained silent.

"I don't understand," he said.

"I know."

"I want to move back home, but I can't as long as you're dreaming about another man."

She nodded.

"But you're going to keep doing the dream sessions anyway?"

"It's something I have to do."

With a wounded look he moved toward the door. "Call me if you change your mind."

"I will," she said. But she knew she wouldn't change her mind. The dreams were as important to her as air. Maybe more so.

Every day she ate three meals and exercised and tanned by the pool. Her eyes still had circles under them. Apparently that was just a consequence of living between two worlds. But otherwise she looked almost normal.

She called her partners and requested an appointment with them on Monday. She hoped that when they saw how healthy she looked, they would allow her to return to work part-time.

And finally it was Saturday so she could return to Joey.

***

When Meghan opened her eyes she saw Joey walking into her hospital room, carrying Sophie.

"Mama!" Sophie cried.

"There's my big girl!" Meghan replied, blinking back tears. It had only been a few hours since she'd seen her older daughter but it felt like much longer.

Joey put Sophie on the bed so she could see Anna, who was nestled in Meghan's arms. Sophie pulled back the blanket to get a better look. Then she grinned up at Meghan and said, "Baby!"

Meghan was delighted. "Did you teach her that?"

Joey shrugged. "We've been practicing. First I tried Anna, but finally gave up on that."

Meghan laughed. "She'll eventually learn her name, but *Baby* is okay for now!"

The next few weeks were a blur of sleepless nights and days full of caring for babies. It was overwhelming at first, but Meghan adapted quickly. The semester ended and Meghan's professors allowed her to email in final assignments. Summer arrived and Joey started working extra hours with his dad and uncles, still saving up for those tires.

One Saturday the washing machine broke. She hated to tell Joey when he came in late, but she still had several loads of clothes that needed to be washed. So she broke the news to him while he was eating a grilled cheese sandwich.

He finished his sandwich, gulped down a glass of milk, and then got out his toolbox. He pulled the washer away from the wall and started searching for the problem.

Meghan sat on the floor in the laundry room to keep him company.

"I figure by the end of the month I'll have enough money for a set of tires," he told her. "As long as I don't get anything flashy."

"You don't need flashy," she agreed. "Just safe."

He selected a wrench from his toolbox. "Then I figure I can start saving for a down payment on a house."

She was surprised. "We have a house."

"We live here but it really belongs to my dad and his brothers. I want us to have a place of our own. A house where we don't have to add a room every time we have a baby. A house where something isn't always breaking so you won't have to worry about this." He waved to encompass the laundry room, his tools, and the whole repair process.

"Then what will I need you for?"

He gave her a bone-melting smile. "More kids."

Her heart beat a little faster.

He continued, "I figure in two years when I'm finished with school I can get a real job. By then we should have the money for a down payment and can qualify for a mortgage on a house. The girls will be older so you can double up on classes and get through school quick. Maybe once you have new house and a college degree your parents won't think that I've ruined your life."

"I thought we only cared about the goals on our list and that we weren't trying to please anyone else."

"True, but part of the reason those goals are on our list is so your parents can't hold your life against me."

"They don't hold my life against you," she murmured.

"They will if you don't graduate from college and have to spend your life in this broken-down house."

"It's not broken-down," she said. "And in all seriousness, I am very happy with our house *and* my life."

154

"Even if you have a broken washer?"

"Even then."

He looked over at her. "You don't regret giving up medical school?"

"How could medical school compare with our beautiful daughters?"

"So you're not sorry you married me?"

"It was the best decision I've ever made."

He tossed down wrench and wrapped his arms around her. Several kisses later he stood and pulled her to her feet. "Let's go to bed. I'll worry about the washer later."

"But I need to wash clothes!"

"We'll wear dirty clothes."

After a few more kisses, she didn't even think that was a bad idea.

They were making slow progress toward the bedroom when they heard a knock on the back door. They peeked around the doorframe and saw Caldwell's face pressed up against the glass.

Joey groaned. "Pretend we're not here!"

Meghan laughed. "She can see us!"

"Let me in!" Caldwell mouthed.

He released Meghan and picked up his wrench. "I hate her."

Meghan laughed as she opened the door.

When Caldwell walked in Joey stood in the doorway to the laundry room and asked, "Why are you lurking around, looking in people's windows?"

"Why aren't you two answering when someone knocks would be a better question!" she returned. "I pounded on your front door for five minutes."

"Sorry, we didn't hear you," Meghan said.

Caldwell looked between them with a sly smile. "I hope I didn't come at a bad time."

"No, of course not," Meghan assured her. "Joey is fixing the washer and the girls are asleep."

"Well, I just wanted to bring the baby a gift," Caldwell said. "You know – good manners and all."

"Please tell me you didn't bring us another huge Teddy bear," Joey said from the doorway.

"Naw," Caldwell said. "This time I got you a gift card."

"Thank you!" Meghan gave her a hug. "That's very practical."

Caldwell nodded. "And much easier to carry."

"So, do you want to see the baby?" Meghan asked.

Caldwell shrugged. "Not really. Mostly I wanted to see you and be sure you survived a second round of childbirth."

"Well, I did." Meghan held out her arms.

"Yeah, you don't look as bad as I expected," Caldwell said after a critical visual examination.

Joey made a growling noise and returned to his washer repairs.

Meghan pointed at the couch. "Have a seat." Once they were settled she asked, "So, have you been somewhere new and exciting lately? That is if there's anywhere exciting left that you haven't been to already – besides the moon."

Caldwell rolled her eyes. "There are a lot of exciting places I haven't been besides the moon. And actually I dated a guy who works for NASA once. Does that count as space travel?"

"I think it does," Meghan said. "So mark the moon off your list."

Caldwell crossed her tan, thin legs. "I just got back from a trip to Fiji and I'm headed to New York next week. My dad got me a summer job working at the United Nations."

Meghan was impressed. "Wow."

"What have you been doing besides cleaning up baby puke and sleeping with the same man every night?"

"You should give it a try – sleeping with the same man, I mean. I can't really recommend the baby puke."

Caldwell shook her head. "I can't figure out why you seem so happy – living here in this tiny old house with two babies and a crabby husband."

"I heard that!" Joey called from the laundry room.

"Eavesdropper!" Caldwell hollered back.

"Unwelcome guest!" Joey reciprocated.

"Joey's great," Meghan whispered to her friend. "I hope you find someone like him one day."

"Heaven forbid." Caldwell stood. "Well, I'll let the two of you get back to . . . whatever. Hope you buy yourself something fun with that gift card."

Meghan walked Caldwell to the door and gave her a hug. "Thanks. Come back and see me again when you're not in New York or on the moon."

Caldwell waved. "Don't die of boredom while I'm gone."

After Caldwell left, Meghan walked back into the kitchen.

"Did I mention that I hate her?" Joey asked.

"Once or twice," Meghan replied.

He put down his wrench and pulled Meghan into his arms. "Now, where were we?"

She closed her eyes as his lips pressed against hers. And when she opened her eyes, she was back in Dr. Morrow's lab.

**

When Meghan got home after the dream session, she had the regular sadness. It was so hard to be away from her family, especially with a new baby. But she only had to wait until Saturday. Two days. She could do it.

She curled up on the couch and tried to remember every moment of her dream.

Chase called but she didn't answer it. There was nothing new to say and she didn't want to rehash previous arguments. But seeing his name on the caller-ID made her think about something he had said. He claimed that the Joey in her dreams was a fictional character created by Dr. Morrow to be exactly the right man for her. Up to this point she had been satisfied to see Joey only in her dreams. But suddenly she knew she had to find him. She needed to know if the man she loved really existed.

A quick internet search gave her two addresses for Joey. One was in Old Mountain and one was in Marietta, a business listing for Patrone Appraisal Services. Going to his home would be too personal, and might involve confronting a wife or children. So she would have to go to his office.

Just staring at his name she was filled with conflicting emotions. She knew she had to go see him. But then what? Without the dream, would her feelings for him be the same? And how would Joey react to seeing her after so many years? In real life she had refused his marriage proposal and aborted his baby. It was likely that he hated her.

And even if he didn't hate her he was probably married. Then a relationship between them would destroy two marriages. And what if he had children? Then a relationship between them would destroy a whole family. Could she really do that?

While her mind was in turmoil, the doorbell rang. She groaned, assuming it was Chase or worse, her parents, coming to try and save her from herself again. Only the certainty that they would not go away made her decide to answer it. She braced herself for the emotional onslaught. Then she opened the door.

Standing on her front porch was Joey Patrone.

Chapter Twelve

He was older than the boy in her dream. His hair was cut shorter, but his dark brown eyes were the same. He looked haggard and tortured just like she felt. A little whimper escaped her lips. And then she hurled herself into his arms. Their lips met and dreams collided with reality.

Joey moved them inside and kicked the door shut. She put her hands behind his head to hold him close. He tangled his fingers in her hair. Their kisses were filled with sweet longing, restrained passion, and deep affection. When they finally pulled apart she had the answers to at least some of her questions.

"Oh Joey," she said with tears in her eyes. "I love you."

"I know," he whispered. "I love you too."

She led him to the couch and they sat down. She tried to compose herself, but every time she wiped her eyes, fresh tears appeared.

"Let me guess," she said. "You have been doing dream therapy sessions at Dr. Morrow's lab too?"

"Yes."

"So we've been sharing the same dreams?"

Joey ran his fingers through his hair. "Yes. He recruited me when he found out what your pivot point was. Apparently he's never had a dream-couple before. He thought this was a great opportunity to try it. He paid me a small fortune , but I would have done it for free. The chance to reconnect with you even in a dream was just, well, irresistible."

"I can't believe he involved you in my dream without my permission," she said.

"I knew he wasn't being honest with you. I'm sorry."

"You hadn't seen me in ten years so I don't hold you responsible. And I'm more surprised than hurt by Dr. Morrow's deception. What I want to know is how does it work? How can we share the same dream?"

"I only know what he told me," Joey prefaced his explanation.

She nodded. "I understand. Tell me what he said."

"They interviewed us both and the computer used our combined memories to generate a very realistic dream-version of what could have happened. Then they drugged us and used subliminal messaging techniques to project the same dream into both of our malleable subconscious minds."

"The ability to project a computer generated dream into one mind is amazing," Meghan said a little breathlessly. "But to be able to project the same dream into two different minds simultaneously . . . wow."

"I'm not sure if his methods would work so well on anyone else. I believe they were particularly successful in manipulating our feelings because we loved each other before. That gave him something to build on."

This reminded her that while their feelings for each other were real, their dreams were not. "Oh Joey, our children." Meghan rested her head against his chest. "I miss them so much between sessions I can barely function. And you." She caught his hand and brought it to her lips.

"I know. I feel the same way."

Meghan stood up and paced, agitated. "How can you stand to look at me? I killed Sophie!"

He shook his head. "The dream is just something that could have happened. If you had continued with the pregnancy you might have had a miscarriage, or you could have had a boy. But like your mother said in her kitchen that day - at the time our baby was just a little bundle of cells."

"That could have grown into a child if I'd let it."

He shrugged. "I held that against you for a long time, but even before the dreams I'd let go of it. You were just a kid."

She sat back on the couch and put a hand on his cheek. "My husband said you weren't real – that the man in my dreams was something Dr. Morrow created as the perfect match for me."

"I wondered the same thing. That's part of why I had to come."

"Do you really sing in the shower?"

"All the time."

160

"Do you like sappy romantic movies?"

"That will be our little secret."

Meghan clung to him. It was exquisite to feel the warmth of his skin and the beating of his heart while she was wide awake. "What are we going to do? I have a husband who loves me. And I love him – but not like I love you."

"My life is not quite as complicated as yours. I have a girlfriend and she thinks we're getting married. So does my mom. My whole family loves her. And I thought I could be happy spending my life with her – until Dr. Morrow introduced me to his dream-therapy."

"So your mom is okay – she doesn't have cancer?"

"She really did have cancer, but she's been clear for a long time."

"I can keep the events in the dreams separated from reality, but it's the feelings that I have a hard time with. I care about your mother, even though I don't really know her. And Sophie and Anna . . . I can't make my mind accept that they don't exist."

He looked away. "But we do have to accept that. They are part of the dream."

"Now you are a part of my reality too – not just my dreams," Meghan said. "And if we continue to dream together we won't lose the girls completely."

Joey shook his head. "That's the road to madness, Meg."

She couldn't give up. "We can limit ourselves to one dream session a month. That will keep the dream from over-taking our regular lives. It will be like visiting the girls. And when we have real children of our own it might be easier to let them go."

"That would probably be the least painful way – to wean ourselves off of the dream therapy slowly, but we don't have that luxury." Joey's tone was so final. "Dr. Morrow is at least irresponsible if not evil and he has to be stopped."

"Stopped?" Meghan gasped. "If we stop him – then our dream life together . . ."

"Will disappear," he finished for her. "Our children, our home, our goals nailed to the wall of my grandparents' cottage. It will be gone forever."

"Oh Joey," she gasped. "How can we live without the dream?"

"At least we don't have to live without each other," he tried to comfort her. "We can get married and have children. But we won't name them Sophie and Anna. Those children are not real."

"I don't think I can bear to let them go," Meghan whispered.

He clasped her hands. "There is no choice. Think about all the misery and chaos Dr. Morrow will cause if he's allowed to addict the population at large to dream therapy."

"Chase and my parents both said I was addicted, but I didn't want to believe them."

"It's not your fault. The dreams are irresistible," Joey said. "They're like drugs or alcohol - making people lose interest in the things that are real."

"Dr. Morrow purposely made the dreams addictive so that people will keep coming back and paying for more sessions?"

"Maybe that wasn't his original intention, but addiction is a consequence of his dream therapy," Joey said. "The technology he has created is very powerful, with negatives that outweigh any positives. Used in the wrong way by the wrong people, dream therapy could control nations and armies and, well, the world."

"That sounds kind of dramatic."

"A few weeks ago we were regular people leading happy lives. Now look at us."

She couldn't argue this point.

"It's like a legal drug that makes people give up their jobs, spend their life savings, walk away from their spouses." Joey sighed. "And there's more."

Meghan was pretty sure she didn't want to hear it, but she nodded for him to continue.

"Did he tell you that he recruited homeless people, drug addicts, and prostitutes as his first test clients?"

She nodded. "He said he paid them and he pointed out that they did far worse things for money than dream."

"That's just a lame excuse for taking advantage of defenseless people," Joey said. "He experimented on them with reckless disregard for their welfare. And when he was finished, he cut them off from their dreams."

"He couldn't keep letting them dream for free indefinitely," Meghan defended Dr. Morrow. "And he gave them all exit counseling."

"I'm not saying he was obligated to let them dream forever and he may have given exit counseling to some – especially the ones he wanted to star in his sales DVD. But there were many that he just dumped back on the street. And from what I've been able to determine, most of them are now dead."

Her heart pounded. "Dead?" she whispered. "The therapy is lethal?"

"Indirectly," he confirmed. "While I'll admit that my research techniques are not scientific or infallible, based on what I've been able to determine, the suicide rate among Dr. Morrow's original test clients is staggering."

"They were addicted to their dreams and when he cut them off they couldn't stand their real lives, so they killed themselves?"

"It's possible that they just killed themselves when he wouldn't let them dream anymore. We're rational people and we can't stand to think of our dreams coming to an end. It would be worse for people who are emotionally unstable or chemically dependent."

"And we have each other," she murmured. "We can support each other through the emotional detoxification process."

"That's the best possible explanation," Joey told her.

"What could be worse?"

"Experimenting on homeless people and then killing them – and making it look like suicide," Joey said.

"Dr. Morrow wouldn't kill people!" Meghan was sure.

"I hope not," Joey said sincerely. "But his technology is not only dangerous, it's also potentially valuable. Eventually someone will realize that and take it away from him. So we have to consider the possibility that he killed them to keep his secret safe."

Meghan shook her head. "I can't believe that the man I know would purposely kill his test clients."

"Then we will go with the suicide theory, but keep murder as a possibility in the back of your mind."

"Dr. Morrow assured me that his test-clients were better off after the therapy than before."

"Well, that's at least two times he lied to you."

She sighed. "I don't want to believe he's a terrible person."

"Whether he purposely killed people or just let them die doesn't matter," Joey insisted. "His dream therapy technology is lethal and it has to end. We're the only people in a position to stop him."

"What can we do?"

"We can prove that what he does kills people," Joey said. "Then we'll take our case to the police."

"The word that worries me there is 'prove'," Meghan said. "How can we prove anything?"

"I've compiled a list of twenty-five homeless people that I suspect were his test-clients and their death dates."

"You can't confirm that they participated in the dream therapy?"

He shook his head. "Not without access to Dr. Morrow's records. I can't even provide real names – just their street names. If we keep searching among homeless people maybe we can find someone who survived the dream therapy and is able to testify against Morrow."

"That sounds like a long-shot," Meghan said. "Besides Dr. Morrow said he is moving away from homeless clients and using more regular people like us. It seems like that's where we should focus our efforts – identifying them."

"I want him to answer for the homeless people that died," Joey said. "But I agree that more normal people would make better witnesses. The only way we'll find those people will be to get access to his records."

Meghan thought about the lab. It was not only ultra-modern, it was very secure. "That won't be easy."

"We'll think of something." Joey sounded confident.

"I'm a doctor," Meghan said. "And I'm basically unemployed. So I could ask to be part of his staff. I'd have access to his test client list and the dream process."

"Why would he want to hire you? He thinks you're a dream-addict."

"I *am* a dream-addict," she admitted. "But that might not matter if I tell him that I loved dreaming, but I love being a doctor more and don't want to give up my career. I'll say that I know I can't dream anymore but I'm fascinated by the process – by the science, and by his work. If I can convince him that I want to stay near it by helping him, he might let me work there."

"You'd appeal to his pride and vanity," Joey summed this up.

"Basically," she acknowledged. "I'd donate my time and as a former client I might be able to give him some insight and improve the process."

Joey shook his head. "He'd probably be a little suspicious and watch you closely, so you wouldn't have access to much valuable information. And it puts you personally at risk, so I don't think it's something we should even consider."

"What else can we do?"

"Maybe we could get one of his employees to collect information for us."

"Steal information, you mean?"

He nodded. "Yes, steal it."

She considered this. "My technician, Heidi, always seemed mildly disapproving of the dream process so she might be willing to do it. But if Heidi steals client data there's a good chance she'll lose her job. So we'd have to offer a financial incentive."

"Dr. Morrow paid me $25,000 to do the dream sessions with you and I have another $25,000 I can access without mortgaging my home. That gives us $50,000 to use as a bribe."

"We have about that much in savings," Meghan said. "And if we need more I can ask my parents."

Joey shook his head. "I don't want to use any of your money, since it is also your husband's money. And I definitely don't want to ask your parents. I'll mortgage my house if Heidi demands more money."

"If we tell Heidi that Dr. Morrow is about to be arrested, so her job will be gone anyway, she might be willing to help us for the $50,000. And as an added incentive, I'll ask my dad to help her get another job. He does that for Momentum patrons all the time. And he'll be glad to do anything that will get me away from the dream therapy."

"But not if they know I'm involved in the bribery scheme – and that I might be a part of your future."

"No, I won't mention that," she agreed.

"Then that's the deal we'll offer her," Joey said.

"How will we present this proposal to Heidi?"

"We'll go to our dream session on Saturday and afterwards we'll wait for Heidi. When we see her leave the lab we'll follow her, approach her, and convince her to help us."

Meghan nodded. "That sounds perfect."

"I'll get the money tomorrow but we won't give it to her until she gives us the information," Joey said.

"And if we can't convince her to help us?"

"Then we'll go to the police and tell them our story. We'll show them the names of homeless test clients that committed suicide and hope they'll take us seriously."

"Chase is an assistant DA," Meghan said. "He could help us build a case against Dr. Morrow."

"He wouldn't want to help me."

"No, but he hates the dream therapy."

"I'd rather not involve your husband," Joey said. "Let's see what we can work out with Heidi first."

Meghan frowned. "If Dr. Morrow gets arrested, all his dream clients will be cut off abruptly. And based on your research, that could cause them to commit suicide."

"Once we have the list of clients, we'll contact all of them and make sure they get counseling. And all we're doing is speeding up the process anyway. At some point Dr. Morrow will cut them off."

"You think he's a heartless man?"

"I think he's let science overrule his humanity. But I can't hate him because he brought us back together."

Tears filled her eyes again. "What about us? Do we have a future together without the dreams?"

"There's no easy answer," he said. "We can't go back and change the past, so if we stay together we have to take our baggage with us."

"Like the aborted pregnancy?"

He nodded. "That can't be changed. I told you I made my peace with it but my family might not feel the same."

"In real life your parents don't love me like they do in the dream."

"They might learn to some day– but not right away."

"They'll see me as a baby-killer and a home-wrecker."

"And a divorcee," he added. "That's not popular with Catholics either."

"So you're saying they may never accept me."

"Completely?" He shook his head. "Probably not."

"And my parents won't accept you either."

"Many people will be very unhappy if we stay together," he agreed. "And we'll have to live with the pain we've caused all of them."

"How can we do that?" She met her eyes. "How can we not?"

They were quiet for a few minutes, each lost in unpleasant thoughts. Finally Joey said, "Let's leave the future and huge decisions that affect a lot of people alone for right now."

"I'm glad we can attend one last dream session. I know I can't really say goodbye to the girls, but if I know when I start that it's the last time I'll ever see them, maybe it will be easier."

He nodded. "Maybe."

She didn't want to think about the end of their dream, so she stood. "Are you hungry?"

"You cook now?" he asked.

She smiled. "Not really. But I can scramble eggs."

He sat at the kitchen island and watched as she prepared their simple meal. It was unnerving to see him there – in her space, in Chase's space.

"We've got to start taking better care of ourselves," he said. "Morrow's a genius. If we're going to beat him – we'll have to be at the top of our game."

"For the past week or so I've been eating and sleeping," she said. "And now that I know I can see you outside the dream, I think it will be easier for me to concentrate on life."

"I think it will be easier for me too," Joey agreed. "Plus we have a mission now. We have to stop Morrow."

She was less enthusiastic about this. It wasn't that she didn't believe Dr. Morrow had created a technology that was dangerous to individuals and possibly even the world. But she felt personally connected to him, she admired his intelligence, and she was grateful for the opportunity he had given her to go back and at least through dreams, correct the biggest regret of her life.

They ate their eggs side by side. It was like the dream yet different. They loved each other, they were happy to be together. But they didn't belong to each other. And they didn't have two daughters.

"So, tell me about the past ten years," she requested. "Did you play football in college?"

He shook his head. "No, I joined the Army instead. I did a tour in Afghanistan and then went to Georgia Tech."

"You're a real estate appraiser?"

"Yes."

"Do you like it?"

"I liked it better a few years ago before the housing market bottomed out. But I'm still doing okay."

"That's good," Meghan said although his career didn't sound very fulfilling to Meghan, especially in comparison to her medical practice and work at the *Mom*entum clinic.

After the meal they put their dishes in the sink and then Joey pulled her close. His breath stirred her hair, his whisker stubble grazed her cheek, and his body heat radiated into hers.

"I can't believe you're here," she whispered.

He nodded. "It's like a dream come true."

She fingered the top button of his shirt. She had given her heart to him and the rest just seemed like a natural next step.

His hand covered hers, stilling her fingers. "So far you haven't been unfaithful to your husband."

"But we love each other," she argued.

"I want all your options to still be open when you have to make a final decision."

"I don't need options!" she said. "I can't live with Chase when I feel this way about you!"

He turned away. "I don't want you to go too far – so far that there's no turning back."

To avoid an argument, Meghan let the subject drop. She pressed her cheek against his chest. "Will you just hold me then?"

His arms tightened around her and he whispered, "If I could, I'd never let you go."

She fell asleep to the reassuring sound of his heartbeat.

***

When Meghan woke up on Thursday morning she was in her bed. She hurried out of her bedroom terrified that Joey had left during the night – or worse, that she'd dreamed the whole thing.

But she found him in the kitchen, sitting in the same chair Chase favored, working on his laptop. He looked tired so she knew he hadn't slept much.

"Good morning," he greeted her with a smile.

She walked up behind his chair and put her arms around him. "Good morning yourself." Against the warm skin of his neck she asked, "Do you want some breakfast?"

"I helped myself to some cereal," he said. "You need to eat too, since that's your number one goal."

"You've seen my list on the mirror?" she guessed.

He nodded. "That's what Morrow's dream therapy does – it makes you have to think about doing the simplest things."

She poured herself a bowl of Frosted Mini-Wheats and sat down across from him. While she ate she asked, "So, what have you been working on?"

"I've identified twenty-five homeless people that I believe were test clients and who are now dead from suicide. And there are several others who are missing and could also be dead."

"Homeless people are transient by nature and their mortality rate is probably pretty high anyway," she pointed out.

"True," he agreed.

"And we've agreed that the homeless test-clients won't be good witnesses."

"But even if their testimony isn't useful, the sheer number of people who were treated irresponsibly and then abandoned proves that Morrow is unethical."

Meghan nodded. "If we can prove they were associated with Dr. Morrow's research, twenty-five dead homeless people should be enough to get attention from the police."

"I want to try and find more," he said. "We'll go tonight after dark since that's when they're most likely to talk to us. But since homeless people are not our best potential witnesses, I've been trying to think of a way to find normal clients – who have real names and addresses."

"What have you come up with?" she asked.

In response he posed what seemed like a strange question. "Do you watch tennis?"

She shook her head. "No."

"Well, last night I was searching the internet for people who acted out of character and I found a clip from the US Open. A woman named Gina Lightsey charged the court during the title match and tried to grab one of the players, Ty Randall. She said she loved him and that they had a child together. Randall denied even knowing the woman. The clip was replayed for several days on all the sports shows and even on some news reports. Everyone assumed that she was crazy or on drugs. But there were no illegal drugs found in her system. And she was quoted as saying – 'It can't all be a dream.'"

Meghan's heart pounded. "She was a dream therapy client?"

He nodded. "I found another article that said until a few months before the US Open, Gina had been a successful real estate agent in Florida. Her only connection to the tennis player was that she showed him a house two years ago when he was looking for a vacation home."

Meghan said, "That was her pivot point?"

"I think so. Maybe he asked her out and she turned him down."

"So she dreamed she married a tennis star – as part of Dr. Morrow's therapy?"

"This is just a guess," Joey reminded her. "But it makes sense. If she participated in dream therapy, she returned to her pivot point and she made a choice that put her on the road toward a relationship with the tennis player. They married and had a child. Then she confused the dream with reality and walked onto the tennis court during a match."

170

It sounded plausible except for logistics. "But she lives in Florida."

"The article said she was from Atlanta originally and she has a sister who still lives here. So I called all the Lightseys listed in the phonebook and found her sister - Leah."

"Does she know where Gina is?"

He nodded. "In a Florida mental hospital. The sister said treatment in the hospital was part of the deal she worked out with the district attorney in Florida to avoid criminal charges in the US Open incident. She has no proof that her sister was participating in dream therapy with Dr. Morrow – but that's what Gina told her."

"Can we talk to Gina?"

"The sister says she's not allowed to have visitors other than immediate family and anyway they keep her heavily sedated because of repeated suicide attempts."

"So even though she fits the pattern perfectly, it's a dead end?"

"Probably," he said. "But Gina Lightsey wasn't an isolated case. I've got more."

"More what?"

Joey held up a stack of newspaper articles. "These are articles from all over the southeast about people who broke in to houses or stole cars or tried to drive off in boats that didn't belong to them. But when they were arrested, they claimed that the house or car or yacht was theirs."

"They got confused between their dream life and their real life?"

He nodded. "I think some of them at least were dream clients."

"What does that mean?"

"It means if we can connect any of these people with Morrow we might have credible witnesses who can testify against him."

"How will we connect them to Dr. Morrow?"

"I'd rather not call and ask them directly since some of them may still be participating in the dream-therapy and they might tell Morrow that we're investigating him."

"Then how can we connect them to him?"

"We need access bank accounts, phone bills, credit card statements, things like that."

"The police could get access to all those records," she said.

"We have to have a stronger case *before* we turn it over to the police," Joey said. "You can't accuse a Nobel Prize winning scientist of multiple murders without some kind of proof. Not if you want to be taken seriously."

She sighed. "I guess that's true."

"Why don't we go to my office where we can spread out?" he suggested. "We'll take each article, find out what we can about the people involved, and determine if they were dream-clients. That should take us all day. Then when it gets dark we'll look for test-clients among the homeless community."

"So, what are we going to do today?"

"First, I'll get the money to bribe Heidi."

She nodded.

"Then I thought we'd go to my office. I can show you the information I've collected. And then maybe we can drive to into downtown where the homeless people gather and try to find a dream-therapy survivor."

Meghan took a quick shower. She rushed through dressing and drying her hair, nervous about having Joey out of her sight.

When she walked back into the living room, Joey was waiting by the door. "Ready?" he asked.

She nodded. "Let's go."

When she walked outside she saw Joey's old truck, the same one he'd driven in high school, parked in front of the condo.

"You kept your truck!" she breathed.

He nodded. "I did buy new tires, though."

She smiled as he opened the door for her to climb in. She slid across the familiar vinyl seats and felt both melancholy and nostalgic. After putting on the seatbelt she looked out the windshield. It was almost like being in another time – or in her dream.

They went to the bank and Meghan waited in the truck while Joey liquidated his money market account. When he returned to the truck he was carrying the money in a large envelope. He placed it on her lap.

"It's doesn't look like as much as I thought it would," she told him.

"I hope it's enough to interest Heidi," he said. Then he eased the truck into the flow of traffic.

They drove to Joey's office, which was part of a modern looking strip mall. The inside was sparse but neat. There were four desks, all facing the door. Each had a computer and a telephone on it.

"I used to have a staff," he told her. "I had to let them all go. But business is picking up so maybe I'll be able to hire them back soon."

He sat down at the first desk and turned on the computer. While he typed commands on the keyboard her eyes were drawn to the framed pictures on his desk. There was one of his parents, looking older than she expected. The other was of a girl in her early twenties with long brown hair. She was pretty, but not beautiful. Meghan took no pleasure in the fact that she was more attractive than Joey's girlfriend.

"Why don't you take those articles and spread them out on desks," Joey suggested. "Then we can each take turns researching them one at a time."

She did as he suggested and kept the last one, the case of a man who interrupted a wedding to say that the bride had been his wife for ten years. She took her article to the desk beside Joey and entered the names of the man and his 'wife' into an internet search engine.

They worked for several hours and by the time Joey said it was time to stop, they had come up with twelve names of people in Georgia who were arrested, or otherwise reported, for strange behavior. They had some details on each situation beyond the article in the newspaper, but there was no obvious connection to Dr. Morrow.

"It's almost time to go for a nice little walk through streets crowded with homeless people."

"I can hardly wait," she teased.

"I need to take a shower and change clothes." He moved toward the back of the office. "There's a vending machine back here if you want something."

She followed him to a little lounge area and got a Coke and a pack of crackers. Then she returned to the front and waited at his desk. He returned a few minutes later dressed in tattered jeans and a faded shirt. His hair was damp and curling on the ends. She could barely take her eyes off him.

He misunderstood the reason for her stares. "I know these clothes are ugly, but this is the disguise I wear to blend in with homeless people," he explained.

"You look fine," she managed.

Then he handed her an old jacket and a baseball cap. "Try these on."

"My disguise?" she guessed.

He nodded. "It's the best I could do."

They rode in his truck to downtown Atlanta and parked in a deck near the civic center. Then they walked up and down the streets, asking the homeless if they'd heard of a doctor who paid people to dream.

Finally they found a panhandler named Bucket who claimed to know about Dr. Morrow.

Joey showed him a picture of Dr. Morrow. "Is this him?"

Bucket shrugged a thin shoulder. "Could be."

Meghan couldn't tell if he was being cagey or just had a bad memory.

"We want to talk to some of the people who took part in his dream project. Can you point any of them out to me?"

"Naw, once they bought into the dream machine – they never came back here."

"They moved on to a better life?"

He shrugged. "More likely they checked out of life – permanently. And then the doctor would come looking for more folks."

Meghan and Joey exchanged a glance.

"Why didn't you tell the police?"

"Naw. Nobody cares if a few people from the street go missing," Bucket claimed. "Especially the police."

"We care," Meghan claimed.

Bucket studied her with his rheumy eyes for a few seconds. Then he nodded. "I can tell you a couple of street names – don't know if that will help you find 'em."

"Anything you can tell us will be appreciated."

Bucket gave them the names of four people. All had bragged about being paid to dream and none had been seen in the area lately.

They continued to walk around for another hour without finding much of substance. Finally Joey took Meghan back to her condo.

"Will you stay here with me?" she asked when they got inside.

"I'll stay tonight," was all Joey promised.

She changed into pajamas and then sat beside Joey on the couch. He was looking through the newspaper articles again. She leaned her head against his shoulder and closed her eyes.

Meghan had just dozed off when she heard a noise by the door. She opened her eyes and although the room was dark, she could see Joey put a finger to his lips, requesting silence. Then he slid off the edge of the couch and stood just as the front door opened.

The light was flipped on and Meghan saw Chase standing in the doorway.

He took in the scene – his eyes moving from her on the couch in her pajamas to Joey standing beside her. He came to the obvious, if erroneous, conclusion and charged toward Joey.

"Chase, stop!" Meghan screamed.

He ignored her completely.

She saw Joey spread his feet and brace for impact. Chase's punch caught him in the left jaw with a sickening thud. Joey's head snapped back but he held his ground.

Meghan was screaming at them both. Neither man acknowledged her.

Chase drew back his fist for another punch, but this time Joey caught his arm.

"The first one was free because even though I'm not guilty of anything - you didn't know that. But if you try to hit me again, I'll knock you unconscious."

Chase was a brilliant, well-educated man. But he was not a fighter. So he wisely pulled his arm free of Joey's grasp and stepped back. "What do you mean you're not guilty of anything?" he yelled. "You were spending the night in my house with *my* wife!"

175

Meghan heard the pain in his voice, mingled with the anger. She saw the blood on his knuckles from probably the first punch he'd ever thrown. It was all her fault and she despised herself.

"I was staying here, but Meghan hasn't been unfaithful to you."

Meghan wasn't sure this was totally true. In her heart, she'd left Chase weeks ago.

Chase stared back in disbelief. "You seriously expect me to buy that?"

"You know about the dream sessions," Joey tried again. "Dr. Morrow had me dreaming with Meghan – so we have feelings for each other, but we haven't acted on them."

Now Chase added confusion to the expressions warring for control of his features. "You were both dreaming at the same time? The same dream? And you didn't know it?"

"I knew it," Joey said. "Meghan didn't."

"That's unbelievable."

"It's true." Joey pointed toward the couch. "Let's sit down and talk about it."

For a second Meghan thought Chase was going to refuse, but finally he walked over and sat down.

Once they were all seated in an awkward little group, Chase said, "So what are you saying?"

"We fell in love in our dreams," Meghan explained.

All the color drained from Chase's face. "And you still feel the same way when you're awake?"

Meghan and Joey nodded in unison.

Chase asked Meghan. "Do you want a divorce?"

"I don't know what I want," she told him. "I don't want to hurt anyone."

From the look on Chase's face, she knew it was too late for that.

"I'm sorry," she whispered.

She expected an angry response from Chase, but what he said surprised her.

He leaned closer and said earnestly, "Please don't make a rash decision about the future. Wait until you've been away from the dream therapy for awhile."

"My feelings won't change. I feel the same when I'm dreaming or awake."

Chase gestured vaguely at Joey. "Until a few weeks ago he was just a part of your past. It can be that way again!"

She didn't want to go back a life without Joey. She didn't want to lose the feelings she had for him. But to spare Chase's feelings, she just nodded. "I will consider everything very carefully before I make a final decision."

"And you'll stop the dream sessions?" Chase pressed.

She nodded. "We are going to have one final session on Saturday – just for an hour. And then we'll stop. We'll sort out our feelings slowly and carefully and decide what the future holds."

Chase seemed relieved. "I think that's wise. There's no need to rush." Then he turned to Joey. "But you can't live here while things get sorted out. I have to draw the line there."

Joey nodded. "I won't spend the night here again. Let me get my laptop."

Meghan started to follow Joey and then stopped and looked back at Chase. She had put herself physically between the two men.

Chase was watching her. She knew he expected an apology and he definitely deserved one. But saying she was sorry would be a lie. She loved Joey in a way that she had never loved Chase. There was no point in giving him false hope.

Finally he looked away. "I just came by to get my raincoat." Chase walked into their bedroom and came back out a few seconds later. Ignoring Joey, who was still in the kitchen, he asked her, "Can I call you?"

"Of course," she said, but she didn't walk him to the door. She just watched as he let himself out.

Joey returned with his laptop and walked toward the door.

"Are you going home?" she asked.

He shook his head. "Girlfriend is there."

She didn't need him to explain to her why this would be awkward.

"I'll stay at the office. I left my card on the kitchen table in case you need me."

She nodded.

"I'll call you tomorrow," he promised.

177

As he kissed her goodbye she could see the bruise forming along his jaw-line. Filled with guilt she locked the door behind him. Then feeling lost and alone, she crawled back into bed and did her best to recapture the dream.

Chapter Thirteen

Meghan spent a sleepless night tossing and turning and worrying. So on Friday she was tired as well as lonely. She felt adrift without anything to anchor her. She had no job, no Joey, no children, no purpose. She had given up everything in the real world and was about to put an end to her dreams. Was she leaving herself with nothing?

Joey called around noon to tell her he had a couple of appraisals to do and would come over later with a pizza for dinner. That gave her the incentive to take a shower and get dressed.

It was well past dark by the time he got there and Meghan was beginning to worry. When he arrived she pulled him into the condo and put the pizza on a table by the door. Then she wrapped her arms around him and pressed her cheek against his.

"I missed you," she whispered as tears slipped from her eyes. "I hate it when we're apart."

"Don't cry. I can't stand to see you sad."

"When we're together there's always an edge of sadness," she whispered. "I guess there always will be."

He didn't deny it. Instead he kissed her forehead and pointed to the pizza. "Let's eat. You'll feel better after that."

She doubted it, but she didn't argue.

During their dinner he said, "I spent last night and most of today typing up our list of 'normal' client possibilities and the data we've collected on each one. I think it looks pretty impressive. And once we have Heidi's testimony and the client list – we'll be ready to take it all to the police."

She gave him a wan smile. "Let's have a look."

He pushed a stack of papers toward her.

She picked the top page up and was reading it when the doorbell rang.

"Expecting anyone?" he asked.

She shook her head.

"I hope it's not your husband coming to try and beat me up again," he muttered.

"Nobody is going to beat you up," she said as she walked to the door. But honestly she was afraid it might be Chase, or worse her parents. Instead it was Caldwell. She was wearing tattered jeans, a plain white T-shirt, and sunglasses. Since she was always on the cutting edge of fashion Meghan could only assume that grungy was back in style.

"Well, this is a surprise," Meghan said.

"It's rude of me to drop in without calling first. You don't have to tell me."

Meghan frowned. "I wasn't scolding you. Come in."

Caldwell walked inside and saw Joey standing in the kitchen. "Ah, here's your dreaming co-star."

Joey nodded in minimal greeting. "Caldwell."

"You've aged well, Patrone," she said. "I guess I can see why Meghan can't quit you."

Meghan saw his jaw tighten and quickly intervened. "So, Caldwell, why are you here?"

"First, I owe you an apology." Caldwell removed her sunglasses, exposing red-rimmed eyes.

"You've been crying!" Meghan said in alarm. In the entire nearly twenty-five years they had known each other she'd never seen Caldwell shed a single tear. "What's the matter?"

Caldwell squared her thin shoulders and looked at Meghan. "I might as well come clean. I went out to the lake house earlier tonight to see Chase. He let me in and we had a few drinks. I sympathized with him over this whole dream thing and then I kissed him. He didn't seem to mind that so I asked him if he wanted to sleep with me."

Meghan gasped.

"I know its so cliché! I'm more embarrassed than ashamed." Caldwell walked over and sat down on the couch. "I've always had a thing for him – ever since the two of you started dating. But even I wouldn't sink low enough to break up your marriage."

She cut her eyes over at Joey and he cursed under his breath.

"But now that you're with Patrone, I figured Chase was fair game."

"Oh Caldwell," Meghan said.

"You know how I am," she went on. "I'm always looking for something new. Sleeping with my best friend's husband is one of the few things I haven't done. And Chase is so cute. But there isn't any excuse for my behavior."

"I don't know what to say."

She sniffled. "He declined my offer – if that makes you feel any better."

"It doesn't." Meghan was shocked and hurt by Caldwell's behavior. Chase was not 'fair game', at least not yet. But she was glad that he had not taken advantage of her. While Caldwell acted tough Meghan knew she was much more vulnerable than she seemed.

"I'm sorry," Caldwell was continuing. "I know you hate me." Her voice quivered. "But it won't happen again. I promise."

Meghan sat down and put an arm around her. "I don't hate you. But I really advise you to stay away from Chase. The two of us are at odds and I don't want you to get caught in the middle."

Caldwell nodded. "Which brings me to the other reason I'm here. And once I tell you this, I'll never have a chance with Chase – even if you two get divorced."

Meghan frowned. "Tell me what?"

"When I was at Chase's place I overheard him making some phone calls. He's setting the two of you up at the dream session tomorrow."

"Setting us up for what?' Joey asked.

Caldwell sighed. "He's arranged with Meghan's parents to make a big donation to Dr. Morrow's research organization. And in return, Dr. Morrow is going to change your dream."

Meghan grasped her friend's hand. "Change it how?"

She shrugged. "I didn't hear the details but the gist of it is that when you wake up from your dream you won't be in love with Patrone anymore and Chase will get you back. Everything will be like it used to be. Sort of."

Meghan was so angry and so frightened she could barely breathe. "I can't believe my parents would conspire against me like this."

"They think you're crazy," Caldwell said blithely. "They're doing it for your own good."

Meghan stared blankly at Caldwell, trying to make sense of what she had just said. "They thought I would benefit from being brainwashed?"

"It's not brainwashing exactly," Caldwell hedged.

"They're just trying to get you away from me," Joey said. "Like before."

Meghan turned to him. "But before they made their argument out in the open and let me decide. This time they are sneaking around behind my back."

Joey sighed. "Like Caldwell said, they think they are helping you. And I guess under these circumstances they feel justified."

Meghan rubbed her temple where a headache was forming. "And Chase. He's the epitome of honesty and justice for all. How could he sink so low?"

"I guess the thought of losing you pushed him over the edge."

"And how could Dr. Morrow change our feelings for each other – even if they changed our dream?"

"Maybe they were going to reset the dream, take you back to your pivot point and make us unhappy this time," Joey proposed.

Meghan shook her head. "That wouldn't work. It wouldn't erase my memories of the other dreams."

"Maybe Morrow was going to turn me into a total creep and have me break your heart. We fell in love in the dream so I guess we could fall out of love in one. Then at least when you woke up you'd be confused and conflicted. And you might give your husband another chance."

Meghan shivered. "I can't believe they want me to be confused and conflicted."

"Well, one thing's for sure," Joey said. "We can't go to our dream session tomorrow."

"That's a disappointment," Meghan drastically understated her feelings.

"In fact, it might be a good idea for the two of you to disappear for awhile," Caldwell suggested. "When they find out you skipped on the corrective dream session, Chase and your parents are going to be furious. And they'll probably cook up some new, diabolical plan to break the two of you up. But I don't want to know where you're going. They might get it out of me."

Meghan hugged her lifetime friend. "We won't tell you our plans. But thank you for coming to warn us."

"We're still friends?"

Meghan nodded. "Always – as long as you don't try to steal Joey away from me."

Caldwell gave her a weak smile. "That would be a waste of time. Patrone has always hated me."

"I don't hate you," Joey denied. "But I wouldn't let you kiss me."

Caldwell rolled her eyes.

"Then our friendship is safe," Meghan said.

Once Caldwell was gone, Meghan turned to Joey. "Do you think we should leave?"

He nodded. "The sooner the better. Pack the essentials and then we'll go."

She pulled a small suitcase from the coat closet. "Where are we going?"

He ran his fingers through his hair. "I don't know yet."

***

Meghan was an emotional wreck as she packed. She knew she shouldn't be devastated by Chase's betrayal or surprised by her parents' interference. But it hurt that she couldn't trust Chase and that her parents had chosen his side over hers.

She was nervous about their efforts to build a case against Dr. Morrow. She didn't really want to be responsible for ending his dream-therapy research and possibly putting him in jail, assuming they could prove he was doing anything wrong.

And she was truly grief-stricken that they couldn't do one last dream session. The thought that she would never see Sophie and Anna again was almost unbearable. So she closed her mind to all the things that worried her and concentrated on packing.

Joey was waiting by the front door when she returned. He turned off all the lights and they left through the back door. They drove to his office where he packed some clothes in an old gym bag.

"We'll need to leave our phones here," he told her. "They have GPS and someone could use them to track us."

183

Meghan handed him her phone and watched as he put it with his in a desk drawer.

Then they went outside, climbed into the old truck, and headed south.

When they left Atlanta Meghan asked, "Did you decide where we should go?"

He risked a quick glance at her. "Any place is as good as the next as long as we're not here. So I figured we go to Savannah."

Her heart pounded. "Where we went on our dream honeymoon?"

"We should probably stay in a different hotel," Joey said. "Since we're not married and we won't be . . . honeymooning."

She smiled at him. "That's a shame, but it will be nice to be there together at least – in real life."

It was almost two o'clock in the morning when arrived in Savannah. As they passed the hotel where they spent their dream honeymoon, Joey reached across the seat and took her hand in his. Meghan sighed, remembering, and knowing that he was remembering too.

They found a rundown motel on the edge of town. Joey had Meghan stay in the truck while he checked in. Then they spent what was left of the night trying to sleep – him on one double bed and her on the other.

Meghan snuggled under the cool, dampish sheets and looked across the room at Joey. Moonlight filtered in through the hotel window and shone down on his face. Relaxed in sleep he seemed younger, like her dream Joey. Slowly his eyes opened and smiled at her. In spite of all the problems that were swirling around them, she felt content.

"I love you," she whispered.

"Oh Meg," he returned. "You know I love you too. Now go to sleep."

With a smile on her face, she closed her eyes.

***

When she woke up it was morning and Joey was sitting at the desk, working on his laptop. His hair was wet from a shower and he was wearing fresh clothes.

She pushed into a sitting position and looked at the clock. It was almost noon.

He smiled and said, "Good morning, Sleepyhead."

She stretched. "Good morning."

He pointed at an assortment of snack cakes and a case of bottled water on the counter by the bathroom sink. "I went to the gas station across the street and got us some food."

She walked over and unwrapped a Twinkie. "Looks nutritious."

"We've missed our dream session and our chance to approach Heidi."

She nodded. "So much for that plan."

"Will Dr. Morrow be suspicious?"

"Naw," Joey said. "He'll probably guess that we found out about the plot to change our dream, but he won't guess that we're trying to build a case against him."

"Do you think Chase will realize that Caldwell warned us," Meghan asked.

"Oh yeah," Joey answered. "I mean, who else could it have been?"

"Poor Caldwell."

She looked over his shoulder at the information on his computer screen. "How much more time do we need to get our case ready to give to the police?"

"I don't know." Joey sounded discouraged. "We have a bunch of missing homeless people that a guy named Bucket *says* were working with Morrow."

"And Bucket won't make a very good witness."

"He'd be a terrible witness, assuming we could ever even find him again," Joey confirmed.

"But we have some normal people with at least a vague connection to Dr. Morrow who committed suicide," she said. "And the woman who attacked the tennis player – Gina Lightsey. Her sister who can testify that she was a dream client."

He nodded. "But the sister's word is not proof, Meg. If I walk into a police station with what we've got now I'm not sure I could get an over-worked officer to even listen to our story, let alone look into it."

185

She frowned. "Even if we don't have proof, what we do know is at least suspicious."

"But we're asking the police to believe that a Nobel Prize-winning doctor is a criminal and we're leaving the burden of proof on them."

Meghan rubbed her temples. "So we have to get more?"

He nodded. "Definitely."

"I want to get this turned over to the police so that we can concentrate on the decisions we need to make in our personal lives."

He looked very sober. "Yes, we do need to make some decisions."

She clasped his hand in hers. "I've already made one decision. I want you in my life. Now that I have you back, I won't let you go."

He wouldn't meet her eyes. "Can you honestly say that you don't miss practicing medicine?"

"I miss it," she admitted. "Especially miss my work at *Mom*entum. But I don't have to give up either one to be with you."

"I hope not." He stood and stretched. "I need a break. Would you like to go out and act like tourists?"

"I'd love to," she assured him.

He drove his truck several miles from their hotel and parked in a crowded lot near a public pier. They made their way slowly down the sidewalk, holding hands and window-shopping.

When the sun started to set and the dinner crowd arrived, they mingled in. They bought fish tacos and they ate on the beach.

Then they took off their shoes and walked along the sand, pretending they didn't have a care in the world.

"I almost feel like a honeymooner," he said finally.

"I wish we were," she whispered.

They held each other, bathed in moonlight, while the surf bubbled around their feet.

With her cheek pressed against his, she said, "I wish we could go somewhere and get married right now."

"Maybe it's for the best that we can't," he said with a wry smile. "With our luck you'd probably be pregnant before the end of the week."

She knew he was trying to lighten the mood, so she played along. "If we were really married, I'd gladly have a baby every year." But she couldn't quite pull off the joke. Tears spilled onto her cheeks.

He kissed her forehead, but he didn't have any words to comfort her. They stood arm in arm watching the waves crash in.

Eventually he pulled back. "Let's go to the hotel." Then he took her hand and they walked back up to his truck.

***

On Sunday morning they ate the last of the Twinkies for breakfast. Then Joey sat down in front of his laptop. "It's so frustrating to be here accomplishing nothing. We're too far away from the homeless people to look for more of Morrow's victims. We don't have access to the records of victims we've already identified. I feel like we're wasting time."

"Then let's go back to Atlanta," she suggested.

"Your parents and your husband are there and it doesn't seem wise to be near them since they've already tried to brainwash you."

"What more can they do?"

He shrugged. "They could try to separate us."

She frowned. That was not a risk she was willing to take. "We'd have to sneak in, then. We won't go to your office or my condo."

"We need internet access and privacy and proximity to the homeless population in downtown Atlanta."

"We can go to the *Mom*entum offices. The clinic is closed on Sunday so no one will be there. We can sleep on the couches in the waiting room and as long as we leave before any of the volunteers arrive tomorrow, know one will know we were there. No one will think to look for us there because my parents and Chase think I've been kicked off the *Mom*entum staff."

Joey winced. "You have been kicked off the clinic staff."

187

"Exactly. But I still have keys. And the best part is we have a subscription with a company that does background checks. We use them to make sure our prospective patrons aren't felons. But maybe we could run the names of our non-homeless suspected clients through. The reports may not show a connection with Dr. Morrow, but if we have more information about them – we might be able to find the connection ourselves."

He smiled. "What are we waiting for?"

She stood. "At least it won't take us long to pack."

They made it back to Atlanta around one o'clock on Sunday afternoon. Joey drove around the *Mom*entum offices a few times to be sure it was deserted. Then he parked his truck and they entered the building through the back door.

Meghan walked past the cubicles and led Joey into Barrie's office.

She sat in front of the computer and opened the online submission form for the background company. "Give me a name," she told him.

He provided one and then asked, "How long will it take?"

"I'll ask for an expedited report," she said. "So we should have it in a couple of hours."

"Can we submit more than one name at a time?"

"We can try. Give me another name."

Joey looked over his list. "Simon Perkins."

She typed it in and pushed 'submit'. "Give me a few more."

Once they were all entered and submitted, Joey asked, "What now?"

She leaned back against Barrie's desk chair. "Now, we wait."

They watched the screen together for awhile. Then Meghan stood. "My Twinkie breakfast seems like a distant memory. You want something out of the vending machines?"

They walked to the employee break room and got a variety of non-nutritious food. They ate in Barrie's office while keeping a close eye on the computer screen. Time seemed to crawl by. An hour passed and Meghan was about to give up hope when Joey pointed at the screen.

"You've got a message."

She walked over and looked at the computer. "5 Results Available".

After exchanging a smile with Joey, she pressed 'print'. Then she sat down in front of the computer and said, "Give me five more names."

They had basic background information for twenty of the possible victims from Joey's 'normal' list before a warning message ended their research.

When the words "Limit Reached – Administrative Override Necessary to Continue" flashed in red letters across the screen, Meghan said, "I think that's our cue to leave. That message may have been sent to the phone or email of the clinic's administrator. So we can't spend the night here. We'll have to get another crummy hotel."

She cleared the computer's history and turned it off. Joey picked up the pages they'd printed and added them to his list. Then they left the office, turning off the lights and closing the door behind them.

It was dark when they walked outside. They were walking across the parking lot toward Joey's truck when someone called Meghan's name.

"Dr. Collins!"

She turned automatically and saw Quentin Jackson and his sons walking toward the *Mom*entum office.

"What are you all doing here on a Sunday night?" she asked them.

"Seresta is meeting us here," Quentin told her. "She wants to look over my English homework before I turn it in tomorrow."

Meghan smiled. "Seresta is thorough – that's for sure."

Sedrick pulled on her arm. "Dr. Collins! We saw you on TV!"

Meghan was surprised, but assumed he'd seen a re-run of her Today in Atlanta interview about her Woman of the Year award. "You saw me on television?" Meghan asked. "Did I look nervous?"

Sedrick frowned. "No, it was just your picture. And his!"

She followed the direction of his finger. He was pointing at Joey. Concerned, she turned to Quentin, who looked extremely uncomfortable.

"It was during the local news," Quentin informed her. "They said you'd been kidnapped." He cut his eyes at Joey. "By him."

Meghan was confused. "I haven't been kidnapped by anyone and certainly not by Joey! I don't know why the news would be saying that!"

Quentin said, "Your parents said you had a mental breakdown and that he is armed and dangerous. Your mother was crying and begging him to let you go. She said they would pay a ransom." He looked away. "They're offering a reward. If anyone sees you they're supposed to call the police."

Horrified, Meghan looked up at Joey.

"We underestimated your parents," he said. "They didn't just give up when they found out their dream session trickery wasn't going to work."

"Are we going to call the police, Dad?" Sedrick wanted to know. "Because we saw Dr. Collins and that's what it said on TV!"

Meghan lowered her voice and spoke just to Quentin. "I'm not crazy and I haven't been kidnapped. I left my husband and he's trying to force me to come back."

Quentin nodded. "I know you're not crazy, but I don't need any trouble."

And Meghan knew he could use the reward money more than most people. "I'm sorry to put you in a bad position."

Joey took her arm. "We'd better get out of here."

"If you're sure you don't need help, I won't say anything," Quentin told her as she started walking away with Joey. "You had my back, I got yours."

She smiled at him. "Thank you. And don't worry about me. I'll get all this straightened out and see you at the clinic soon."

Quentin nodded, but he didn't look convinced.

She waved at Sedrick and they hurried to Joey's truck. Quentin stared after them solemnly.

As they were leaving the parking lot, Penelope passed them headed in the opposite direction, toward the clinic. They made eye-contact and Meghan saw shock register on her assistant's face.

"You'd better drive fast," Meghan told Joey. "That was my assistant. She's a regular volunteer at *Mom*entum and was probably sent to check out that warning message from the investigation firm. And I'm sure she's calling the police as we speak."

He sighed. "Since she thinks you've been kidnapped."

"She looks for any opportunity to impress the partners," Meghan said. "And she's in love with Chase – so she'll be more than happy to help him."

"It seems like everyone is in love with your husband."

"Except me," she said sadly.

Joey glanced over at her, but didn't comment.

"I can't believe Chase would lie to the police just to stop us from being together. And that my parents would lie right along with him."

"I can," Joey said. "If the situations were reversed and I was married to you – I'd do anything to keep you from leaving me for another guy. And maybe they really do think I kidnapped you."

She frowned. "They do not."

"Well, not at gunpoint or anything," he conceded. "But they believe you are emotionally disturbed because of the dream therapy. So I can see how they might convince themselves that I pressured you into leaving with me."

"And I'm too crazy to resist if I didn't want to go?"

"In their opinion – yes," Joey said. "When we left I didn't think it was necessary for you to contact them let them, but looking back, maybe that was a mistake."

"We could find a pay phone and call them now," she suggested. "Then they can tell the police it was all a mistake . . ."

"But what if they don't believe you?" Joey asked.

"Well, obviously then we have no choice but to go to a police station and tell them that I wasn't kidnapped," Meghan said. "And we might as well deliver our evidence against Dr. Morrow at the same time."

He nodded. "That might work – if we had enough evidence against him. But we don't."

"Can we get the evidence we need if we hide out a little longer?"

"I think so," he replied.

"But now that our pictures are in the news and there's a reward offered, it's going to be hard to find a place that is safe."

"I know a place," he said. "And someone who will help us."

She could hear the reluctance in his voice. "Someone who will risk trouble with the police?"

"Yes."

"But you hate to ask them?"

He sighed. "You have no idea how badly I hate to ask."

She turned to him in alarm. "Who is it?"

"My brother Matt. He's a priest of an inner-city parish. I know he'll hide us, even if it means trouble for him."

Meghan was glad that Matt had grown up to become a priest. She knew Paula was particularly proud of this and Matt had always been interested in serving others. Although it was hard not to superimpose feelings she had about the dream-Matt onto the real Matt that she barely knew ten years before.

"I'm sorry that we have to ask," she said. "But I'm glad he's in a position to help us."

***

As hey drove into downtown Atlanta, the signs on stores and restaurants reflected the different nationalities and cultures that called the city home. Meghan noticed that the signs had been Spanish for some time when Joey parked the truck. Then they walked for several blocks. Meghan felt vulnerable and conspicuous.

Finally Joey stopped in front of a soup kitchen

Meghan was surprised. "I thought we were going to your brother's church," she whispered.

Joey shook his head. "Since I'm a suspected kidnapper, the police might be watching the church. But this soup kitchen is one of the charities his parish sponsors."

The times of operation were printed on the door of the soup kitchen and the dinner meal had ended almost an hour before. There was a light on in the back and they could see a couple of people cleaning up. Joey led her around to an alley that ran behind the building. Then he knocked on the back door.

They had to wait a few minutes, but finally they heard someone coming. The door opened a crack, still secured by an industrial-strength chain. An elderly Latino woman spoke in heavily-accented English, "We are closed. There is a little food left. I will give you a plate – but next time you come early!"

Joey said, "I need to see the priest – the father that runs this place. Is he here?"

The old woman was instantly wary. "The priest has no time to serve soup! Go to the church if you want to have confession."

"I can't," he whispered. "My sins are too black to carry into a church."

She chewed her lip, presumably trying to decide if Joey was a serial killer or a repentant sinner. Her indecision was apparent.

So Joey pressed his advantage. "Please ask him to come."

She nodded curtly and closed the door. They heard her go through a series of locks. Meghan assumed this was a precaution against the serial killer possibility.

While they waited Meghan heard scrabbling in the garbage.

"It's nothing to be scared of," Joey whispered. "Just rats."

She shivered even though the night was warm.

The woman returned to the door and unlocked everything except the chain. "Father Patrone is coming quick. Now you eat while you wait." She passed them Styrofoam containers through a cutout in the door a little larger than the type used for mail.

After the old woman was gone, Meghan stared at the container in her hands. "I don't feel right eating this food when we can afford to buy our own."

"It would be rude to refuse – not to mention wasteful." He opened his container. There was a turkey sandwich, a cup of vegetable soup and a cookie. After a bite of the sandwich he nodded. "Not bad."

Meghan shook her head. She was standing in a dark alley, holding food from a soup kitchen. Her husband and parents had told the world she was mentally unstable. Her picture was on the television news and the front page of the newspaper. Joey was accused of kidnapping. Her life was a mess.

Oblivious to her despair, Joey finished his meal and discarded the empty container in the dumpster. Then a filthy old man staggered out of the shadows and asked for money.

Meghan handed the man her dinner instead.

He mumbled his gratitude and shuffled off into the darkness.

Meghan stared after him. Even with all her work at *Momentum* she had never seen hopelessness on this level. Then the vagrant disappeared from her view and she saw a tall figure approaching. He passed under a dim streetlight and she could see dark brown hair and a priest's collar. So this was Matt, all grown up.

He stepped into the little circle of light by the backdoor to the soup kitchen.

Joey held out his hand. "Father Patrone."

Matt pulled his brother into his arms.

Meghan stood awkwardly, separately aside and watched the reunion.

When the brothers moved apart, Matt said, "The whole family is worried sick about you."

"I know. I sent Dad a text telling them everything would be okay – but I didn't expect them to believe it."

"Can I call them?" Matt asked.

Joey shook his head. "You can't let anyone know you've had contact with me."

Matt waved at Meghan. "Obviously she's not with you against her will. Why doesn't she just tell the police so they will drop the kidnapping investigation?"

"It's complicated." Joey looked nervously up and down the dark alley. "Her husband and parents think she's crazy and that I'm coercing her. So if we go to the police we're afraid I'll end up in jail and she'll be in a mental institution."

Matt glanced at Meghan. "Is she crazy and are you coercing her?"

"No to both questions," Joey said.

"And what can I do for you?"

"We need a place to stay – just for a day or so."

"You can stay in my quarters at the church," Matt offered.

Joey shook his head. "The police might be watching for me there."

Matt pointed at the soup kitchen. "Then you can stay here."

Joey nodded. "That would be good. Thank you."

Matt knocked on the back door. The lock routine started in reverse and finally the old woman opened the door. When she saw Matt she muttered under her breath and then ushered them into the small kitchen. It smelled of bleach and grease and incompatible spices.

Matt made introductions. The old woman who had fed them was the cook named Carmen and her helper was Raul. They nodded back stiffly as Matt described Joey and Meghan as, "My brother and his friend."

Then Matt led the 'friends' through the kitchen down a hallway and into a single room. There was a couch against one wall and a bed against the other. In the far corner was a door that opened into a small bathroom.

They sat on the couch and Meghan looked around uneasily. "Are you sure it's safe here? If your kitchen staff recognized us they might call the police."

Matt seemed annoyed – whether by her actual comment of the necessity of speaking to her directly, she couldn't tell. "These people would not call the police for any reason. They are hiding just like you."

"They are in the country illegally?" she guessed.

He nodded, looking even more annoyed.

"I'm very torn on the subject of illegal immigrants," she rushed to assure him. "But I'm surprised that the Catholic Church allows you to employ them. And feed them."

"The Church has trained me to care for people who can't care for themselves." He gave her a pointed look. "Like you."

"But we're innocent."

"Their families were starving in Mexico so they came here to survive. Does that make *them* guilty?"

At first his hostility confused her. Her memories of Matt were of a kind, sensitive teenager. He was always a little shy around her, but unfailingly pleasant. Then she remembered that in real life to Matt she was a baby-killer, a presumed adulterer – dragging his brother down the same road of mortal-sin. So she sat back in the kitchen chair, relinquishing the conversation to Joey.

Matt faced his brother. "Now, tell me what is going on."

Joey took a deep breath and told his brother everything – Meghan's meeting with Dr. Morrow and her interest in his dream therapy. He described how Dr. Morrow had sought him out, proposed that he secretly dream along with Meghan. And he explained that over the course of the past month they had developed a dream life together. He briefly described their face to face meeting at the condo and the subsequent confrontation with Chase. He finished with Caldwell's warning that their next dream session was a trap.

Despite the fantastic nature of these disclosures, Matt didn't question their truthfulness. Instead he asked, "So what would have happened if you had attended your last dream session?"

"We're not sure, but we can assume that it wouldn't have been good – at least not for my future with Meghan."

Matt cut his eyes over at her briefly. "So the kidnapping is a complete fabrication? There is no basis for it whatsoever?"

"Of course not," Meghan said.

"And what about this Dr. Morrow? Is he part of the kidnapping accusations?"

"We don't know for sure," Joey said. "We think his involvement is limited to rigging our dream session for a price. But if Dr. Morrow suspects that we're on to him, he'll *kill* us if he gets the chance. That's another reason we have to hide. Because that would allow Dr. Morrow to continue using homeless people as guinea pigs and addicting people to his therapy, and ruining their lives."

Matt exhaled. "This is a police matter. They need to arrest him, question his employees, and seize his records."

"That would be ideal," Joey agreed. "But convincing the police to do that at this point will be difficult since we can't even approach them without getting arrested."

"So what are you going to do?" Matt asked. "Hide indefinitely?"

"We are hiding but we're also trying to build a case against Morrow – one that will convince the police to investigate him. If you think this will get you in trouble with the Church, we'll find somewhere else to stay."

Matt shook his head. "I don't want you to leave."

Meghan saw Joey relax. It had been difficult for him to ask his brother for help, but being refused would have been much worse.

"Now what else can I do to help you?"

Joey told Matt about Gina Lightsey who thought she had a relationship with the tennis player, Ty Randall. "She has a sister who could give us information, but since we're fugitives . . ."

"You want me to go see her?" Matt guessed.

"I believe she would trust you." Joey said. "If she has any copies of her sister's phone records or cancelled checks – things like that would help our case."

Matt nodded. "I'll go tomorrow morning and see what I can find out."

"Right now we're going to go out and talk to some homeless people."

"We're going to try and get more possible victims?" Meghan asked. "The list we've already got is too large."

Joey explained, "Since the homeless people won't make good witnesses, even if we can find them, I just want names. I'm hoping the sheer numbers will help shock the police into action."

Matt said, "I have a good relationship with the homeless people in this area. If I go along there's a better chance that they'll talk to you – and maybe even tell you the truth."

"That would help a lot," Joey said. "But once you start asking questions about people associated with Morrow you might draw negative attention to yourself."

"I'm not scared."

"I wanted to limit your involvement," Joey told his brother. "Mom will kill me if anything happens to you."

"Mom would want me to help you," Matt replied. "And you can't limit my involvement. I'm in it all the way. Now let's hit the streets."

Chapter Fourteen

This time as they walked among the homeless people, Matt did most of the talking with Joey making an occasional comment. Meghan hung back, more of an observer than a participant.

They added a few names to their list of probably test-clients. But when they got back to the soup kitchen, Joey seemed discouraged. "We may never be able to compile enough real evidence to convince the police that there is a case here."

"Maybe you're misjudging the police. If we go to a police station, once they see that I am with you voluntarily, the kidnapping charges will be dropped. We can show them what we've found and tell them what we suspect. Then it will be up to them to prove the case."

"If your parents and husband and Dr. Morrow, a Nobel prize winning scientist, claim you're mentally ill – the police will be inclined to believe them. Especially after the way we've acted for the past few weeks."

She thought about the partners at the medical practice and how they had looked at her on the day she began her leave of absence, the way Barrie at *Mom*entum had requested that she stay away, and how Penelope had looked when they crossed paths briefly that morning. Yes, they would believe the worst about her.

"If we can't prove our innocence then we'll just run away," Meghan proposed. "We could go to another country – a place where a doctor is so valuable that they won't ask too many questions. We could help others and live a happy life – together."

"You would separate yourself from your parents *forever*? And expect me to do the same with my parents? My brothers too?"

"Well, I guess – if that's the only way we can be together."

"What if we do have children? You want them to live in the conditions you just described? And you want them to grow up without ever knowing their grandparents or uncles?"

She was surprised by the ferocity of his tone, and a little hurt. "Of course I don't want that. But if that's the only way – I'm just trying to find a way for us to be happy."

"I'm not sure there is a way for us to be happy," he said. "We've hurt so many people already – and we'll hurt more before we're through."

"I'm sorry," she whispered, feeling very responsible for everything that had happened.

He put his arm around her. "No, I'm sorry. I don't mean to be so negative. But I got an email from Phoebe today. She demanded that I come home."

"And if you don't?"

"Then she says we're through."

Meghan couldn't pretend to be unhappy about this news. She wanted Joey to break up with his girlfriend. But she understood that he regretted the pain he'd caused Phoebe. She felt guilty about Chase's pain too – although that feeling had decreased since he labeled her crazy and accused Joey of kidnapping.

"She's completely innocent in this," Joey continued. "She loved and trusted me. And now I've broken her heart."

"It wasn't your fault," Meghan tried to comfort him.

"That doesn't make me feel any better."

She knew his feelings toward Phoebe were reasonable and in no way reduced his love for her, but it was a painful topic. So to give him some space, she walked as far away as possible inside the small room. She looked out the window into the alley. The view matched her mood, dark and depressing.

Finally he came up behind her, put his arms around her waist. He pulled her close against him. She leaned back, savoring the warmth, the contact, the reassurance. Everything was in turmoil and a happy future seemed impossible. But they loved each other. On some level – surely that was enough?

She turned and pressed her face against his neck. "I miss our children," she whispered in the darkness. "I want to be safe and comfortable in our little cottage. Even if we can't afford to put new tires on your truck."

"You have to try and stop thinking about the dream," Joey advised. "Every time we slip back into dream memories we're giving Morrow control over us."

"I know all that – intellectually. But I can't help longing for it."

He sighed. "I know. Me too."

"Maybe we can still feel close to the kids tonight if we dream about them at the same time."

There was a brief pause and then Joey said, "I dream about them every night."

His lips found hers, hungry and desperate. She kissed him back, reaching for the closeness they had in the dreams. His lips moved from her mouth to her neck and she looked toward the sagging mattress a few feet away. Maybe if their relationship moved to a more intimate level they would be meshed so completely that they could not be separated. It felt right, it seemed inevitable. She could overcome his reservations and his determination to keep her 'options' open, as if she had any interest in a life that didn't involve him.

Then there was a knock on the door – soft but insistent. Joey leaped back and stared at her, breathing hard. His expression was something between regret and relief. He walked to the door and pulled it open. Carmen was standing in the small hallway.

"You must go!" her tone was strident. "The police found your car and know you are near! They are looking in every house. They will be here soon! Father Patrone says you leave now. I will wait by the back door."

Joey stuffed his laptop into his backpack while Meghan did the same with hers. In less than a minute they walked into the hallway. When they reached the back door Carmen was there as she had promised.

She wrapped a roughly woven scarf around Meghan's head and handed a battered cowboy hat to Joey. "Keep your eyes down and follow me," she instructed. Then she opened the door and stepped out into the alley.

Meghan was terrified and only the sure knowledge that it was more dangerous to stay, convinced her to plunge herself into the sinister darkness. They joined the other people who were using the alley as a means of escape.

They dashed from alley to alley, sometimes stepping inside businesses for a moment and then passing on. Carmen had a phone pressed to her ear, getting reports on where the police were and what direction they were headed. Sometimes they went through houses instead of around them. When the occupants saw Carmen and heard Father Patrone's name, they admitted them wordlessly.

Meghan was too terrified. It wasn't just that her life as she knew it was at stake and that if caught, she could end up in a mental hospital. She was more concerned for Joey, who meant nothing to Chase or her parents. They would not protect him from Dr. Morrow. And she hated being afraid of the police and suspicious of every stranger she saw.

Finally they ended up at a Chinese laundry. Meghan assumed this meant that they had managed to get outside the boundaries of the Latino neighborhood.

Panting, she followed Joey in to a large room with a garage door that opened onto the street. Several vans with Chinese letters on them were being loaded with deliveries for the day. Carmen waved them toward a van and motioned for them to climb in. They obeyed without hesitation.

They moved to the front-most part of the van where a panel was pushed back, revealing a small space that could be separated off from the rest like a hidden compartment.

"Sit, sit!" Carmen instructed.

There was a small bench on each side of the compartment, so they each took one and sat down facing each other with their knees touching. The escape plan was evident – if not particularly imaginative – and Meghan was less than optimistic about its success.

Carmen was joined at the back of the laundry truck by an equally old man. The way he looked at Carmen and his steadying hand at her elbow spoke of many devoted years together. Without having to be told, Meghan knew he was Carmen's husband.

From her seat on the laundry bags the old woman turned to them and said, "Father Patrone paid the driver to take us away. But because of the reward he cannot be trusted."

Meghan asked, "You and your husband are going with us?"

Carmen stared at her for an uncomfortable few seconds. Then she nodded and closed the panel so that they were hidden.

They listened as the door of the van was slammed shut. They heard the sound of squealing chains as the garage door was opened. Then the van eased forward and bumped onto the road.

They were pulled from side to side as the van started or stopped. It was cramped and uncomfortable but Meghan was thankful to be making their escape.

Then they heard the siren approaching from a distance. Meghan willed herself not to panic, but as the screeching sound grew closer, she couldn't help it. The stakes were very high and as she sat in the hidden compartment she faced the fact that very soon she could be in a mental hospital, unable to defend herself. Her medical career would be over. Her future with Joey would never happen. Her very essence could be destroyed, snuffed out by Dr. Morrow and his mind altering drugs. She started to tremble.

Joey squeezed her hands, offering encouragement or commiseration or both.

Finally the siren was so loud that the walls of the van were vibrating. For a few seconds Meghan held out a small hope that the sirens would pass by them. But then the van came to a sudden halt and she her hopes died.

There was shouting outside, some in English and some in Chinese. Then the panel that separated them from Carmen and her husband was pushed open a small crack.

Carmen leaned close and whispered, "When the door is opened they will find us and not think to search anymore. Get out at the fifth stop from here when the driver is not looking. There is a diner on the corner. Our son will find you there." She passed a small key to Joey. "Lock the panel."

He nodded solemnly.

"They are going to take you?" Meghan repeated stupidly.

"That is why we came," Carmen said. "To take attention from you."

Tears sprang to Meghan's eyes. "Why would you would do that for us?"

"I do nothing for you," the old woman said. "I do it for Father Patrone." Then she pushed the panel firmly closed, hiding Meghan and Joey from view. Joey reached up and locked the panel.

Seconds later they heard the back door of the van open.

"Please!" they heard Carmen say. "Do not shoot us! We are unarmed! We surrender."

"Get down, now!" the voice commanded.

"We live here for thirty years! We raise our family here and we cannot leave them!"

"You'll have to sort that out with the immigration folks." The policeman sounded tired and disinterested as if he'd heard it all before. There were scuffling sounds as the elderly couple left the van.

"Look around and make sure these two are the only passengers," the policeman's voice said.

Meghan held her breath, as they felt someone climb in. Laundry bags were tossed around as the van was searched, but the panel was not disturbed. Finally the van's back doors were slammed closed and after a volley of angry Chinese, the van crept forward.

Meghan peered at Joey. He looked devastated.

"I can't believe I sat here and let two old people get arrested," Joey said.

"You did it for me," she said, feeling worse than before.

He brought his eyes up to meet hers.

"We'll help them. I have connections." She hoped this was not an idle promise, but at the moment all her money and her influential friends were part of her old life – the one she had abandoned.

They kept count of the stops the van made and after the fourth one, Joey opened the panel. He moved a few laundry bags aside to clear a path to the door, and then stepped back in their hiding spot. They waited nervously as the driver got out at the fifth stop. While he was delivering the fresh laundry, Meghan and Joey slipped out and hid in the alley between buildings. Once the laundry van was gone, they moved as quickly as they dared to the diner on the corner where they would meet Carmen's son.

They walked to the back of the diner and found an empty booth. Joey ordered breakfast for both of them.

"I don't think I could eat anything," she whispered once the waitress had walked away.

He nodded. "I only ordered to be inconspicuous. I'm not hungry either."

Their food was delivered a few minutes later by a middle-aged Latino man. In addition to the plates of greasy-looking food, he also gave them a single key.

"My car is parked out back," he told them softly. "It is an old brown Mazda. When you are through with it, throw the key away and park in a towing zone. It is registered to me so I will be notified by the city to get it from the impound yard. I will say that it was stolen."

Joey didn't object to this. Apparently since he was wanted for worse crimes, he thought a count of grand larceny wouldn't matter. "We will take care of your car," Joey said. "And thank you."

"What about your parents?" Meghan asked.

He shook his head. "I don't know yet."

"We have some money and I know some people – good lawyers – who can help them. Just tell Father Patrone what you need," Meghan told him. "We'll arrange assistance through him."

He nodded. Then he gave them the bad news that the reward for information leading to Joey's arrest and Meghan's safe return had been increased to a million dollars. "Almost anyone would turn you in for that much money. Especially if they think you are guilty of a crime."

"I understand," Joey said.

As Carmen's son walked away Meghan wondered if he was warning them that even he might turn them in. His parents were in jeopardy because of them. She couldn't blame him if he did.

They waited for a few minutes before leaving the diner.

A fine drizzle was falling, making their situation a little more miserable. They walked down two blocks and circled back, just to be sure no one was following them. When they reached the parking lot behind the diner they found the car waiting for them. It was in worse shape than Meghan expected, but it started on the first try.

Then Joey drove while Meghan watched the sun rise over the city through the car's bug-splattered windshield.

When they were far from Matt's parish and the Chinese laundry and the diner, he parked in front of a grocery store and turned to face her. "I think we got away."

Meghan sighed with relief. "Where are we going now?"

"It will be light soon so we need to get off the street, but we can't go to a hotel because that would involve providing identification and now that there is so much money on our heads."

"Someone would recognize us and call the police," she finished the sentence for him.

"Yes," he said.

"We can't go to anyone we trust, like family and friends, because the police will be watching them."

He nodded. "And because of the reward we also have to worry about private investigators and bounty hunters and even amateurs who will be looking for us just to get rich."

"Maybe we could use some of Heidi's bribe money to buy a camper off Craigslist and go hide out in a state park," Meghan suggested.

"A camper will be expensive – even if it's an old one – and since we can't get jobs to earn more money, we need to preserve what we've got. Besides, if we're hiding in the woods we're not making any progress on our case against Morrow."

She sighed. "I'm trying not to feel hopeless."

He smiled. "Don't give up hope yet."

His smile disappeared a few minutes later when Meghan turned on the radio. The local news reported that Joey's car had been found in the Atlanta area – in a Latino neighborhood where his brother was the local priest. Police were conducting a search and Joey was believed to be armed and extremely dangerous. The reporter ended the spot by saying the police had Father Matthew Patrone, the fugitive's brother, in custody.

"How could they arrest Matt?" Meghan cried.

"For helping us," Joey answered. "That makes him an accessory to a crime."

"A crime that hasn't been committed," Meghan muttered bitterly. "We can't let him go to jail because of us! I'll have to try and explain."

Joey shook his head. "There's nothing we can do for Matt right now. He has friends in the community and the Church will back him up. Maybe he can get out of this without us."

"And if not?"

"Then I'll turn myself in," he said. "But that is the last resort."

Meghan hated the wait and see approach. "Maybe we could skip the police and go straight to the FBI. We know that one of his dream clients was from Florida – that makes him a national problem."

"The FBI would be even quicker than the police to dismiss our case. Then they'd turn us over to the police, who would throw me in jail and put you in a sanitarium while Dr. Morrow continues his evil practices."

Meghan wrung her hands. "It *is* hopeless! We can't help Matt! We can't even help ourselves! It's not safe for us anywhere."

Joey spread his arms. "What do you want me to do?"

She burst into tears.

He gathered her in his arms. "Don't cry. Please. I can handle anything but that."

"In our dreams we never fight."

"That's because our dreams weren't real."

She sniffled. "What are we going to do, really?"

"I know someone who might help us, or hide us at least," he told her slowly. "But you should know up front that he operates outside the law."

"At the moment, so do we."

"I'm serious," he said. "He's anti-government, anti-business, almost anti-American. He's a spammer and a hacker – maybe even a thief. He's paranoid and unstable and I wouldn't go to him if we had any other choice."

"How do you even know such a person?"

"We served together in Afghanistan and I saved his life. I was just doing my job – but he thinks he owes me. And since we need help, I guess that's a good thing."

"And this obligation will keep him from turning you in for a million dollars?" she was skeptical.

"I think it will. Besides he couldn't go to the police even if he wanted to since there are outstanding warrants for his arrest. I think he'll be intrigued by this whole thing with Dr. Morrow and love the chance to prove he's smarter than a Nobel Prize winning scientist. And he has the computers and technological know-how to help us research our case."

She shrugged. "If you trust him, then I say we go there."

Joey seemed relieved. "If I can pick up an unsecured Wi-Fi, I'll email and let him know we're coming. Otherwise he might shoot us on sight."

This was a sobering thought.

Joey pulled out his laptop and borrowed the grocery store's public wireless to send the email. Then he closed his laptop and looked at her. "Now prepare yourself – you're about to see something like you've never seen before."

She frowned. "Where does he live?"

"That's more bad news," he muttered as put the car in gear. "You'll pretty much have to see it to believe it."

She sat back against the car seat and watched as the Joey drove into a part of town she'd never been to. It was an old, rundown industrial area. It was hard to imagine anyone living there, even a crazy ex-soldier. Finally Joey stopped in front of a dilapidated warehouse. "This is where my friend lives."

Meghan stared at the rusted corrugated metal structure. "Here?' she clarified.

"I told you he has to keep a low profile to keep from getting arrested."

She returned her gaze to the building. It was more than ugly – it didn't even seem sound. "I didn't know it was possible to get your profile this low."

"Actually, I'm not positive he's here," Joey admitted. "He has to move from time to time to keep from being arrested."

She was more concerned about being shot. "Are you going to check and see if he answered your email?"

He shook his head. "No, I probably can't find any wireless out here and I wouldn't want to risk it if I could."

Joey opened his door and got out of the car. Meghan did the same. Then they walked up toward the main entrance. The asphalt was crumbling was strewn with broken glass and leaves in various stages of decay so Meghan stepped with care. The door was secured with three rusted padlocks – which seemed unnecessary since it was hard to imagine anyone wanting to break in. The whole place had an aura of neglect and abandonment.

"I think your criminal friend is gone," she whispered. "In fact I don't think anyone has been here for a long time."

"That's just camouflage," Joey said, "to throw off the police or anyone else who is looking for him."

She gave him a skeptical look as he grabbed her hand and led her around the corner of the building.

They saw another door but Joey didn't stop there. They continued around the building, past two more doors, and finally came to a set of decrepit steps that led up to a loading dock. Joey tested the first step for soundness and then walked up, waving for her to follow him.

The loading dock looked like the rest of the building – vacant and desolate. She expected Joey to say that his friend had obviously changed locations. But instead he walked over and pounded his fist against the wall. To her surprise, in response to his 'knock' a piece of metal slid back about a foot – just enough room for them to pass through if they turned sideways.

Joey moved toward the makeshift door, but Meghan resisted. "Are we seriously going in there?" she hissed at him.

"We seriously are." He put a little pressure on her hand.

Against her better judgment, she walked through the hole.

Once they were inside the metal strip slammed back into place behind them, leaving them in total darkness. Meghan clutched Joey's arm and blinked, willing her eyes to adjust to the absence of light. After a few seconds her vision improved and she could see a dim shape standing a few feet away from them.

After a brief pause the shape stepped forward and turned on a flashlight. "That you Patrone?"

As she squinted against the bright light, she felt Joey relax. "Hey, Emmett."

"I got your email and came up to welcome you. What brings you to these parts?"

"You said if I ever needed anything all I had to do was ask," Joey replied.

Emmett moved in closer, towering over them. With the illumination from the flashlight, Meghan could see their host for the first time. He was wearing faded military fatigues and scuffed combat boots. He was bald, but compensated for the lack of hair on his head with a bushy red beard. His dark eyes were large and protruded slightly. He was terrifying and Meghan shivered.

Emmett pointed the flashlight at Joey and said, "So, you're taking me up on my offer?"

Joey nodded. "We're in trouble."

"Yeah, I watch the news," Emmett replied.

For a few seconds they just stood there. Emmett didn't refuse to help them or demand more details about their situation, but he didn't welcome them either. Finally, Emmett turned and the arc of illumination from the flashlight went with him. "Come in and we'll talk," he said.

Joey followed Emmett, pulling a reluctant Meghan along by the hand. They continued across the warehouse, weaving through barrels and stacks of empty crates. Joey kept Meghan close and Emmett in sight. On the other side of the warehouse, Emmett opened a trapdoor in the floor.

Meghan looked down into the gaping nothingness and whimpered.

"There's a ladder along the wall." Emmett shined the light into the hole. "Hold on tight, though. It's slippery." Then he swung down and descended from view.

"Do you want me to go next?" Joey asked.

Meghan did not want to go next, but she also didn't want to be left alone in the creepy warehouse – even for a minute. So she shook her head. "I'll go next."

She walked gingerly to the edge of the hole and looked down. With the aid of the flashlight below, she could see walls of mildewed concrete and the rusted ladder. She put one foot on the first rung. Then grasping the handles, she lowered herself. She went down further and further. She was sweating and her hands felt slimy. She wanted to cry, but she didn't.

Finally her feet touched the ground. She stepped away from the ladder to give Joey room and bumped into Emmett.

"I'm sorry!" she said. She moved back toward the ladder and collided with Joey as he hopped off.

Emmett laughed. "Your lady friend is a little skittish."

"She hasn't spent a lot of time in underground bunkers," Joey said. He put his hands on her shoulders. "It's okay."

She took a deep breath and nodded.

Then they followed Emmett into a large pipe. Water splashed up around their feet as they walked. It smelled like a forest after weeks of rain – dank and musty, but not terrible. Meghan hoped that meant the pipes they were walking in drained something other than sewage.

They took several turns, moving from pipe to pipe until Meghan was completely turned around. In addition to her sense of direction, she also lost track of time and didn't know how long they had been walking when they finally emerged from the drainage system and stepped into a small room.

It seemed very bright after the time they'd spent underground, so Meghan had to shield her eyes. Once she adjusted to the light she glanced at Emmett. Now that he wasn't surrounded by sinister darkness, he looked a little less terrifying. So she relaxed.

Against the far wall was a large utility sink. Emmett pointed in that direction. "We'll wash our hands before we go in."

The men stood back, allowing Meghan to go first. She approached the sink with trepidation. After a brief glance back at Joey, she scrubbed her hands and splashed some water on her face. A glance into the small mirror on the wall confirmed her suspicions. She looked awful.

Once her hands were clean she pulled off a few sheets of paper towel from the dispenser and stepped back so the men could make use of the sink. Joey washed up quickly and returned to her side. He held out his hand and she clasped it gratefully.

When Emmett joined them they walked through a door and into a large room. Except for the fact that it had no windows – it could have been an office anywhere. It was nicely furnished and each wall had a large picture of a landscape – presumably to simulate the outdoors. State of the art computer equipment was set up all around the room, but there was nothing personal. No pictures of kids or snapshots of Emmett with his Army buddies. No sports memorabilia. Nothing.

Meghan was relieved and alarmed at the same time. It was almost as if they had crossed into an alternate universe, an underworld. A place where normal people didn't come. Her mind reeled as she accepted that she was in serious trouble.

"I'm going to have to check you for wires and weapons," Emmett said.

Joey nodded as if this were to be expected.

Emmett used a wand to scan them. Then he patted Joey down. He turned to her and apologized in advance. "I'm sorry, but I'll have to search you too."

She held out her arms. "I have nothing to hide."

He stared at her for a few seconds and then nodded. "I'm going to trust you."

She was grateful to be spared this humiliation. "Thank you."

Emmett pointed at some chairs in front of his desk and addressed Joey. "You two sit down and tell me what's really going on because obviously this lady is not being forced to go anywhere with you!"

Chapter Fifteen

Meghan held Joey's hand tight as he took a deep breath and began their story.

He told his old friend about their past history together, Meghan's meeting with Dr. Morrow and her interest in his dream therapy. He described how Dr. Morrow had sought him out and proposed that he dream along with Meghan – without her knowledge. He explained that over the course of the past month they had developed a dream life together – complete with a home and two children.

"So you dreamed the same dream?" Emmett asked.

"As close as we have been able to determine, yes," Joey said.

Emmett shook his head. "Wow."

Joey went on to describe their reunion at her house ten years later, where they discovered their deep emotional attachment to each other.

Emmett held up a hand. "Wait. So you fell in love through the dreams and then those feelings continued when you were awake?"

"Our feelings were the same in real life as in the dreams," Joey confirmed, "When we met a few days ago it was as if the past ten years hadn't even happened. We feel like we've been married for years."

"But in real life you're both married to other people?"

"I'm married," Meghan told him. "Joey is just engaged – or he was."

"So you haven't seen each other for ten years but you're back in love just like that." Emmett snapped his fingers. "Crazy."

"It is crazy," Joey agreed. "That's part of what makes the dream-therapy so dangerous. Almost from the beginning I had concerns about Dr. Morrow and this new technology he's developed. So I started researching and found out that contrary to what we were told, many of Dr. Morrow's former 'test-clients' now have mental problems."

"The therapy does something to their minds and makes them mental?"

"We hope not," Meghan answered. "Since that would mean we are at risk."

"We think it's when they have to stop the therapy that the mental problems happen," Joey said. "Because the feelings they have in their dreams are so real, they can't adjust back to regular life. Many of his test clients even committed suicide or disappeared. We're trying to track them down, but it's not easy."

"We knew we had to stop our dream sessions, although we didn't want to. We were addicted," Meghan told him. "I was worse than Joey, I think. Probably because I was allowed to change a decision to have an abortion when I was eighteen. In the dreams my baby lived."

"So that made you more desperate to hold on to the fantasy," Emmett said.

Meghan didn't like his reference to their dream-life as 'fantasy', but she nodded. "Before I started the dream therapy I was a very successful pediatrician."

"You were Atlanta's Woman of the Year," Emmett said. "I saw you on TV."

She sighed. "Yes. But the dreams overtook my life and I was unable to function at work. I didn't eat or bathe or anything except think about the dreams."

"Just like a real addict," Emmett said.

She nodded. "I was a *real* addict. My husband left me, my parents were hurt and confused and the partners at my medical practice put me on leave. I even gave up the charity I started – all for a chance to dream about a life that doesn't exist."

Joey resumed the explanation. "What Meghan is trying to say is that we are relatively normal, rational people and the dreams almost destroyed us. This technology ruins lives and could potentially destroy the world."

"The world?" Emmett's already prominent eyes bulged a little more.

"Once someone is hooked on the dream therapy, whoever has power over their next session controls them," Joey said. "Imagine what would happen if the dreamer was a world leader and the person controlling the dreams wanted to create anarchy."

"But maybe some people wouldn't be as susceptible as you and your girlfriend were," Emmett argued. "Maybe it affected both of you so strongly because of the baby you could have had – but didn't."

"Maybe," Joey was willing to concede. "But even if that's true, the technology is still dangerous on a large scale."

Meghan contributed, "And even if you don't believe the world is at risk, Dr. Morrow is at least guilty of gross neglect of his test-clients. His lab should be closed down until some safety procedures are in place. And there probably needs to be some oversight by the government or medical community."

"So to protect other people from suffering the way we have, we decided to collect evidence and build a case against Morrow. Then Meghan's husband paid us a surprise visit. He misunderstood the situation and punched me in the jaw." Joey rubbed the side of his face where bruising was still noticeable under his whisker stubble.

"Can't say I blame the guy," Emmett said. "I mean you stole his wife – in a dream!"

"I didn't blame him," Joey agreed.

"My husband doesn't understand," Meghan contributed. "He thought if I would just stop the dreams that I would forget about Joey and come back to him. But even with out the dreams, my feelings have changed. I love Joey now."

"So you won't dream any more?" Emmett asked.

She nodded. "It was the hardest thing I've ever done since it meant I can never see our daughters again." Her voice caught and she pressed her fingers to her lips to keep from crying.

Emmett looked between them. "These two kids don't really exist?"

"Yes," Joey admitted with a sigh. "It's hard to explain to someone who hasn't experienced it – but the dreams were very vivid and they covered a long period of time – years. So we developed an emotional attachment to the dream-children that will probably be with us forever."

"We were going to have one last dream session," Meghan told him. "We knew we wouldn't exactly be able to say goodbye to the girls, but we hoped to gain some closure. Then my best friend told us that my husband and parents had made a deal with Dr. Morrow. Our dream wasn't going to be like the others. Dr. Morrow was going to manipulate the dream to make me stop loving Joey so I would want to go back to my husband."

Emmett shook his head. "Man, this is heavy. So let me guess. When you skipped and your husband couldn't break you and Patrone up through a dream, he told the police you'd been kidnapped."

"Yes," Meghan confirmed. "I can't go to the police and just explain what happened because they think I'm crazy."

Joey said, "They've even offered a million dollar reward for her safe return!"

Emmett whistled. "Her husband means business."

"He does," Joey agreed grimly. "And I can't say I blame him. If he'd stolen Meghan away from me – well, I'd pull out all the stops too."

Emmett leaned back in his chair. "And what can I do for you – besides give you a place to hide?"

"We do need a place to stay," Joey said. "But if you take us in, eventually the police might find your office."

Emmett looked around the room and the fluorescent lights reflected off his balding head. "I'd hate to lose this location. It's got a good vibe. But I'll risk it. After all, you did save my life."

"I just did my job, Emmett," Joey corrected him. "You are not obligated to help us."

Emmett grinned. "Well then I guess if I help you – you'll owe me."

Joey nodded. "I guess I will."

"Besides, I can't let you get all the glory for saving the world."

"I'll share the glory – *if* we save the world," Joey promised.

"And I don't have to worry about you stealing my wife. She left years ago."

"I'm sorry," Meghan said.

"I don't even miss her," Emmett claimed.

But she wasn't sure it was true.

"I have an extra bedroom you can use. It's not like a hotel or anything, but it's clean."

Meghan saw Joey relax and realized that he hadn't been sure Emmett would help them. And apparently he had no plan B.

Emmett rubbed his hands together. "Now, show me what you've got on this evil doctor."

***

Joey explained, "We're not trying to single-handedly save the world. We want to turn this whole thing over to the police. But we know if there isn't enough substance to the case when we do – it will never get fully investigated."

"Too much career-risk involved in accusing a Nobel Prize winner of criminal neglect and possibly murder," Emmett said.

Joey nodded. "We don't have access to Dr. Morrow's client list, of course, so we're trying to back into it. We canvassed the homeless population near his lab and got several names of people who were probably involved, most of which were also chemically dependent."

"They are also almost all either dead or missing," Meghan added.

"Then they are useless to you," Emmett said. "What else have you got?"

"Morrow showed us a DVD documentary to promote his therapy," Joey continued. "It followed three clients through the process and ends with all of them living improved lives. If we can identify those people and find out what happened to them . . ."

"I have access to databases that identify people using photographs," Emmett interrupted. "Do you have a copy of that DVD?"

Joey shook his head. "Unfortunately, no."

Emmett raised his eyebrows. "Well, then you can forget that too. Anything else?"

Joey sighed. "We've identified a few other 'normal' people who we believe participated in the dream therapy. One in particular, is a woman name Gina Lightsey."

217

"She's in a mental hospital, sedated to keep her from harming herself," Meghan said. "But she has a sister who confirmed on the phone that Gina was associated with Dr. Morrow's lab. Joey's brother, Matt, was going to talk to her sister for us today, but now he's in policy custody."

Emmett shook his head. "Wow, you two just can't catch a break."

"We have this list of names." Joey tapped on the pages in front of them. "And we have background checks on twenty of them. If we put all the information in and cross reference it with what we know about Morrow, maybe we'll find a connection or two."

"Maybe," Emmett conceded.

"We need access to phone records and bank records too."

"We can't illegally access bank and phone records for forty people without drawing attention," Emmett said. "Besides, any information we collect without a warrant is inadmissible in court – which will be a problem for the police when you turn this over to them."

"Could we take just a couple of our names and try to tie them to Morrow using illegal means so we'd have something to show the police?" Meghan suggested. "Then they could obtain information on the other suspected test clients legally."

"I guess that's all we can do," Emmett said. "So you two sit there and watch me work my magic."

It took Emmett almost an hour just to scan in all the reports, but once he had the data in his computer he was able to start organizing it. There were several vague connections between various suspected test clients – riding the same bus, attending the same adult education classes, children in the same schools or daycare. But Emmett dismissed this as unimpressive.

"That might be how they learned about Morrow's therapy – through another test client at school or on the bus," Meghan pointed out.

"But that's hard to prove," Emmett said. "And it doesn't prove your case. Pick two 'normal' people and I'll try to get their bank and phone records. If we find a connection there – I think you're in business."

They chose two names and with Emmett's help, and the use of his computers, were able to confirm that both received regular phone calls from Dr. Morrow's lab.

"Probably appointment reminders," Emmett said. "But there are no compensation checks coming into their accounts so they must be volunteering – not paid dream clients."

"Can you find out anything about their lives?" Meghan asked. "Like if they are still working at their jobs or if they've been fired?"

They watched while Emmett investigated the two people further. "One is still getting a regular paycheck from the airport. The other has been diagnosed with severe anxiety attacks and she is on short term disability."

"Should we contact them to confirm their participation?" Joey asked.

"They are still dreaming regularly and if they cooperate with us, they will put an end to their dreams," Meghan pointed out.

"It would be hard to convince them under those circumstances," Joey agreed.

"I think it would be a big mistake to approach these folks anyway," Emmett gave his opinion. "If you go to some of Morrow's satisfied customers with a bunch of crazy accusations and ask them to bite the hand that feeds them their dreams, they are going to tell you to get away from them. And you've lost the only advantage you have – the element of surprise."

The hopeless feeling returned as Meghan asked, "Then what can we do?"

"Go see the sister of the mental patient. You don't have to convince her that Morrow is dangerous and unethical – she knows that already. See what she can tell you. Ask for any phone or bank records that belong to her sister."

Joey nodded. "I guess you're right. That's our only option."

"Okay, right now we're going to eat because I'm starving," Emmett said. "Then we're going to get some sleep because even geniuses like me need rest occasionally. And in the morning we're going to figure out how to approach the sister."

Meghan was too tired to argue.

Emmett stood and walked toward the kitchen. "Now, I'll make you some dinner."

After they ate Emmett led Meghan to his spare room, which had a small bathroom attached. She took a long shower and then changed into her pajamas.

When she walked out of the bathroom she found Joey setting up a cot in the hallway by her bedroom door.

"Why don't you put your cot in here?" she asked him.

He tilted his head toward the kitchen where Emmett was cleaning up from their meal. "I don't want him to get the wrong idea."

She sat on his cot. "You'll stay right here though, all night?"

He sat beside her. "I promise."

"It's too dangerous for you to leave the bunker to meet with Gina's sister," Meghan said. "Can't we ask Emmett to do it?"

Joey shook his head. "Emmett won't be able to argue the case well enough because he hasn't experienced the dreams. And I don't want to put that much responsibility on him."

Meghan sighed. "And he's so strange looking Gina's sister would probably run from him before he said a word."

Joey looked toward the kitchen again. "Shhhh!"

"It's so dangerous," she said.

"I'll be okay. And I won't be gone long."

She shuddered at the thought of Joey putting himself at risk, and the thought of staying in the underground bunker alone with Emmett. "And what if Gina's sister won't talk to the police?"

"We'll face that if and when we get there." He stood and pulled her to her feet. "Now go to bed before Emmett gets mad at us."

She kissed him and then walked back into the bedroom. Too tired even to feel lonely, she climbed onto the bed and fell asleep.

***

The next morning Joey left the bunker driving Emmett's car, headed for a meeting with Gina Lightsey's sister – Leah.

Emmett worked quietly at his computer, presumably filling inboxes with anti-government spam, while Meghan paced nervously around his office. She felt frustrated and confined and afraid.

Emmett turned on the television and suggested that she try to watch it. "You're making me nervous," he said.

She apologized and sat down in front of the TV. Then she flipped channels continuously, terrified that she would see a 'breaking news' update telling viewers that Joey had been caught and arrested.

At lunch Emmett offered her a microwave dinner, but she was too nervous to eat. The waiting was torture.

It was almost one o'clock that afternoon when Emmett told her that Joey had returned. She ran to the door to greet him. Running her hands over his face and arms, she reassured herself that he was really back and he was okay.

"So," she asked. "How did it go?"

"Gina's sister, Leah, wants Dr. Morrow stopped and she is willing to talk to the police, but she doesn't know anything except what her sister told her. She's never been in the lab or met Morrow."

"Hearsay testimony," Emmett muttered.

"She gave me Gina's phone bills and there are calls to and from Morrow's lab."

"Combined with our other information that might be enough to convince the police to open an investigation," Meghan said.

"It's still weak," Emmett said. "You'd need a very sympathetic judge to issue a warrant with so little. And considering that the suspect is a Nobel Prize winner – well I don't think there are any judges that sympathetic."

"Really all we need is one cop who will listen to us and believe us and then take the investigation from there," Joey said.

Emmett frowned. "I don't trust the police – none of them. Using the press would be a better option – trying the case on television. You'd get a more fair trial that way."

"But then the whole world would know about Dr. Morrow and his dream-therapy research," Megan pointed out. "We're trying to prevent that from becoming common knowledge."

Joey shook his head. "Taking this to the press is definitely out."

"But I'm nervous about trusting the police too," Meghan said. "It would be one thing to rot in a mental institution knowing Dr. Morrow had been stopped. But if he was continuing his research unrestrained . . ."

Joey spread his hands. "But we can't keep running, hiding, and hoping the police don't find us."

"You can stay here for awhile," Emmett said.

Joey ran his fingers through his hair in obvious frustration. "We'll get more evidence. Once we have a strong enough case . . ."

"No," Meghan interrupted him. "We can't get a stronger case without risking our safety. And taking what we've found to a random, low-level policeman is never going to work."

"You got a better idea?" Emmett asked.

Meghan nodded as the only reasonable path came to her mind with clarity "Yes. I know what we have to do."

Joey studied her warily. "Why do I think I'm not going to like it?"

"You're not," she confirmed. "But if you'll give it some consideration, you'll agree that we really have no choice."

"What is your idea?" Joey asked.

"We've agreed that if we try to go to anyone – the press, the police, the FBI – no one will believe us because they've seen the news and, well, our story is so fantastical."

"I barely believe you and I know never trust the news," Emmett added helpfully.

She gave him a doleful look before she continued. "But there are two people who *know* we are telling the truth. I don't count my parents because instead of trusting in me, they always assume I'm wrong and start working on a way to 'help' me."

"So the only two people who know you're sane and that I didn't kidnap you, are Dr. Morrow and your husband," Joey said.

"Right," Meghan said. "I think it's safe to say we can't go to Dr. Morrow, so we'll have to go to Chase."

Emmett laughed. "Wow, talk about twisted!"

Both Joey and Meghan ignored this comment.

"He'll turn me right over to the police," Joey said.

"Not if we approach him right," Meghan disagreed. "Not if he thinks he has a chance to get me back by helping us."

Joey rubbed the bridge of his nose. "Is there anyone we won't trick, any lie we won't tell?"

She did feel guilty, but she was getting used to that. "Chase started the whole kidnapping thing," she reminded him. "So I don't feel too bad about misleading him."

"He loves you," Joey said wearily.

Meghan was encouraged that Joey hadn't refused to even consider her idea. His willingness to discuss it meant he was open to the possibility.

"That's why approaching him will work," Meghan pressed. "And he believes that it's possible for me to forget you. We'll use that to our advantage. Chase has the connections to get a case against Dr. Morrow started with the police. He is the only person who can help us stop Dr. Morrow."

Joey spread his hands. "How can we ask him to help us?"

"To save the world, man," Emmett said. "She's right. That's what you've got to do."

"It's just crazy," Joey tried again to dismiss the idea.

Emmett smiled. "I don't know. I kind of like it. Might be just crazy enough to work."

Joey looked at his friend. "Seriously?"

Emmett shrugged. "You're out of options. And like she said – her husband is in a position to make the case against Morrow stick."

Joey sighed. "If I did decide to risk asking your husband for help – and I'm not saying that I will – but if I did, how would we do it? The police will be watching your condo and his office. I'd be arrested and you'd be institutionalized before we ever got near him."

Meghan considered this for a few seconds. Then she said, "He moved into his parents' lake house a few weeks ago – when I refused to stop my dream sessions. We could go there and wait for him. We he gets there tonight, we'll talk to him – away from the police and television cameras and other distractions."

"I doubt he's still staying there," Joey said. "It makes sense that he would move back to your condo since its closer to his work."

She frowned. "If he's doesn't come to the lake house tonight we'll get him to come there tomorrow."

"How?" Joey asked.

She waved a hand dismissively. "We'll figure that out later. But if we're waiting when he gets there, we can present out case to him. And if he refuses to help us, we'll leave before he can call the police. I don't see how we'd be any worse off then than we are now."

Joey acknowledged this with a little nod. "So what would we tell him, exactly?"

"Everything we've learned about Dr. Morrow and his dream-therapy. We'll tell him about the suicides and the lack of concern for test-clients. He already knows how powerful the dreams are and it wouldn't take much to convince him that in the wrong hands the therapy could be disastrous. Once he understands that Dr. Morrow poses a threat to the entire world he won't turn us down."

"What if he insists that as a condition for his cooperation, you have to do a dream session and your pivot point is the day you decided to try the dream therapy? If you made a different choice we never would have gotten back together and you'd be perfectly happy with him."

She shook her head. "I would never trust Dr. Morrow again. If he had another chance to play with my mind – he might find a way erase my memories. Erase you."

Some of the tension left his face. "So you won't really do it, but you'll tell him you will, just to get his cooperation?"

"If he makes another dream session a condition for his cooperation, I won't actually lie to him," Meghan said. "I'll tell him that I'm very confused and that I don't know exactly how everything will work out once we stop Dr. Morrow. I'll say that if he helps us I'll keep an open mind. I want to encourage him without giving him false hope. You know where my heart is. But this is bigger than just the two of us."

Joey leaned closer. "What would you choose if you didn't have to consider anyone else? What do you really want?"

"I want the dream," she told him. "But since I can't have that, I want whatever life we're able to build together."

"Even knowing all the people we'll hurt along the way?"

She nodded. "I can't imagine my life any other way except with you."

Joey's shoulders relaxed and he shot Emmett an embarrassed glance. "Sorry to subject you to that personal discussion, but I just have to know where I stand."

"You stand with me," she said. "No matter what."

"So we'll go to the lake house owned by your husband's parents and see if we can convince him to help us."

She nodded. "I think that's our best option."

Emmett was grinning at them. "I've heard of people making strange alliances, but this may be the strangest ever."

224

***

When they were ready to leave they found Emmett standing by the rear exit, scratching his bald head.

"I feel a little nervous about you two striking off on your own," he said. "I've been cooped up in here for too long, so I've decided it's time for a road trip."

"You're coming with us?" Meghan asked.

He nodded. "I like to live on the edge."

"You've done enough to help us," Joey said. "We don't want to involve you more than we already have."

Emmett frowned. "So much can go wrong with a good plan and this one ain't all that good. You need backup and all you got is me."

"I would feel better if you came along," Meghan said, earning herself a scowl from Joey. "There's always the chance that Chase will try to call the police."

"I can handle your husband," Joey muttered.

Emmett laughed. "Yeah, I can tell by that big bruise on your jaw!"

"It was a cheap shot," Joey insisted with a smile.

Meghan was not amused. "This is serious," she told them. "And whether you like it or not, Joey, we need Emmett."

"Okay," Joey agreed.

Emmett grinned. "I'll follow a few miles behind you and park where I can see the lake house." He opened a desk drawer and pulled out a plastic bag full of small, clear discs and two cell phones. "These phones are disposables so they can't be traced to you. But that changes when you call someone. So don't call anybody but me. My number is programmed in."

Joey took one phone and passed the other to Meghan.

Then Emmett handed him the plastic bag. "When you get inside, put some bugs around so I can monitor what goes on in the house. That way if things go south, I can get you out of there before the cops show up."

Joey stared at surveillance equipment. "I guess this is a good idea."

"Now let's go." Emmett led them out of his office but turned the wrong way down the hall, taking them away from the drainage pipe tunnels they had used when they arrived.

"Where are we going?" Meghan asked in confusion.

"Let me guess," Joey said with a smirk. "You have another entrance to this bunker."

Emmett grinned. "Yes, I do."

"One that doesn't involve the sewer or a slimy ladder or a falling down warehouse?" Meghan added.

"Yeah." Then he opened the door to a nice, modern garage where two vehicles were parked. I save this one for *invited* guests."

***

They all climbed into Emmett's old Jeep that was so old it really should have been in a museum somewhere. He drove Meghan and Joey to the car they had borrowed from Carmen's son. Then they drove to the lake house with Emmett right behind them.

There was almost an acre of woods on both sides of the house that effectively separated it from the closest neighbors. Joey parked behind the house so Chase wouldn't see the car and know that someone was there until he was inside the house.

Meghan entered the code on the door. The lock slipped back and she opened the door. They waved to Emmett, who was waiting to be sure they were safely inside before he went to find a vantage point where he could watch over them. Then she took Joey's hand and led him into the house.

Chase's parents had owned the place for decades and to Meghan's knowledge it had never been updated. But it had a simple, rustic charm and she felt safe there – almost at home.

She walked from room to room looking for signs that Chase was in residence. His shaving kit was on the counter in the bathroom and there were dirty clothes in the hamper. That's really all she needed to know. But she walked into the kitchen and checked the refrigerator just to be sure. There was food inside, including milk.

"Chase is living here," she told Joey. "He wouldn't leave laundry in the hamper or milk in the refrigerator if he was going to be gone for more than just the day."

Joey nodded. "Good."

"You need to call Emmett."

Joey talked to Emmett, who was parked on a nearby hill overlooking the lake. He directed them in the placement of the listening devices. Then they all settled down to wait for Chase.

***

As evening fell Meghan stood by the front windows, oblivious to the spectacular sunset. She concentrated only on the road that led up to the house, anticipating the moment when she would see Chase's car round the curve. It was a something she looked forward to and dreaded at the same time.

The sun disappeared behind the horizon and darkness settled, but no car approached the house. She had almost given up hope when Joey pointed out the window. She turned to see lights in the distance, moving slowly and steadily closer.

Meghan's heart pounded. This might be the most important moment of her life. She had two men in her life. Both of them wanted to help her, but only Chase could – and by doing so he would lose her forever. Somehow she had to convince him. It promised to be high drama on the peaceful lake.

Joey called Emmett. "We have a car coming toward us."

"Yeah," Emmett's voice replied through the phone's speaker. "I ran the license plates. The car is registered to Chase Collins."

Meghan clasped her hands together and tried to prepare herself mentally and emotionally for seeing her husband again.

At Emmett's suggestion they positioned themselves on either side of the door so they could prevent Chase from leaving, if he should be so inclined, before they explained their presence in his lake house.

Once they were in place her eyes moved to the door, riveted. They heard the car park outside followed by sounds of Chase's approach.

Meghan felt a great sense of responsibility. It would be up to her to secure Chase's cooperation. If she was unsuccessful, they would have to leave and face a future without much hope.

She held her breath as the code was entered on the lock and the door swung open. Chase stepped inside and when she saw him, all fear left her and she moved out of the shadows.

Shock registered on his face when he saw her. Then he whispered, "Meghan?" His tone was hesitant as if he weren't completely sure she was real.

"Hey, Chase," she replied softly.

He held out his arms and she moved into them. He held her close, trembling a little. She had expected that she would feel guilty at this point, for leading him to believe that she had come back to him. But instead she just felt comfort and peace. No matter what else happened, she and Chase should not be enemies.

Then Chase saw Joey. He stiffened and said, "What's going on here?"

And if the situation wasn't already awkward enough, then Caldwell sailed through the door. "I couldn't find my . . ." her voice trailed off when she saw that Chase was not alone.

"Caldwell?" Meghan said in surprise.

"Hey," Caldwell replied with a little wave.

"I thought you were going to resist your attraction to Chase." Meghan couldn't keep the annoyance from her voice.

Caldwell smiled. "Well, you know I've never had any self-control. But Chase's got enough for both of us, so don't worry. Although I don't know why you care since you're with him." She gestured toward Joey.

"Things are still the same between me and Joey," Meghan said to Chase more than Caldwell. "We have feelings for each other, but we haven't acted on them. And we won't until things are settled."

Chase looked relieved and she knew she had to capitalize on the moment.

"Please come into the living room and sit down so we can explain why we are here."

Chase didn't look happy, but he allowed her to lead him to the couch. Meghan sat beside him, close without actually touching.

"First of all, you have to tell the police I wasn't kidnapped. They are holding Joey's brother in jail and an elderly Latino couple may be deported all because of that outrageous lie. I can't believe you did that!"

Chase shook his head. "You aren't going to make me feel guilty. *I'm* the victim here."

"We're all victims here," Joey said. "We're Dr. Morrow's victims."

"I may not have made the choices you wanted me to make," Meghan said calmly. "But it was wrong of you to try and control me through lies."

He nodded. "I know it was extreme to accuse Patrone of kidnapping, but it was all I could think of. The dreams have affected you mentally and emotionally. I had to protect you – even from yourself."

"I can't blame you," Joey said. "If the situations were reversed I'd probably do the same."

Caldwell walked to the small bar area near the kitchen. "I'm going to fix myself a drink. Does anybody else want one?"

The others shook their heads.

"Fine," Caldwell replied. "I'll just drink enough for all of us." Caldwell poured herself a drink and then carried it to the other couch along with the bottle, presumably for refills. Then she stared out at the lake and sipped her drink, ignoring the discussion going on in the room.

"I understand your motivations," Meghan told Chase, keeping her goal of cooperation in sight. "And I agree that we could both benefit from some counseling. I promise that if you'll help us, I'll go with you to a marriage counselor."

Chase frowned. "You want my help to do what?"

"To stop Dr. Morrow from infecting the world with his dangerous dream-therapy."

"When you say stop him . . ."

"I mean have him arrested, his records seized, and the technology he's developed secured before it can fall into the wrong hands."

Chase was still frowning. "You want Dr. Morrow arrested?"

She nodded. "You've seen first hand how destructive his dream-therapy can be. And when we tell you everything, well, I think you'll agree that he has to be stopped."

"But if he's arrested then you'll never be able to dream again," he said.

"That's another benefit of your cooperation. My dreams will be over."

Chase didn't refuse outright to hear what they had to say, so Meghan took this as passive agreement. With Joey's help she told Chase everything they knew and suspected about Dr. Morrow and his dream therapy. During the course of their discussion Chase's attitude changed from skeptical to almost-convinced.

Meghan concluded with, "This technology is too powerful to exist unrestricted. And Dr. Morrow has already proved through his unethical practices that he can't be trusted."

"Who could be trusted with the power to control the world?" Chase asked.

"The government, I guess," Meghan said.

"The government isn't an entity with characteristics like integrity," Chase said. "It's a collection of people – many of whom might be seduced by the idea of controlling something that could make them rich and powerful."

This was something Meghan had not considered. "So we can't trust the government either?"

Chase sighed. "There are good, trustworthy people in the government. It's possible that we could build a case against Dr. Morrow and present it to one of them. What kind of evidence do you have?"

"We have our testimonies," Meghan pointed out.

"Besides that," Chase said dismissively.

Joey showed him the list of homeless clients and their staggering death rate. He showed him the list of normal people, including Gina Lightsey, and the connections they'd been able to make with Dr. Morrow. "And Gina's sister is willing to testify – although she has no firsthand knowledge."

Chase shook his head. "This is laughable."

Joey didn't argue. "Morrow was smart enough to use disposable people – and since a side-effect of the therapy seems to be suicide, it's hard to find witnesses. But we know that what we are saying is true."

"You have to believe us," Meghan pleaded.

"I believe you," Chase said. "And I understand the dangers of Dr. Morrow's dream therapy on a small or large scale. I'm just saying we don't have enough hard evidence to make a case. If I took this to my boss, he'd throw me out of his office – even if I wasn't accusing a Nobel Prize winning doctor."

"But you could get more hard evidence if you had a warrant," Joey said.

Chase shook his head. "You have to have something to get a warrant and that's not going to happen with what you've got here."

"So what can we do?" Meghan asked.

"Something desperate," Chase suggested. "Like trick Dr. Morrow into incriminating himself."

Joey perked up a little at this remark. "How?"

Chase thought for a minute and then said, "I could call Dr. Morrow and tell him Meghan has come home and, to help her adjust back to real life, we want to do a dream session together."

Joey and Meghan exchanged a quick glance. Then Joey looked back at Chase. "Go on."

"I'll say that we want to use the dream he set up for me earlier, one that resets your pivot point to a day before your other dream sessions."

"In the new dream I choose not to do the dream therapy at all?" she guessed.

"Yes," Chase acknowledged. "My hope was that after seeing how happy we could be you'd be willing to give him up."

Meghan knew she couldn't do another dream session - at least not with Chase and definitely not if the goal was to make her give up her feelings for Joey. So she shook her head. "I can't."

"We won't actually do the session," Chase replied impatiently. "But that's how we'll get into his lab. I'll be wearing a wire so we can record everything he says."

"He might not believe that I would voluntarily give up my other dreams," Meghan said.

"Then I'll tell him you don't know the content of the new dream. You think it's a continuation of your old dream with Patrone. But I want to show you a happy path with me. Maybe we'd have children too, like you did with Patrone." He paused to clear his throat.

Meghan had to look away. Seeing Chase's pain was terrible. Knowing she was responsible for it was worse.

"Then I'll say I wouldn't mind if Patrone was out of the picture – maybe even ask if there's some way to make that happen through the dreams and see what he says. If he offers to give him suicidal thoughts, we've got attempted murder."

"That sounds dangerous for Joey," Meghan expressed concern.

Joey shook his head. "I'll be okay. Keep going."

"If he offers to kill you, I'll have it on tape."

"Would that be enough to get him arrested?" Meghan asked.

"No, nothing we collect without a warrant will be admissible in court, but it might be enough to convince the DA that we have a case," Chase said.

"And once the DA is onboard, we can actually come to our session – giving Morrow the chance to attempt my murder," Joey contributed. "And that should be enough to arrest Morrow."

Chase nodded. "Now we just need to find someone who will sell us surveillance equipment."

Joey said, "I know a guy who can provide us with all of that."

Meghan felt so much better. They were working together with Chase and they had a plan that didn't include Joey risking his life. "Will you get in trouble with the DA for wearing an illegal wire and setting Dr. Morrow up?"

Chase shrugged. "The worst that will happen is that I'll get fired."

Meghan hated that he was risking his career for her. She didn't want him to love her so much. He needed to move on, like she had.

Joey said, "When will you contact Morrow?"

Chase pulled out his phone. "I'll call him right now. When should I set it up?"

"Try for now," Joey said. "He's usually at the lab late and if we handle this at night we won't have to deal with any of his employees."

"What about the surveillance equipment?"

Joey held up his phone. "I'll be working on that while you talk to Morrow. I think I can convince my friend to deliver it here."

Meghan listened as Joey and Chase made their calls. Joey's didn't take very long since Emmett already knew what they needed and just had to tell Joey how quickly he could get it there. Once his call was over, they both concentrated on Chase's.

First he explained that Meghan had come home. "She's not very happy," he said into the phone. "She still misses Patrone but I'm sure if she and I could dream together – she could forget him. So I told her she's going to have one more dream session with him, but really I want you to do the two of us. I'd like to use the same dream you prepared for last Saturday – with just a couple of tweaks."

Chase paused for Dr. Morrow to respond. Meghan noticed that he was careful to keep his eyes averted from her as he spoke.

Then he said, "Good. I'd like to set it up as soon as possible. Can I come in tonight and tell you the changes and then plan the dream session for Wednesday?"

Chase listened for a few seconds and then he turned off his phone. He looked at Meghan and said, "He's still at the lab so he said I could come tonight. Then the dream session is scheduled for Wednesday at nine."

Meghan looked away. Nine o'clock on Wednesday was her usual time to dream about Joey and Sophie and Anna. "Thank you."

He accepted her gratitude with a nod.

Joey ignored the tension between them and said, "A friend of mine is bringing us a wire and the equipment to monitor it. As soon as he gets here we'll hook you up and you can go to the lab."

"While we wait, I'll call the police and tell them Meghan wasn't kidnapped," Chase said.

Joey frowned. "Right now that's kind of old news, but if you announce that she's back and was never kidnapped in the first place it will draw a lot of media attention. Let's just leave it as it is until we have Morrow."

"What about your parents?" Chase asked Meghan.

She was still very upset with her parents. "What about them?"

"Are you going to let them know you're safe?"

She shook her head. "They can wait until after we have Dr. Morrow too."

Chase didn't look pleased. "Can I at least let them know I've heard from you?"

She nodded. "But that's it – no details. I don't trust them."

Chapter Sixteen

It was almost an hour later when Emmett knocked on the door. He walked in and Meghan introduced Chase and would have introduced Caldwell if she hadn't fallen into an alcohol-induced slumber on the couch.

Emmett displayed the wire and the battery pack. Then he suggested that Chase change into something loose.

Chase left and returned a few minutes later a bulky old sweatshirt. There were dark circles under his eyes and he had a weary aura about him. Meghan was tired of feeling guilty, but there was no escape. She was responsible for his unhappiness.

Emmett said "I'll need you to lift up your shirt."

Chase reached for the hem of his sweatshirt.

Even though she was his wife, Meghan didn't feel comfortable watching any process that involved Chase being semi-undressed. So she went over and sat on the couch by Caldwell.

A few minutes later Chase and Joey walked into the living room. Chase's sweatshirt was back in place and it didn't look any different than it had before. "You're wearing the wire?"

He nodded.

"It doesn't show."

"That's the idea," Joey said.

Caldwell snored slightly.

Chase asked, "Are you going to wait here or do you have to stay close to me to record what Dr. Morrow says?"

"We can monitor and record everything you pick up on that mike from a distance," Emmett told him. "So we'll stay here."

"Then I'll come back when my meeting with Dr. Morrow is over." Chase walked toward the door and then glanced at Meghan, like he was expecting something. An apology, maybe? A hug? Promises about the future?

Since she wasn't prepared to give him any of those things, she just said, "Thank you."

He nodded and opened the front door.

235

After Chase was gone Emmett set up three laptops on the kitchen table.

"What's all this?" Meghan asked.

"I'm spying on your husband – listening to his phone calls, watching his heat signature, and monitoring a tracking device I put on his car." Emmett looked up at her and grinned. "That's how we're going to figure out if he can be trusted."

Meghan didn't like the idea of spying on Chase, but she understood the necessity. When she got a blanket and covered Caldwell, Emmett suggested that she get some rest too.

"Patrone and I have to keep an eye on your husband, but there's no reason for all of us to stare at the computers."

"I'm too nervous to sleep," she told him. "But I can't thank you enough for all you've done. Honestly, by the time this is over Joey is going to owe you so many favors he'll never get out of your debt."

Emmett grinned. "I won't hold it against my old Army buddy. It's all in a part of saving the world."

***

Meghan sat by Caldwell's feet and listened to the sounds coming from the 'bug' in Chase's car. She wanted to trust him but felt tense – afraid he really might call the police and turn them in. But the only call he made was to her parents to let them know he'd heard from her and she was okay. Then there was only music from the radio and the hum of the engine.

Emmett announced that he would be making checks around the perimeter of the lake house property on the half hour. His first check was at seven o'clock and he left Joey in charge of the computer monitoring while he went outside.

A few minutes later there was a knock on the door. Assuming it was Emmett, Joey walked over and opened it. Standing on the small front porch was a man wearing a black T-shirt with FBI printed across the front.

Joey cursed under his breath and Meghan couldn't repress a little squeal. This woke Caldwell, who sat up rubbing her eyes in confusion.

The man on the porch said, "I'm Agent Weeks and I'd like to have a word with you." The gun he held pointed directly at them indicated that he wasn't going to take 'no' for an answer.

Joey stepped back to admit the agent.

Meghan joined them by the door. Assuming that Chase had somehow guessed that his car was bugged and had either texted or emailed the police, she said, "I guess my husband told you we were here."

The agent nodded. "Inadvertently. We've been monitoring his phone calls and heard him tell Dr. Pierce Morrow that you had come home."

"And I'm not crazy or on drugs," Meghan added. "I wasn't even kidnapped. Chase and parents made up that lie to force me out of hiding."

Agent Weeks nodded again. "We know all about the set up."

Meghan was intensely relieved. "Can you explain that to the police for us so that we don't have to worry about Joey getting arrested?"

The agent shrugged as if the kidnapping charges were only a minor detail to him. "In due time. Right now we need to talk about Morrow and his deal to sell a weapon to terrorists."

Meghan was stunned by this comment.

"Weapon? Terrorists?" Caldwell repeated from the couch where she had been sleeping before the FBI agent arrived.

Agent Weeks nodded. "From what we have gathered, Dr. Morrow developed some weapon technology and he's arranged to sell it to a very dangerous group for a large amount of money. We want to stop the sale, obviously, but want to know more about the weapon before we make a move. Your names have been mentioned in the negotiations. So we have been looking for you – just like the rest of Atlanta thanks to the reward your parents offered."

Megan and Joey exchanged a quick glance. Then she said, "The only technology we've been involved with at Dr. Morrow's lab is dream therapy."

"Dreams?" the agent said with a frown. "How could dream therapy be a weapon?"

And in that moment the possible threats Dr. Morrow's technology posed to the world became reality.

"I think we know." Meghan decided to leave out most of the personal information about their dream therapy and just concentrate on the technology itself. "Dr. Morrow has developed a way to impose dreams on the sleeping mind."

"What kind of dreams?" Agent Weeks asked.

"Any kind," Meghan replied. "They are very vivid and completely realistic, so when the dream-client wakes up they seem more like memories."

"And how does this qualify as a weapon that would attract attention from terrorist groups?"

"It is very dangerous technology," Meghan said. "In the wrong hands it could be used to eliminate races of people through subliminal suggestions that they commit suicide as soon as the dream is over."

"That would work?"

"It has worked," Megan confirmed. "We have a list of thirty dead homeless people to prove it."

"We don't know if their suicides were the result of a planted subliminal suggestion or just the result of having to quit the therapy cold-turkey," Joey said. "But either way, the test-clients are just as dead."

"And it's not just suicides," Meghan told the agent. "The dreams could incite riots or cause a person to murder people of a different nationality or those who have a certain political view."

Joey added, "The dream can change their feelings, their opinions, and even their actions."

"It will make them do things they don't want to do?" Agent Weeks asked.

"It could make them *want* to do things they never would have considered without the dreams," Meghan clarified. "It's also very addictive. If the terrorists wanted to control a world leader they could introduce him to dream therapy and then require that he do whatever they wanted in order to continue the dream sessions."

Agent Weeks was grim-faced by the time they finished. "How many dream sessions can he conduct at once?"

"I'm not sure," Meghan replied. "He has several rooms, but he may not have the equipment and personnel to operate them all at once."

"We know for sure he can do two people at the same time," Joey stated the obvious."

"How controlled would the conditions have to be?" Agent Weeks asked. "I mean, could he set up a session in an airport or in a car?"

"The conditions were very controlled for us, but they probably don't have to be," Meghan said. "Since the client is sedated the risk for dream-interruption is minimal."

"So say the terrorists wanted to set up a mobile mini-lab inside a van, they could do that?"

Meghan nodded. "I think so."

"This is worse than we thought," the agent said. "Much harder to defend against and secure. You folks have a seat while I call my supervisor. He will want to talk to you. Then we'll have to set up a plan to stop the sale and catch the terrorists."

"We have a plan to stop Morrow," Joey said.

Agent Weeks shook his head. "The FBI is taking it over from here."

Meghan felt a huge sense of relief. They could turn the whole situation over to professionals. She could stop worrying about Dr. Morrow and his patients and the threat his dream technology posed to the world. Instead she could concentrate on her life and decide what parts of it she wanted to keep and what parts she wanted to let go.

"Can I call my husband?" She pulled out the disposable phone Emmett had given her.

Agent Weeks held out his hand. "You can't call anyone and I'll need you to give me your phones, both of you."

Meghan passed hers over. Joey and Caldwell did the same.

She was about to mention Emmett so that the agent wouldn't shoot him by mistake when Joey caught her eye and shook his head slightly. With a frown, she nodded.

"Now just sit here and relax." The agent walked into the closest bedroom and Meghan looked at Joey.

"Why didn't you want me to tell him about Emmett?" she whispered. "What if he sees Emmett walking around outside, thinks he is a terrorist, and shoots him?"

Joey cut his eyes toward the bedroom where Agent Weeks was talking on the phone. "The fact that Emmett hasn't come in tells me that he doesn't want Agent Weeks to know he's here."

This was an alarming thought. Meghan had more questions, but before she could pose any of them, Caldwell spoke.

"I feel sick. How long is this going to take?" she wanted to know.

"You'll have to ask the FBI agent when he comes back," Meghan replied. "In case you haven't noticed, he's the one in charge."

***

Meghan got Caldwell a Coke from the refrigerator, hoping that would settle her friend's stomach. Then she returned to her seat on the couch. She was more than tired. She was drained emotionally and physically. Leaning her head back against the couch she closed her eyes and pictured the faces of her dream-girls, Sophie and Anna. She smiled as tears stung her eyes.

Suddenly Caldwell shook her arm and hissed, "Wake up!"

Annoyed, Meghan opened her eyes and fixed Caldwell with an angry glare. Unmoved by her anger, Caldwell pointed toward the kitchen. Meghan turned and saw Emmett's face in the small window over the sink. His large bugging eyes seemed huge as he put a finger to his mouth instructing her to be quiet. She gave him a slight nod.

Joey was angled toward the bedroom where Agent Weeks had gone. Meghan put a hand on his arm to get his attention. Then she directed him toward Emmett.

"What is he doing?" Meghan whispered.

"He's preparing us," Joey said.

Meghan frowned. "For what?"

"Whatever it is, I can just about guarantee you won't like it," he muttered.

Seconds later they saw Emmett slip inside the house. Pressed against the wall, he inched along to the door of the bedroom where Agent Weeks was talking on the phone. Emmett held out a little mirror so he could see inside the room. Then with amazing grace and stealth for someone his size, he swung into the room. They heard a thud and seconds later Emmett came out dragging Agent Weeks with him.

"What are you doing?" Joey demanded.

Emmett dumped the agent unceremoniously on the floor and pulled a roll of duct tape from his pocket. Then he systematically wrapped tape around the agent's wrists, knees and ankles.

"Thanks to those listening devices I had you put around here I've been listening to his phone calls," Emmett replied calmly. "I don't know if he's an FBI agent or not, but he didn't call his supervisor. He's been talking to the terrorists. Apparently they decided not to buy the technology. They are going to kidnap Morrow and steal his records and all his equipment."

"They are going to take over the lab?" Meghan repeated. "When?"

"Soon," Emmett replied as he worked. "We have to get there before they do."

"Are we going to call the police and have them meet us at the lab?" Meghan asked hopefully.

Emmett finished with Agent Weeks, or whoever he was, and stood. "If we didn't think we could convince the police before, why would they believe us now?"

Joey's shoulders sagged. "They wouldn't. We'd end up in jail and the terrorists would have control of the dream technology and Dr. Morrow."

Emmett nodded his agreement and waved for them to follow him outside. They climbed into his ancient Jeep.

"So what are we doing?" Caldwell wanted to know. "Going to get Chase?"

"We're going to try and save the world," Emmett replied as he drove off so fast he sent dirt and gravel flying.

Meghan clutched the seat, almost as scared of Emmett's driving as she was with the prospect of a confrontation with terrorists.

"I'm going to be sick," Caldwell predicted.

Meghan reached over and rolled down her window. "If you have to throw up, do it outside." Then she turned her attention to Emmett and Joey. "So will we try and talk Dr. Morrow into deleting his data and research before the terrorists take it away from him?"

"Too late for that." Emmett swerved along the road, scraping tree limbs and nearly sideswiping fences. "We'll have to destroy it."

"Destroy the technology?" Meghan asked, unsure of how this could be accomplished.

"Destroy it all," Emmett corrected. "The lab, his equipment, his records – everything."

"I hate to ask this," Joey began and he really did sound reluctant. "But how are we going to do that?"

"We'll use my Jeep as a bomb and blow the place up."

"Blow up the lab?" Caldwell repeated.

Emmett glanced over at is old Army buddy. "I hate to lose this Jeep, since it still has years of good use. But I don't see any other way."

"You think you can blow up an entire building with this *Jeep*?" Joey asked.

"My Jeep has two gas tanks and I am a munitions expert, if you'll remember."

"What I remember is the time you tried to blow up a vehicle and you almost got yourself killed!" Joey responded. "That's when I had to save your life – which is what got you into this whole mess in the first place. So you might want to reconsider!"

"I made a little miscalculation with that truck!" Emmett hollered back. "Detonating vehicles is not an exact science!"

Meghan looked to Joey for his response, unsure who was right or what side she was on. She knew they had to put Dr. Morrow's technology out of the reach of terrorists. But blowing up the lab with Emmett's Jeep seemed drastic and maybe even impossible.

Finally Emmett won the argument with, "You got a better idea?"

Joey sat back against the car seat. "No."

Emmett grinned. "Then it's bombs away!"

Meghan glanced at Caldwell. She was white as a sheet.

Chapter Seventeen

"Are we sure Morrow and the husband are the only two people in the building?" Emmett asked as they drove at an alarming rate of speed.

"We'll have to double check when we get there and make sure everyone is out before you blow up your Jeep," Joey said.

"Where are we going to take Dr. Morrow after his lab is destroyed?" Meghan wanted to know. "We can't let him fall into the hands of the terrorists and we don't know who to trust."

Emmett said, "I have an underground bunker in the Blue Ridge Mountains. We'll destroy the lab, take Morrow there, and hide him until we can figure out what to do with him."

"Are how are we going to get our Jeep bomb into the lab without Morrow calling the cops?" Joey asked.

Emmett frowned, considering this. Finally he said, "We'll have to sneak in."

"Sneak in a Jeep?" Joey repeated with obvious skepticism.

"Chase is already there, meeting with Dr. Morrow," Meghan reminded them. "Maybe he can help us."

Emmett nodded. "That's how we'll do it." He glanced at Meghan. "You will have to go in alone and tell your husband to hit Morrow in the chin. Like he hit Patrone except harder and more chin – less jaw."

Meghan processed the information slowly. "You want Chase to *hit* Dr. Morrow?"

"Yes," Emmett said. "You'll go in alone so no one will be suspicious. Once Morrow is knocked out we'll drive the truck in, through a window if necessary. We'll clear everyone out, set the Jeep on fire, and run."

"You want me to walk in there and tell Chase to hit Dr. Morrow in the chin?" Meghan clarified.

"Whisper it," Emmett corrected her. "He's supposed to surprise the doctor with his punch."

Meghan stared back incredulously. "You're *serious*?"

243

"He's completely serious," Joey assured her. "A little crazy, but serious."

"This may not seem like much of a plan, but it's all we've got," Emmett argued. "We did stuff like this all the time in Afghanistan and it actually worked pretty well."

Joey shook his head. "I don't think it will work here. The success of your plan hinges on Chase Collins' ability to knock Morrow out and I'm not sure he can. He gave me his best shot and I didn't even blink."

Meghan thought this remark was less than honest and she could have used the bruise on Joey's jaw to prove Chase's strength, but she had a more pressing concern. "I don't think I can convince Chase to hit Dr. Morrow by whispering a couple of words. He's just not like that – physical and irrational, I mean."

"You could take in my gun and convince him to cooperate that way," Emmett suggested.

"I've never even held a handgun in my entire life," she told him.

Joey shook her head. "That won't work then. She'd end up shooting herself."

Meghan was both relieved and insulted by this remark.

Caldwell said, "How about mace?" She pulled a little container out of her purse. "Meghan could walk in and spray Dr. Morrow's eyes. That will give her time to explain things to Chase and get his cooperation."

Emmett gave her a look very much like respect. "You have mace? Now that's what I call being prepared for anything."

"I move in some dangerous circles." Caldwell turned to Meghan. "I'll do it if you don't want to."

"I'll do it." Meghan took the little canister from her friend. "I just spray it in his face?"

Emmett nodded. "He won't be unconscious, just coughing and choking."

"But incapacitated enough that we won't have to worry about him sounding an alarm," Joey said.

"Explain the situation to your husband quick," Emmett told her. Then he pulled out his roll of duct tape. "And get him to help you tie Morrow up. We'll give you two minutes to get the place secured and then we're coming in."

"What if someone else is there besides Dr. Morrow?" Meghan asked. "How will I keep them from calling the police?"

The men stared at each other for a few seconds.

"I don't know," Emmett admitted.

"I'll go in with Meghan," Caldwell offered. "I've accompanied her to a couple of dream sessions so they shouldn't be surprised to see me. Then while Meghan maces Dr. Morrow, I'll handle anyone else who's there."

"How will you do that?" Joey asked. "Meghan will have the mace."

Caldwell said, "I know how to handle a gun, so give it to me. And I don't have a problem with giving someone a good punch to the chin either."

***

When they got to the lab, Chase's car was the only one parked in front. Another car, presumably Dr. Morrow's, was parked in the back lot.

"It looks quiet," Joey said. "But how can we be sure the terrorists didn't beat us here?"

"There's no way to know for sure," Emmett said. "But we don't have any time to waste. If you run into trouble in there, fire the gun at the ceiling. We'll come in right away."

Emmett parked in the back lot. Then he turned and spoke to the women over the seat. "Walk in there like nothing is wrong. Meghan, you go straight back to Morrow's office and spray him with the mace. Caldwell, you look around for any employees."

"There's a loading dock," Joey pointed out. "We can drive the Jeep in that way."

Emmett turned to Caldwell. "Once you're sure there's nobody else there – or you've got them at gunpoint – try to open the loading dock door."

Caldwell nodded.

Joey put his hands on both sides of Meghan's face and kissed her. "Be careful."

"I will," she promised. Then she followed Caldwell out of the Jeep and walked around to the front of the building.

Meghan had a bad moment when she pushed open the big wooden door. It was something she associated with her dreams, with Joey, and with her children. She shook off the sentimentality that would only cloud her vision and moved briskly inside. After locking the door behind Caldwell, they proceeded down the hall toward Dr. Morrow's office.

"I don't see anyone else yet," Caldwell whispered.

"Check all the session rooms, the pharmacy, cafeteria, even the bathrooms," Meghan suggested as she stepped up to the office door. She waited until Caldwell had passed by, and then turned the knob.

Dr. Morrow stood as she walked in. "Meghan," he said when he saw her. "This is a surprise."

Both the doctor and Chase looked equally stunned by her sudden appearance.

"I know that Chase is going to reset my pivot point," she said. "And I'm okay with that." She looked around the room, assessing the situation. "I realize I have to give up my dream and live in the real world. I think doing a dream session together will help me make the transition. But I want to be a part of the dream creation process."

Dr. Morrow looked relieved. Chase did not.

"Come on in." Dr. Morrow stepped forward to close the door behind her. She decided she should act while he was by the door, rather than wait until he returned to his chair by the desk where he might be able to push an alarm or get to the phone. So she took a deep breath, raised her hand, and sprayed the mace directly into his face.

His eyes widened in pain and surprise. She sprayed him again.

With a groan put his hands over his face as he fell to his knees.

"Meghan!" Chase cried in alarm. "What the . . ."

"It's okay," she whispered as she dropped to the floor beside the flailing doctor. She pulled the duct tape from her purse and said, "Come over here and keep him still so I can tie him up."

After a moment's hesitation, Chase joined her and restrained the doctor. She wound tape around his ankles as tightly as she dared.

"What's going on?" Chase demanded.

246

"He made a deal to sell his technology to terrorists," Meghan explained, moving to his knees. "They could get here any minute. We have to destroy the lab and get him out of here before they arrive."

Chase looked pale, but he held Dr. Morrow more tightly. "Is Patrone with you?"

She nodded. "And Caldwell and an Army friend of his. They are going to use a Jeep to blow up the lab."

There was a noise at the door and Meghan looked up to see Caldwell holding Emmett's gun like an outlaw with a six-shooter. She said, "I opened the loading dock door and locked all the others."

Meghan nodded as she pressed tape against Dr. Morrow's mouth. "That's good.

Caldwell tilted her head toward Dr. Morrow. "Why don't you go ahead and mace him again just for good measure."

"Do not mace him for no reason!" Chase insisted.

Caldwell tapped Dr. Morrow's leg with the toe of her shoe. "Well, just remember it's an option."

"Would you quit acting like Bonnie without a Clyde!" Meghan told her friend sternly. "This is a serious situation."

Caldwell blew on the tip of the gun and tucked it into the belt at her waist with an irreverent smile. "You're no fun."

"Now will somebody please tell me what happened?" Chase asked.

"A man posing as an FBI agent came to the lake house after you left," Meghan told him. "He was asking questions about the dream therapy. He called it a 'weapon' and wanted to know if it would be possible to set up mobile labs in vans."

Emmett and Joey rushed in at this point and each one was carrying a gas can.

"Okay," Emmett said. "We've got to get this place blazing before we run out of time. I'll erase all the computer hard drives since some of the data on them might survive the fire. I presume they are networked so I can wipe them all clean from one location." He sat down and began typing commands into Dr. Morrow's computer. "Patrone, you start sprinkling the front of the building with gasoline. We'll set a few fires before we blow up the car to make sure that everything burns."

Joey hurried up toward the front.

"Where will we go when we leave here?" Chase asked.

"I have a place where we can hide out," Emmett said without looking up from the computer.

Joey rushed back in. "I've got gas spread around the front lobby. You want me to light it?"

Emmett shook his head. "Not yet. Let's get Dr. Morrow and the women out of here first." He glanced over his shoulder at Chase. "Collins, here are the GPS coordinates for my cabin. We'll meet there." He stood and gave a piece of paper to Chase. Then he said to Joey, "Come on Patrone. Let's get this party started."

Chase put the GPS coordinates into his pocket and his hands under Dr. Morrow's arms. The he dragged the doctor through the door. Caldwell followed him into the hallway.

Emmett pulled out some matches and moved toward the front of the building. "We'll start lighting fires up here and then work our way to the loading dock."

"I'm not leaving without Joey!" Meghan cried.

Emmett looked at her with a frown. "I thought I told you to get out of here!" He turned to Joey. "Get rid of her fast. I'm torching the lobby."

After Emmett left, Joey put his hands on her shoulders. "You have to go, Meg. Emmett and I are soldiers. We know how to handle this. You'll just be a distraction I don't need." To soften his harsh words he drew her into his arms and kissed her. Then he stepped back and gave her a little push down the hall. "Now get out of here!"

She didn't want to leave him, but she also didn't want to distract him from the dangerous work of blowing up the lab. So after one last look at Joey she rushed to catch up with Chase.

He was struggling to drag Dr. Morrow. "Maybe you two could help me a little," he gasped.

"I'll get the doors," Caldwell offered.

Meghan grabbed Dr. Morrow's feet.

They heard Emmett whoop and seconds later smoke drifted into the hallway. Caldwell coughed and Meghan's eyes watered.

"Hurry!" Caldwell encouraged.

She rushed ahead to the door marked 'Exit' and pushed it open. In the distance they could hear sirens approaching. Dr. Morrow fought Chase as he was dragged out onto the parking lot. A vicious kick took Meghan by surprise and she fell, scraping her knees and hands on the rough concrete.

She wiped the blood from her hands onto her pants and wrapped them back around Dr. Morrow's ankles. This time she held on tighter.

Chase dropped Dr. Morrow beside his car and opened the doors with the remote. Then he said, "Help me get him in the backseat."

Caldwell opened the door while Meghan lifted Dr. Morrow's feet and Chase pushed his body into the car. The doctor stared at them with red, resentful eyes.

"Strap him in!" Chase said.

Meghan did as he instructed.

"Now you two sit back here with him and don't let him open a door." Chase's eyes moved to the gun tucked in Caldwell's belt. "And maybe you should give that to me."

Reluctantly, she handed it over and climbed into the backseat beside Dr. Morrow.

As Meghan got in on the opposite side she looked back at the lab where smoke was oozing out from the edges of the rear exit.

"Joey and Emmett need to hurry!" she cried.

"They know what they are doing," Chase said. Then he got in under the wheel and they drove away.

Meghan twisted in her seat so she could keep her eyes on the smoking lab for as long as possible. Finally it was blocked from her view by other structures. She wrung her hands, too scared to even cry.

When they were a few miles away they heard the explosion. Meghan turned in her seat and saw the black smoke rising in the distance.

"We have to go back and make sure they got out okay!" she cried.

Chase shook his head. "My instructions were to take you to the cabin in the Blue Ridge Mountains where you'll be safe and that's what I'm going to do. Because protecting you is the most important thing to me *and* Patrone."

"But what if they were trapped inside?" she whispered.

"Then there's nothing we could do for them now anyway."

Meghan leaned her head against the car seat and tears seeped from her eyes. Joey could not be dead. He could not be lost to her again. She wouldn't even let her mind contemplate either possibility. But they were apart and she felt so incomplete, so alone. She glanced at Chase and realized that this was how he had been feeling for weeks, ever since she started the dream therapy. She looked at Caldwell, who couldn't sustain a relationship for more than a few weeks. She looked at Dr. Morrow, who had now lost what was left of his wife with the destruction of his dream lab. She was sorry for them all.

As they were leaving Atlanta, Chase got a text. He read it and then put his phone back into his shirt pocket.

"That was Patrone," he said. "They made it out."

Meghan pressed her hands to her mouth, feeling weak with relief. Joey was safe. Everything was going to be okay.

While they were driving Chase turned on the radio and found a news report about the fire in downtown Atlanta. They announced that renowned doctor Pierce Morrow had been killed in the blast and that Dr. Meghan Collins and her husband, assistant DA Chase Collins, were missing and feared dead. Suspected kidnapper Joseph Patrone was being sought by the police in connection with the arson and murder.

Meghan's chest tightened with anxiety. "Why did they have to blame it on Joey?"

"We'll get that straightened out," Chase assured her.

"They didn't even mention me," Caldwell said. "Figures."

Meghan was still worried about Joey. "He could get shot before we get a chance to notify the police! I guess I can go on Good Morning America and tell the whole country at once that he's is innocent."

"Why would they believe you?" Caldwell asked. "The whole world thinks you're crazy."

Meghan cut her eyes over at Chase. "Yes, thanks for that."

He shrugged. "I was just trying to help you." He pulled out his phone. "And I'm texting your parents to let them know you're not missing or dead. They've suffered enough."

"Don't text while you drive!" Caldwell objected. "It's dangerous."

Compared to everything they'd experienced over the past few hours, texting while driving seemed almost safe.

"Hand me your phone and I'll text Meghan's parents in your name," Caldwell instructed.

Chase passed his phone over the seat to her.

"Ah," she said as her fingers wrapped around the phone. "The most terrible part of this whole thing was being separated from my phone."

Meghan rolled her eyes. "You have a distorted sense of what's terrible."

Caldwell just smiled and kept texting.

It was the early hours of the morning when they reached Emmett's bunker. He'd said it was 'underground' but actually it was built into the side of a mountain. Chase parked the car in the woods and Meghan found the key where Emmett said it would be. Then they led Dr. Morrow inside.

It was small to the point of being cramped, musty because of poor air circulation, and a little shabby. But it was someplace no one would think to look for them and so Meghan was grateful to be there.

Chase deposited Dr. Morrow on a couch. Caldwell searched the kitchen for alcohol and Meghan decided to take a shower so she'd be looking her best when Joey arrived. Or at least look better than she did at that moment.

Then she realized that she didn't have a single personal item with her. She had no backpack, no laptop, no money, no change of clothes, no identification, no toothbrush. Some things had been left behind at the condo, some at Emmett's place, some at the lake house until she was now completely without possession. So she forgot about the shower.

Chase walked into the kitchen. "I'm starving," he said as he pulled a can of soup from a shelf. "Do you want some soup?"

"No." She was too nervous to eat and sitting at the table sharing a can of soup sounded too domestic – something a husband and wife would do. And she didn't want to leave any doubt that for her and Chase, those days were over.

She walked from to the front window, watching for any sign of a car.

Chase heated up his soup and sat at the kitchen counter to eat. This annoyed Meghan, even though she knew it was unreasonable. Chase was not obligated to wait for Joey to get there before he ate. But she couldn't help how she felt.

Caldwell walked into the kitchen and pointed toward Dr. Morrow with her glass of bourbon and Coke. "Are we going to leave him tied up?"

The doctor was sitting on the couch, staring straight ahead. There were tears on his cheeks, whether from the mace or grief, it was impossible to tell.

Chase sighed. "I guess not." He walked over and untaped Dr. Morrow's hands and mouth.

The doctor wiped his lips with the back of his hand and then asked, "Are you going to explain why you destroyed my lab and kidnapped me?"

"We had no choice," Chase said. "It's the only way to keep your dream technology from falling into the wrong hands."

"Which means *any* hands," Meghan added. "Even someone who intended no harm could do a lot of damage with it since suicide is a common side-effect."

"Suicide?" Dr. Morrow repeated.

"We've tracked the suicide rate among your homeless test-clients and it is astronomical. Whether it was intended or an unavoidable, the people are still dead."

Dr. Morrow seemed stunned. "I didn't know the suicide rate was so high."

Meghan looked at Chase. Then she asked, "How could you possibly not realize that most of your test-clients committed suicide? Didn't you do any follow-up?"

"We did some," Dr. Morrow said, "but it was hard to keep up with homeless people. If they didn't show up for counseling sessions, we just moved on. I didn't have the time or resources to track them down."

"So there was no real follow-up for hundreds of people you tested?"

"It was irresponsible," Morrow admitted. "I was negligent. There's nothing I can do for the people who are dead, but perhaps I can fix the survivors. If only you hadn't destroyed my lab and all my research!"

"You weren't trying to help your emotionally damaged test-clients," Meghan said. "You were going to sell your technology to terrorists! You were going to put the world as we know it in jeopardy!"

"I made no such deal!" he said. "I swear!"

He seemed sincere and Meghan faltered.

"The FBI said they intercepted messages between you and terrorists," she told him.

"They lied to you," Dr. Morrow insisted. "Please believe me. I would never sell my technology or purposely kill my test-clients. And if I can fix the suicide problem, the dream therapy will be safe."

"It won't ever be safe!" Meghan disagreed. "People become addicted and desperate. They will do anything for the chance to return to their dream. If terrorists had your lab they could use it to control world leaders or create a whole army of mindless zombies."

Dr. Morrow put a shaking hand to his head. "But without the lab, my wife is lost to me."

"Your wife is dead," Meghan said bluntly. "She's been dead for a decade. It's just her memory that you keep alive with your dreams."

"She seems so real," he whispered.

"Even if we hadn't destroyed your lab, the technology would have been taken away from you. So you would have lost your connection with your wife anyway."

"How can I bear it?" he asked.

"The same way I do," Meghan said. "Your wife *is* dead, but your love for her is not. You can still dream about her. You don't need dream therapy for that."

He nodded. "It's just so hard to face the thought that I will never *see* her again."

"I know," Meghan said. "I've lost my daughters and my dream-life with Joey. But we'll go on and build a real life together."

Out of the corner of her eye she saw Chase pale, but she couldn't back down.

"It's real life that matters," she insisted.

Dr. Morrow nodded, his eyes heavy with grief.

Meghan stood. "Now let me get you some of Chase's soup."

***

Finally as the sun was coming up, Meghan saw a car approaching in the distance. With her heart in her throat she yanked open the door and ran into the yard as a car she'd never seen before came to a stop. Peering around the blinding headlights she saw Emmett get out. He started walking toward her. She looked back at the car, expecting to see Joey. But he didn't.

She reached Emmett and breathlessly demanded, "Where is Joey?"

He looked down at his feet. "Joey didn't come."

"But he's coming soon?"

Emmett shook his head. "No, he's not coming. Not ever."

Her lungs constricted and for a few seconds she couldn't breathe. The lack of oxygen caused her vision to blur and she staggered backwards.

Chase was there to steady her.

She looked up into his solemn eyes. "You knew," she whispered. "You knew Joey wasn't coming."

Chase nodded. "He told me."

She clutched his arms. "When? When did you have this conversation where important decisions were made about me and my life?"

"Last night when he was taping the wire on me," Chase said. "And it wasn't about you and your life. It was about Joey and his."

Chase never referred to Joey by his first name. This camaraderie between the men in her life was almost as alarming as Joey's unexpected absence.

"You conspired with him behind my back," she accused. "You helped him betray me."

"He didn't betray you," Chase responded patiently. "He did what he thought was right. And he asked me to give you this." He pulled an envelope out of his pocket.

She was furious with both of them – but only Chase was there to face her wrath. "This will not work," she hissed at him. "If you thought that once Joey deserted me I'd come back to you – well you were very wrong. I want a divorce. I want you out of my house. I hope I never see you again."

He flinched at each verbal assault, but he didn't argue or contradict her.

She snatched the envelope from his hand and stormed into the house. Her chest was heaving and she was so angry her entire body hurt. She tore open the envelope and scanned the words written in Joey's scrawl. She knew that at some point in the future she would read over the letter carefully, lovingly, savoring every phrase. But not right now.

The gist was that the dream wasn't real and while their feelings for each other were, the life they had together did not exist. In order to be with him she would have to give up everything and there was no guarantee that she would be happy. He could not be responsible for ending her marriage and hurting so many people when there was a chance that some day she would look back and regret the decision. So they would keep their dream and go back to the real world. He loved her, but he had promised himself that he would never put what he wanted before what was best for her again.

After refolding the letter, she put it back into the envelope. Her initial wild anger had settled into a cold, controlled fury.

Caldwell, Emmett, and Chase had come into the living room and were watching her warily.

"I need keys to a vehicle," she told them. "I don't care which one."

"What are you going to do?" Chase asked.

"I'm going to find Joey, of course."

"That's not the way he wanted it," Emmett said.

"I don't care," she replied succinctly. "Chase and Joey don't get to make all the choices about my life."

Chase nodded. "Okay, I'll take you back to Atlanta and help you find him."

"I didn't ask for your help," she said. "I am perfectly capable of driving myself."

"I know you can drive yourself," he replied. "But you need to get things straightened out with the police. If you go alone, they might not believe anything you say. If I go with you . . ."

He had a point but she didn't want to admit this so she just smirked at him.

Chase said, "I'll tell them I thought you'd been kidnapped, but really you just don't love me anymore."

He might have been hoping for a little sympathy with this remark but she didn't have any to spare. "That let's Joey off the hook for my kidnapping and our murders," she said. "But what about Dr. Morrow? We want everyone to think he's dead, but we don't want them to think Joey did it."

"I'll tell them that I was there and witnessed the whole thing. I'll say Dr. Morrow went crazy and burned the place down. I'll swear he died in the flames he set."

"Do you think they will believe you?"

"The police have no reason not to," Chase pointed out.

"So Joey won't be a fugitive anymore?" Meghan confirmed.

Chase nodded. "Right."

"I guess that's a good enough reason to put up with your company for a few hours," she muttered ungraciously. She turned to Caldwell and Emmett. "Goodbye and thanks for your help." Then she walked out the door.

As she hurried across the front yard she heard Chase behind her with the car keys jingling in his hand.

About the Author

BETSY BRANNON GREEN was born in Salt Lake City, Utah, but she has lived most of her life in the South. She currently lives in Bessemer, Alabama with her husband, Butch, and her youngest son, Clay. She is the author of several books. For more information visit her website at www.betsybrannongreen.net.

Made in the USA
San Bernardino, CA
15 November 2012